D0494531
CITY AND COUNTY
WITHDRAWN
LIBRARIES

IF I HAD TWO LIVES

Abbigail N. Rosewood

IF I HAD TWO LIVES

Europa Editions
8 Blackstock Mews
London N4 2BT
www.europaeditions.co.uk

First Publication 2019 by Europa Editions

A catalogue record for this title is available from the British Library
ISBN 978-1-78770-159-5

Rosewood, Abbigail N.
If I Had Two Lives

Book design by Emanuele Ragnisco
www.mekkanografici.com

Cover photo: Pexels

Prepress by Grafica Punto Print – Rome

Printed at Grafica Veneta, Trebaseleghe (PD), Italy

For my mother

IF I HAD TWO LIVES

Part One

1

In front of the wall soldiers used for rope climbing practice, a little girl was stacking four rows of red bricks. At first glance, I thought that she was building her own fortress, but as I watched, I realized her task was more complicated. She carried the bricks diligently, one by one from a pile of debris across the courtyard. She added one to the first tower, fifteen blocks high, and another to the much shorter second tower. Skipping the third row, which was already the same height as the first, she counted to twenty before prancing away to gather more materials. The new brick was added to the last row.

Together the brick columns looked like guns aimed at the sky.

She was absorbed and didn't notice the other children—all boys—were gathering at the metal gate to peer at me, the newcomer.

The boys were careful not to lean on the electric fence, though one of them dared me to grab the wire to see how long I could hold on. I didn't sense any particular hostility in their challenge because I was worn out by the car trip. The boys' eyes shimmered with want and delight at my blue backpack. They ogled my clothing, which was made of finer fabric than their own faded burlap.

They seemed disappointed that I was a girl. I felt betrayed by the soft texture of my dress, hand-woven from bamboo fabric. My cheeks were hot. If I hadn't worn a dress, my hair—a bowl cut popular with boys and girls at the time—would have disguised me for a while.

My soldier, the one who had driven me here in the van—I already thought of him as my own—was talking to another man in the same uniform. They looked exactly alike, buzz cut and pine green uniform, except the other man had a shotgun and my soldier didn't. I thought he must have been armed too, probably a handgun, tucked away where I couldn't see it.

The one with a shotgun was not willing to open the gate for us. My soldier said something to him. I tried to listen to their conversation, but could only pick out a few words.

"Arrangement . . . "

"Yes."

"Let them know."

The gate opened. My soldier and I got back in the car and he drove forward. Once we were inside, I got out of the car again, my fingers gripping the straps on my backpack. I concentrated on looking at my toes. It was a feeling I would come to know more deeply as an adult—the suspicion that I didn't belong. My soldier took my hand and walked us away from the van toward the rope-climbing wall. The little girl, her face streaked with orange-colored dust, waved to me silently when we walked pass. I didn't wave back at her, only let out a long breath I'd been holding.

Our building at the camp was constructed in 1889. The walls were white inside and out, like many national buildings. It had large arched windows on both floors. During the French war, it had been used to host parties for French officials and their guests. After the French left, their architecture remained as pockets of memories and a reminder to the Vietnamese that their lives were both precious and meaningless. Since then it had housed many political refugees including writers, artists, businessmen and women.

Though its paint had become tawny over the years, our building's grandiose architecture stood apart from the other buildings at the camp, square and rectangular boxes designed to be cost-efficient. Sandy colored tarps swathed everything inside the camp—tanks, equipment, lawns. Even the branches of banana leaves used to weave into roofs were delivered to the camp already dry and brown. It reminded me of the desert. I felt as though a ball of heat was lodged in my throat. From the first day of being there, I wanted to leave. I longed for a field of uninterrupted green grass, though I'd only ever seen that kind of landscape in comic books.

My mother left our before-home in 1993 and had been living at the camp for four years before I came. I was seven-years-old when I could join her. She was waiting on the veranda as my soldier and I walked up. She wore a cream dress that dragged on the floor, the dress's laced hem torn and smudged with dirt. She was barefoot, using her toes to kick the dress's extra fabric to the side as she walked. In one hand, she held a pen and clicked it repeatedly as though she was warning someone of an imminent danger. I was in awe and afraid at the sight of her—she looked like the building we were in—its natural child—dusty, beautiful, neglected.

"Get some tamarind paste for dinner, will you?" she glanced at me while talking to my soldier. "But, what do you want to eat?" she asked me, though she didn't wait for an answer before grabbing my suitcase and ushering us inside. My soldier nodded, turned and left.

"Do you remember the night I left?" she asked as we entered the building, "Of course you don't. You were too young." I looked up to the ceiling, where paint bubbled and cracked, probably from rain leaking through the roof. A chandelier hung in the middle, its crystal teardrops blackened by moth carcasses. Our footsteps echoed as we walked. "If I'd stayed, they would have taken me. You wouldn't have been safe either," she continued. I didn't tell her that I remembered the night she left and still often dreamt of it.

In the foyer, she turned to face me and gestured as though she was about to hug me. Then she dropped her arms by her sides. I wondered if she were my real mother. She used to joke that she would get kidnapped and replaced with a clone. We'd come up with a secret number so I could tell if she'd been replaced. I had the urge to ask her what the number was, but I was afraid she wouldn't remember.

I realized I still hadn't said a word since we reunited. I didn't want to say the wrong thing and be taken from her. In the car on the way to the camp, my soldier had stressed how hard it was to bring me here. He said that technically the camp was a semi-permanent facility for soldiers in training, but over the years it had been used for many missions because of its strategic location—cut off from the rest of the country by both streams and mountains. I didn't see the view because I was in the backseat and there was no window. He warned me not to talk to anyone else at the camp beside himself, especially soldiers, since I was a young girl and they were not-quite boys and not-yet men. He seemed to exclude himself from this group. I blushed when he said he would shield me from any danger as long as I promised I would be on my best behavior.

Mother stood an arm's length distance from me. She held her chin in her hand, her head slightly tilted to one side. Perhaps she too was wondering whether or not I was really her daughter.

As though to fill the space between us, she tried to explain why she'd had to leave. Mother had worked as an energy consultant. She had negotiated contracts with Sweden and Japan, bringing electricity to hundreds of districts in Vietnam. Maybe because she was a small woman, fifty-five kilos and one hundred and sixty centimeters tall, nobody paid attention to her first successes, but before long she became a thorn to corrupt officials who were used to buying defunct equipment, installing useless energy plants, and keeping the money to themselves.

After her business partner got arrested, my mother began to worry about her safety. The possibility of being eliminated or imprisoned on false charges became real. An old colleague who worked for the government warned my mother that complaints about her had reached the Prime Minister's ear. She sought help from a childhood friend who was then a lieutenant in the army. He explained that the President and the Prime Minister disagreed on a number of issues—the President wanting more foreign investors while the Prime Minister would rather pocket the investors' money than work for "a bunch of dogs" who upturned their noses and looked down at Vietnamese people. Mother's childhood friend—the lieutenant—was able to get her a safe place to stay inside a military camp with the condition that she backed the President in the next election. The Prime Minister was unlikely to interfere with the army, which was under the President's command.

I listened without speaking. Though she didn't say it, I felt as though she was unloading information on my seven-year-old self as a way of apologizing for having left our before-home four years ago when I was still wetting my bed. Suddenly, I felt that familiar heat between my legs and had to squeeze them together to keep from peeing in my underwear.

According to Mother, there were other families under protection inside the camp but they were scattered and we wouldn't see them. We went into a room on the ground floor. In the middle of the room was a long, rectangular, wooden table with rounded corners. There were at least fifteen chairs. In the corner was a glass armoire that looked as though it hadn't been opened in years, which displayed delicate china and bottles of alcohol. On the wall facing the door hung a picture of Ho Chi Minh, the colors faded almost to white. Underneath it were his five most famous lessons, which I recognized because my before-school had the same words painted in all classrooms.

My mother sat at the end of the table. Because she hadn't told me to come closer to her, I took a seat four chairs away from her. A layer of fine dust coated the tabletop. I drew a cloud with my finger.

She stood back up and went to the armoire, opened a drawer I hadn't noticed was there, and picked up two cassette tapes. She held one out to me, sticking her finger inside the reel and started to unwind it. "I was going to send them, but the lieutenant told me there was a way to bring you here for a visit." She dropped the tapes in my lap and pressed my temples between her palms, lifting up my face.

During her absence, we had often communicated through recording our voices on tape. Every few months, a soldier would come to my before-home to bring me my mother's words, sometimes on paper, but mostly on cassettes with the sound of waves breaking in the background. Had I actually heard the ocean? Or had I only thought I did because she would vaguely mention a sea, an island . . . At my before-desk, I would listen to her tell me to be good, to listen to my grandfather, to brush my teeth before bed. I would imagine her in a turquoise dress, her features liquid, surfacing and retreating, as constant and elusive as the sea. I had begun to forget what she looked like.

"You can listen to these tapes later, if you like," she said, and closed her eyes for a moment as though to recall her last night at our before-home, "I didn't want to wake you that night, the night I left. I had to go. It was lucky I learned that the Prime Minister's men were coming to arrest me. If that happened, I wouldn't have ever seen you again. I had no choice, I could either accept military protection or be taken from you."

I listened, nodding sporadically to pretend I understood. In reality, her words were jumbled, worse than the bushes of thorns that grew around my before-home. I wanted only to be held, to press my nose in her stomach. She stood up and circled the table, sometimes knocking her knuckles on its surface.

"Please don't give me away again," I said, remembering how frustrated she'd gotten at our before-home whenever she had to spoon-feed me. I would hold the food inside my cheeks, unable to chew while she pushed another spoonful in my mouth and pinched my nose so I would be forced to swallow to breathe. Frequently, I'd throw up my meals and my mother's face would glow red with anger. Once, as she fed me, she'd mumbled repeatedly, *Be better. Why aren't you better? Be better, be better.*

"I'm right here," she said, as though that was enough to erase all the years before. How many nights I'd lain awake, praying for my mother to suddenly materialize beside me. I didn't know what to do now that she was right in front of me. I had the urge to lunge at her, claw at her skin and pull off her flesh to prove she was real.

"I'll be better. I'll be good," I said, "I'll eat my food, I'll—"

"Give you away? I didn't—I did what I had to," she explained. Still I didn't understand what the difference was—when people left you, weren't they also giving you away to the unknown, to a life without them? Suddenly, Mother's voice grew quiet, "I don't know if I made the right choice. Sometimes, I think I'm caught in a political arena, a man's game, when all I wanted was to bring light to the villagers. Seeing those school girls able to study at night inside their own homes—it felt—important." She covered her face, "They arrest everybody, anyone who tries to do his small part, anyone who's honest about the reality of our country."

"When can we go home?" I said, biting my knuckles.

She sat back down and looked at me oddly, seeming disappointed she didn't have a better audience. "Home?" she said as though it was nothing but a strange sound. "When things calm down and I can work again. You should go wash up. The restroom is over there." She pointed her fingers behind her. It made me sad to realize she would not help me bathe or wrap a towel around me and dry me off. I had no memory of her ever having done so. Why did I yearn for something I had no idea of?

I climbed into the tub. The water came out weak and rusty. I rinsed off quickly. When I was done, I looked for her in the upstairs bedroom. She sat at a small desk, absorbed in reading the pages in front of her. I climbed into the single bed. It creaked.

"Is it sleepy time?" I asked so that she would come to bed with me, but I wasn't sleepy. It was just warmer there.

She didn't answer. She squinted at the loose pages before her—the strings of symbols and letters, the empty spaces between them. I wondered if I stood a chance against these abstractions, if they had wholly seized my mother and if it would be up to me to rescue her, to make her mine again. For now, I was content to watch her—the outline of her body assembling and reassembling, straining to match the one in my memory. Even when my lids grew heavy, I kept my eyes on her as though simply by looking I could make sure she wouldn't disappear.

My own scream, distant and familiar, woke me—shivering in a urine-soaked bed. For the third night in a row, I'd peed myself. My new surroundings—the mildewed walls, the flickering fluorescent bulbs, the sound of Mother moving around in the bathroom—scared me even more than the nightmare had. For a few minutes, I sat sunken into the soiled sheets not knowing what to do, my wet pajamas clinging to my thighs and back. I knew how upset Mother would be, so I looked for ways to hide the evidence.

I jumped off the bed, took off my clothes, balled them

together and shoved them under the bed. Doing this made me feel better. Next, I straightened the blankets to cover up the puddle. When I was done, I thought I should turn on the fan to help everything dry. I was untangling our standing fan's electrical cord when a floral scented steam-cloud from the bathroom overtook the bedroom. Momentarily, the air was laced with both the medicinal smell of my urine and the sweet scent of Mother's shampoo.

Mother was wrapped in a purple bathrobe. Her eyes widened at my naked body. I dropped the fan's cord and resisted jumping from fear when it hit the ground. Since I'd already figured out how to bathe and dress myself at our before-home, she had yet to see me without clothes.

"What are you—" she said, the lines on her face already rearranging to the emotion I'd seen the most often on her since I'd arrived at the camp.

I'd seen so little of my mother's body—always clothed in long dresses, except for her face and hands—that even in a moment of fear, I couldn't help staring at her pale knees, her hairless shins, so different compared to the thick and wiry hair on her head.

"Did you—again?" she said. "My god, how many times do I need to tell you not to drink before bed? Do you want to drive your mother to the grave?" While walking toward me, she asked even more questions I didn't know how to answer. I felt my neck retract into my shoulders like a turtle into his shell. My ears burned because I'd been caught in the middle of fabricating a lie.

The first night at the camp, I'd peed during sleep. Mother was still in bed. When the warm liquid seeped underneath the mattress and spread to her side, she twitched her leg and woke me with a kick. I'd tumbled off the bed and cried myself back to sleep on the ceramic tiles. Mother had left with her laptop and papers. The second night, when the same thing happened—my inability to differentiate between dreams and reality causing me to release my bladder—I'd woken up before Mother. I climbed out of bed and stood in the corner of the room watching her sleep, waiting for the inevitable flutter of the eyelids, recognition. It was the slowest time had ever ticked past. Part me of me had wanted her to wake up sooner so that I wouldn't need to wait in fear, another part prayed she would stay asleep forever. When she realized what I'd done, I received two powerful slaps on each side of my face. "Are you going to remember not to do it again? Are you? Are you?" she'd shouted. I touched my right cheek, remembering the way my skin burned like the inside of my mouth when I accidentally ate a hot pepper—a tingly warmth that took over your whole body. I didn't know what she would do now that the mattress was probably ruined for good.

But as she came toward me, the tension in her shoulders seemed to wane and the fierce blacks in her eyes lightened.

"Come." She reached out, took my fingers in her hand. We walked to the bathroom, where she guided me to sit down on the tub while she ran soap under the faucet. I was amazed—hundreds of tiny, shimmering bubbles spilled from Mother's palm. "Were you having a bad dream?" she asked. I nodded. It was the same dream I'd always had—the one of her leaving, but I didn't tell her this. She dipped her hand in the tub, and then put it over the crown of my head as the water droplets rolled off her fingers, down my forehead, the bridge of my nose. "I'm not going anywhere. I promise," she said as though she'd read my mind.

"Do you want to take a bath too?" I said, squeezing soap in my hand and forming a circle with my fingers. Through the ring, I blew a bubble. It floated to the ceiling, suspended there for half a second before popping out of existence. Mother looked at me, a rare half-smile on her lips, seeing for the first time that I was a child. Her child.

She shook her head, "Already showered, but I'll stay until you're done." In truth, she left soon after, remembering an important phone call she had to make. We would never be this close again—my mother's bare shoulders, my own, our slippery fingers under the perfectly warm water. But I knew then as I would many years later that I was hers and would be hers still, even after she would break her promise and send me away on my own.

2

It was summer and I stayed inside often. After a few weeks at the camp, I grew fond of the slate mansard roofs, just as much as the peeling white walls. As soon as I was inside, I was immediately aware of the moist air. A cool, humid, and moldy smell saturated my lungs. I was fond of the perfume of rotting wood, decomposing bricks and cement, similar to the smell of a dead ant pressed under one's finger. Though there were many windows, Mother had taped newspaper over all of them. No light penetrated the building. The few light fixtures we had didn't work. I stood in the middle of the foyer and called up to my mother, the imprisoned princess.

"Princess, it's time to come out of the dark," I called Mother.

"It's not dark anymore. Our room has a light," she answered from the balcony. She looked over her shoulder to the flickering, bluish fluorescent bulb. "You can do your homework now."

"Will Mr. Soldier tutor me?" I said, still in the coarse and brave voice of a prince.

"I'll ask him. Go study your participe passé." Mother carried a stack of loose papers to bed.

I liked studying a language my mother didn't speak. The front of my notebook was neat, obsessively so. I conjugated verbs, copied passages from French and German philosophers whose names I struggled to pronounce. My mother didn't believe in segregating children and adult books. She assigned me to memorize lengthy passages and poems. Somewhere in my brain, she believed, the letters would cling and make sense when the right opportunities came. It was fine not to understand a word as long as I could say it correctly. Mother used the house phone to call my soldier. Apart from ordering him to do things for her, they didn't talk. I didn't remember her ever having a conversation with anyone.

My soldier came in wearing his full uniform, but without the cap. It was the first time I saw his buzz cut. His face was exposed, his expression more relaxed than the first time we met. I wanted to impress him so I recited from heart a passage from a French novel though I didn't understand a word.

"Good girl." My soldier smiled, amused by my obvious struggle. "But for next time, we'll learn about the laws of physics. That would at least be useful for you to memorize. It's important to understand how the world works," he said.

In the evenings, after my soldier left, Mother taught me. She would invent math problems, vocabulary, and grammar exercises to keep me busy. Unlike at my before-school, history lessons were entirely absent. She told me stories about the United States, France, Russia, everywhere but our own country. She was especially fond of conspiracy theories, suspicions about governments blindsiding their citizens, elaborate plots of murder and embezzlement.

I would sing songs I learned at school, praising young boys' and girls' heroic deeds, but Mother said they were communist propaganda. Vietnam, she said, was built on deceit. Still, I'd memorized one about a delivery boy who had gained the trust of American soldiers. He sold them cigarettes, beer, occasionally Vietnamese sausages. One day, the boy strapped bombs around his scrawny body, went to the American campsite, and blew himself up with the enemies who had let their guard down around a child. At my before-school, teachers heralded the unnamed boy's courage. Imagining the boy's delicate body engulfed in flames was attractive to me. I was a timid child, afraid and easily startled, but I saw myself in him. Big things didn't scare me. In this way I was more like my mother.

My mother began to learn a little French alongside me. There was nothing she couldn't be good at if she tried, she would tell me. Her bloated confidence in her intelligence might have been an attempt to make up for its absence in me. Math was my weakest and her favorite subject. One day, while I was trying to inconspicuously count with my fingers, I felt her frustrated shadow behind me. I barely touched the tips of the other fingers with my thumb when the point of a mechanical pencil jabbed repeatedly at the back of my hand.

"How old are you to still be counting with your fingers?" she screamed.

When I heard the slightest change of pitch in her voice, I shivered, trying to hold back my tears. I knew that seeing me cry would upset her even more. Her anger was like a tumor that grew and grew until it overtook every cell in her body. Every mistake I made, no matter how minor, was an affront to her. The more I cried, the angrier she became. I choked on my sobs, hiccupping between breaths. When her voice cracked from being too loud and sharp, I wondered which one of us was hurting more and why. She kicked the legs of my chair with a strength that shocked me. I tumbled on the floor and crawled away from her toward the leg of the bed.

"Tell me the point of teaching someone with a pig's brains!" She flung my textbook at me. It hit the side of my head. She towered over me, her hands shaking by her sides. She squeezed her fingers into a fist. Seeing me crouched in a corner, she said, "It would be different if your father was alive. I was different. I used to never—" She slammed the bedroom door behind her.

When my mother was a girl, she did not think she would fall in love with a man destined for death. Once I asked how long she was married to my father, and she didn't hesitate, "Five years, four months, eleven days." She remembered him with an impossible clarity, as though he was still with us. She did not tuck their time together away like you might with the things that did not align with your understanding of the universe. He was there in her thoughts as she struggled to survive after his death, as she changed into a woman he wouldn't have loved.

When she was gone for a while and I knew I was safe, I crawled under the desk and scribbled angry, incoherent phrases in French in the back of my notebook. I didn't realize then that learning a new language permanently separated you from yourself so that each version was neither a lie nor a whole truth. French allowed me to avenge myself in a way Vietnamese never could. My handwriting here slanted right. There were no expletives because I didn't know any, but writing the words *nosebleed* or *fingers* would tear into me a rage fresher than any real wound and I would have to hold back the urge to rip up those pages. Eventually, my mother discovered those secret pages. She would learn enough French to decipher something I wrote, a rare, fully formed sentence amidst the trembling words of unexpressed rage. She didn't say much except to let me know she'd seen it. Afterward, I would still sometimes turn to the back of my notebook, comforted by its luring emptiness. I didn't need to put ink onto paper. It was enough to know the words had been there.

I turned off the desk lamp and sat motionless in the darkness. I thought that perhaps if Mother couldn't see or hear me, she would be less furious. I asked myself why she would bring me to the camp if she hated me so much. To keep myself from sobbing out loud, I'd learned to slow down my heartbeats. All you need is to stay as still as possible, pretend your body is hardening into stone. I did my best to hold my breath, inhaled and exhaled so slowly and minimally that it appeared I wasn't breathing. In this way, I willed myself into nonexistence. The molecules of my body split away, tossed into space. Bands of twilight had surged through the front entrance of our building. For a moment, I was one of the shimmering specks of dust, circling and recircling each other, buoyed up in space.

One afternoon, while I was studying on my own, I looked out the front door and saw a face flat against the glass pane. It was the little girl who I saw building columns of bricks the day I arrived. I knew instinctively that she had come to find me, and I regretted that I still had so many writing exercises to do. To my surprise, Mother told me to go see what the little girl wanted. Perhaps my mother felt sorry for me. Not long before that day, she'd caught me talking animatedly to my fingers. We had been living at the encampment for two months. I didn't know I was lonely because loneliness required the experience of having had company and then lost it, or having felt oneself visible amongst others. At my before-school, I'd had difficulty making friends, so being alone at the camp was a relief at first. Here people, uniformed and not, came and went from our building all the time, but they often considered me an extension of my mother and ignored my presence.

I jumped down from my chair and took a manga book with me, thinking that the little girl might want to read together.

She had on yellow pajamas, the same pair I wore to bed at night. Seeing her made me blush, like I was looking at myself sleepwalk in the daylight. Without an exchange of words, it was decided that she would lead and I would follow. She was my age, or a year or two older, and was roaming the camp alone.

"Are soldiers protecting your mom too?" I asked as we walked together.

The little girl picked up a stick and traced a line on the ground as she walked. "My mommy's a thief. She took daddy's money and left us," she said.

"Is your dad a soldier?" I thought every man in the camp must be a soldier.

She shook her head. "He works in the kitchen. Where were you before here?"

"In class. My soldier picked me up at school and brought me to visit Mother."

"Are you going back to school? You should stay," she said.

"I don't know. I want to," I said, excited at the prospect of having a friend.

We walked across the courtyard, past an outdoor public shower where I saw soapy and glistening male bodies for the first time. The men spoke in loud and cheerful voices. They stood legs astride, taking up as much room as possible. Though they were in our full view, they did not glance our way once. I thought that she must have taken that path to impress me.

We ended up behind the barracks, facing a field of young green shoots. The large white sun, unveiled by clouds, was so different from the frothy white winter I read about in the translated Russian and British novels my mother left lying around.

"I planted some sugarcanes in this row here," the little girl said. I envied her the ability to claim something so physical, so real.

"What for?" I asked.

"They feed us, dummy. What else?"

"I've never eaten anything like that," I said.

She plucked a leaf and chewed on it, "No, we don't eat it like this. After harvest, we turn the canes into sugar or juice. A cup of sugar cane juice to cure the summer blues, my father says."

I nodded and pretended to understand. Though I'd seen Mother use sugar for cooking, I didn't know where it came from. I wanted to share my new knowledge with her, but then thought better of it. Mother wouldn't be impressed. She had no use for common things.

"Do you eat cheese or butter?" I asked, recalling a description in a novel that made my mouth water.

"What are they? They sound weird."

"No, they're delicious." I lied. I had not tasted either myself.

We sat down on a dirt platform and were silent. I could tell she was entranced by the sounds of cheese and butter just as I had been when I first learned of them. I decided to tell her about snow.

"If I have extra, I'll bring you some," I said, believing that snow was cold, white fluffs that I could put in a box and she could keep. I imagined packing the snow inside my music box, around the miniature ballet dancer who spun round and round.

"You promise?" she said.

I nodded.

"I'll love you forever!" She got up and tried to lift me into the air.

Because she was so thin, she appeared much taller than me though we were about the same height. She tripped and we both fell with me still in her bony embrace, rolling down the sunbaked ground.

I thought about the little girl day and night. I'd never had a friend like her. It wouldn't be until many years later, when I'd find myself wholly alone again in a different country that I'd meet another like her—a woman who could get me to do anything by simply asking. I sometimes wondered if loneliness was a gift, for it intensified every interaction, every small gesture swollen with meaning. At my before-school, kids had begun to avoid me when I started getting called into the principal's office. Men in different uniforms, sometimes green, sometimes black, questioned them about my mother. The other students took notice that I was no longer hit with a ruler when I said the wrong name or date while reciting a lesson or spanked on the bum with a broom when my grades were a few marks short of the perfect ten. Nobody wanted to have anything to do with the girl whose mother was wanted by the police. I tried desperately to rejoin my classmates by doing things that would get me punished. I pinched my table partner who was assigned to sit with me for the year, dumped my lunch meal into the trash, and stayed up talking during naptime. Nothing worked. My misbehaviors continued to be overlooked and my classmates' feelings of envy and hatred strengthened.

At the camp, there was no teacher, principal's office, or other students. The little girl was not interested in my mother. She was interested in me. I knew I would do anything for her.

I got more scrapes and bruises during the summer months. The scabs kept me busy. In between solving a homework problem and thinking of my before-home—the one with the loudest silence, a chorus of singing crickets instead of the clacking footstep of soldiers walking in unison, and an open road, wet with red mud instead of obstructed underground tunnels—I would pick at the dry skin, lifting it to expose a soft pink and slightly wrinkled layer beneath.

When the little girl and I got tired of throwing rocks into the pond and holding funerals for dead bugs, we sat on top of a dunghill and analyzed our wounds. From the hill, we could look out at the rest of the camp, the communal kitchen where the little girl sometimes worked, the pond behind it, rows of tanks and other vehicles, and further east, an open grass field that the soldiers used for marching and playing soccer. The little girl pulled up her pants and pointed to a small, but deep cut in the space between the ankle and instep of her foot.

"This is from when I lived in a forest of nails with a child kidnapper," she winced as if still in pain from the memory.

Though I knew she was making things up, I could not help feeling frightened. The cut was real. "Where is the forest of nails?"

"Are you serious? Who doesn't know about that forest? Children get kidnapped and taken there all the time." She laughed.

"Tell me about it, please."

"I don't think I should. Don't want to scare you," she said.

"Please," I begged.

"It's what it sounds like. Everything is made out of rusty nails, the trees, the grass, the insects, even the sky. If you're not careful, you'll puncture yourself like I did. I was running." It looked like there was a real tear forming at the edge of her eye. Before I could soothe her, she frowned and looked more angry than sad.

"I'm hungry. Do you have food?" she said.

"Who kidnaps the children? Why?"

"He hides in the dark so you never see his face. He asks us to play games. He's very lonely."

"Oh." That didn't sound terrible to me. A dark forest full of bent nails seemed better than this open, cloudless sky. I swallowed to lessen my thirst. Under a maple tree in front of us, a black dog was vigorously scratching and gnawing on its ribs. I suddenly felt itchy and looked down to find a flea crawling on my collarbone toward my neck. The little girl slapped me hard where the brown speck was.

"Ouch!" I cried.

"It's gone."

"Thanks. I guess." I was irritated and started to climb down the hill.

"Hey! Wait up. Where're you going?"

"Home," I said, knowing I didn't really want to go. As soon as my mother saw me, there would be more homework and more punishment. I pressed the bruise on my thigh from our last study session. It was still tender.

"Want to catch that dog for the kitchen?"

"He probably has rabies."

"Come on," she said. "Let's look for a rope."

"Okay, but promise he won't be killed," I said, knowing I wouldn't protect the poor stray if the little girl really wanted to turn him into dinner.

As the little girl approached, the dog bared its teeth, its gums red and its mouth full of saliva. She slapped the side of its head, left then right. The dog snarled and took a few steps backward. The little girl slowly sidestepped so that the dog was to her left and in one swift motion she climbed behind it and held its body tight between her legs. The dog whimpered when she caught its throat. Then it slipped out from her clutch and snapped its fangs on her wrist.

"Enough! Leave it alone," I pleaded.

The little girl didn't listen. She became as wild and incensed as the beast. She lunged at it, punched its ribs, tore out its hair. The dog bit her where it could reach, but its eyes were wet and a half-growl half-whine escaped its throat. It knew it was losing and wanted mercy. The little girl too used her teeth and bit the dog's stomach. It let out a piercing yelp.

"Stop it!" I yelled. The little girl was finally satisfied. She came toward me, still on all fours, her mouth full of dog's hair, her arms and legs scraped in multiple places, her pupils large and glinting. The dog limped away.

"Let's play a game," she said, spitting out dog's hair.

It was hot. We needed something to do. A purpose. I saw the imbalance in our friendship, seeing how it didn't matter what I meant to the little girl because of how much I already needed her.

We hid in a bush and watched soldiers coil up their ropes. The last man climbed down the wall with surprising speed.

"They're done," the little girl said. I picked dry grass from my hair and followed her. By the time we got there, everyone had gone. I remembered the columns of bricks the little girl was building the first day I came to the camp.

"Where are your bricks?" I looked at the pile of bricks across the courtyard.

"They remove them every morning," she said.

"What were you building?"

"A ship. It had just enough room for me. We can make room for you too."

I was grateful for this offer. "Where do we start?"

"We'll have to start from scratch," she said.

We worked until we were both drenched in sweat. In front of my eyes, the courtyard, the trees, the jeeps blurred together. I tumbled backward. Except for a missing helm, the ship was finished. The little girl called to me from inside it.

"Look out! A lava flood is coming our way. Get in here. Now!" she yelled.

I got to my feet quickly and climbed inside, my heart thumping, my throat dried.

The brick vessel was a turning point in our friendship. My life depended on whatever imagined role the little girl gave me.

After that day, in front of my building, she would leave pieces of clues as to what I was to do that day, where I could find her. If we were to meet at the brick wall, she would leave a broken piece of red clay. For other locations, she drew pictures on paper. Her drawings consisted of single objects, like a green door, colored and shaded with such attention to detail that it came to life on the page. The real doorknob seemed to glow once I found it. I would touch it, satisfied. At first, it took me a long time to translate her pictures to the real map of the camp. Following the clues she gave, the barrack grew larger and larger in my mind, and at the same time, I came to know it better, its secret passages, real and imagined, belonging to us alone.

3

One Saturday evening—I knew it was Saturday because the soldiers had gathered outside to play cards—when the weather had cooled and there was a bit of wind, my mother and I walked along the courtyard. She talked to me about the architectural style of the buildings around us. They were predominantly French colonial—timber frame, wide porches, and thin wooden columns—built during the French occupation. Their design is considered by some to be the best in Vietnam. They were similar in style to the old quarters in Hoi An, which were often used as a prime example for art students, something to model their none on. They attracted many tourists because of their displaced nature, like finding volcanic rocks in lake water, or coal in the mouth of oysters.

"Looking at this now you wouldn't think it was a disastrous time for our country. You would ask why we would drive away the people who gave us something so beautiful," my mother said.

The soldiers hooted and cheered all around the quarters. There were sounds of glasses clinking, dogs barking, and droning of news reports from portable radios. My hands were cold and I wanted to grab my mother's, but I couldn't without calling attention to the fact that I was still a child, too young to understand her words and too insignificant compared to her world. I wanted to prolong that moment when she was speaking to me, only to me. I trailed behind her to make my form disappear or at least fade away.

"In all beauty, there is ugliness and the opposite. Like your father's death," she said. "I would still be a housewife if he were still alive. People ask me why I don't focus on raising you, but they don't understand that our fate is bound up with the fate of our nation. In working towards a better future for our country, I'm working towards a better future for you."

"Thank you, Mother," I barely breathed out the words.

My mother's face radiated with a mixture of hope and conviction. My grandfather, a loyal member of the Communist Party, had saturated Mother with Marxist ideologies since she was a child. As an adult, she tried to fuse Grandfather's lessons with her economic ambitions. Constantly she struggled against the Party's teachings, which prohibited the selling and owning of land. After eighteen years of working for the government, she had left to open her own consulting business and eventually help build energy plants. She found many loopholes in the law—even though land couldn't be sold, there was not yet any restriction against the selling of buildings on that land. She wrote proposals and from different corners of the world foreign investors poured in and energy plants were built. Where money multiplied quickly so did controversy. The American war was still fresh in the Vietnamese national consciousness. People asked why they should sell property to foreigners when the Vietnamese people had fought so hard to get back their land. Still, the projects she proposed found great success.

For my mother, it was a simple equation: people who were starving could now work, get paid, spend the money they earned. It was an effective way to repair the aftermath of war. She had not known a case was being built against her from all sides—elected officials, high-ranking Party members. As a reason for her arrest, she was accused of selling sensitive government information to foreign investors.

My mother told me these things because she didn't know how to talk to children, even her own. It took me years to realize she only understood life as grand virtues she must fulfill, like honor and sacrifice. To my smaller inquiries, like why must we cover the windows with newspapers or why are most vegetables green, she would smile blankly and say nothing. Everything ordinary bored her, including me. She would rush through the daily maintenance of life, cussing at the once-again burnt rice and skipping dinners so she could return to her laptop and papers. Her responsibility as a parent stopped at making sure that I ate and studied. I accepted her discipline head-bowed and listened to her words like a mute would, never asking questions for fear she might think me dumb and unworthy even of the little time she could spare. Sometimes when silence didn't work and she accused me of being stubborn, I would oscillate between *Thank you, Mother* and *I'm sorry, Mother.*

We ended our walk behind a group of soldiers with their heads huddled together, engrossed in the game. They had seen their lieutenant talk to my mother, free of his usually severe composure. They politely greeted her but did not invite us to sit down and join them. My mother made a casual remark to the one with the most money chips in front of him that he would need to treat all of us to a whole roasted pig. He admitted he was getting married soon and everyone bellowed with laughter. The idea of a wedding cheered us all up.

My mother and I walked back to our residence. A large cloud was moving with us, uncovering a stretch of sky pulsing with stars. By the time I finished counting them from memory, I was in bed and falling asleep.

The next morning, I looked for my mother in the kitchen. She had gloves on, perusing a bulk of documents: news clippings, photographs, copies and photocopies of pages, contracts stamped with red and blue seals. One of the photographs showed the face of a man I would meet three years later at Ban Gioc waterfall on the northern Vietnam-China border.

What was it that caused me to commit his face to memory? Was I beginning to develop a concept of human aesthetics and had found his features pleasing? Or was it because he resembled another man—my father? Even though he wasn't, he could have been. Remembrances were like slivers of glass, crystal clear until you picked them up and smudged their surface with your fingerprints.

I chewed my food while reading a list of names written on a small piece of paper, thin and soft from having been folded and unfolded many times. These were the people who had faked contracts, pocketed money that was meant for energy plants. Mother planned to expose them for corruption. I tried to memorize the names because her enemies must be mine too.

My mother had forgotten about the steaming fish and cabbage soup. Her rice bowl was nearly full, resting at the edge of the dining table. I held my bowl at waist level with my back to her. I could not separate the fish meat from its skeleton, and was getting rid of my food in a tall vase in the kitchen's corner.

"I'm finished. Can I leave?" I asked her.

"Mm," she said, biting the end of a pen.

I walked across the corridor to the bedroom. I was in a hurry to get back to my manga book, a story about an American archaeology student who was doing research in Egypt. While excavating a rare stone, she was transported to ancient Egypt where she was immediately worshipped for her golden curls and alabaster skin. The King of Egypt fell in love with her because of her extraordinary intelligence and kindness. The King's sister devised plans to destroy the student so she could marry her brother and take back her rightful place as Queen.

When I got to the bedroom, I couldn't find the book. I thought I had put it on the bedside table, but it was not there. I searched everywhere, under the sofa's seats, in my mother's filing cabinet, in the glass armoire filled with dusty teacups. Panic was rising in me when I saw a plastic case under the bed. It looked like a small valise. I pulled it out and opened it. Inside it was a pistol, all black except for the wooden grip. I took it from its case. It was as heavy as the bricks the little girl and I used to build our ship. I knew what it was. I'd never been close enough to the shooting range to see how it worked, but I'd heard the sound of gunfire, a lot like thunder, which made you feel both scared and brave for being close to it. I thought about taking it to the kitchen and pointing it at my mother, but couldn't predict where that might lead us. I thought instead I could bring the gun in its case to her and show her I'd found it. The result of that, in my mind, felt underwhelming. I thought about hiding it in a different spot, but that too was troubling because the effect might be too damaging if Mother needed it in the future and couldn't find it quickly enough. In the end, I put it back under the bed. For days after, I felt like a keeper of an enormous secret. It made me exhilarated and sad, powerful and lonely.

The camp went black—for a few minutes, nothing stirred. The electricity had gone out. Even the air seemed afraid to flow through the darkness. I was at the kitchen table with Mother, a cold spoon on my tongue. I opened and closed my eyes, but saw no difference, so I kept them closed. Flies buzzed around me louder than ever, smashing their bodies against plated glass windows. Mother moved from cabinet to cabinet, opening and shutting doors and drawers. Finally, she announced, "No candles." I volunteered to go look for my soldier, who I'd come to believe could solve any problem we might have. "That careless kid. He should have thought of it," Mother said, "Nothing. Not even an oil lamp—go." I ran downstairs and out the door, sensing her ballooning irritation.

I figured there were two places my soldier could be, the

cafeteria or the game room. I checked the cafeteria first, but the soldiers must have already finished eating. "Hello," I said to the empty aluminum tables and benches. The tall ceiling must have absorbed my voice so thoroughly that nothing bounced back. "Hello-o-o-o," I said again, imitating the echoes of mountains.

Mother had warned me once to never step foot into the soldiers' game room. A bunch of young men hooting, smoking, spitting tobacco was inappropriate for a young girl like me. I traced my fingers on the building's wall as I came closer to the entrance. The plaque on the door said *Museum*. I leaned the side of my arms against the wooden doors; they gave in easier than I'd expected. Unlike in the dining hall, every sound here had its own mirrored image. On the walls hung a few crooked paintings, though I couldn't make out their details. I walked slowly, going deeper into the museum's maze, following the sounds of dragging slippers and using floating candle flames as my guide without making myself known. I walked by a group of people, huddled on the floor around a pile of cards and crumpled money. They didn't look up or seem to notice me. I listened to the sounds of glass bottles clinking on tiles, men coughing and clearing their throats, mumbled curses, but conversations were sparse, as if everything said in the dark would inevitably be a secret. I crouched down against a column, where on the other side, a group of men—the only group of men—whispered urgently.

"Don't be so damn cheap—get me this round man," someone said.

"Fuck that. No offense, buddy, but you're a losing bet." I recognized my soldier's voice and turned to look, but it was impossible to tell. The little bit of light from a few candle flames was positioned so only their hands and the cards they were holding were lit. The men's faces were in the shadow.

"So, tell me, that woman and her daughter—Momma's a

hottie, eh? How's her pussy?" the man laughed. "Or maybe you prefer the daughter."

Someone chuckled and I knew it was my soldier. The sound of his laughter was unmistakable. My face burned.

"You're disgusting," my soldier said.

"What? You're telling me you've never fancied—"

"I don't really think of her mother that way. She's beautiful, sure, like an antique vase is beautiful, but—"

More laughter. "You fancy some vases man? You shoot your cum in a flower pot?"

"What exactly are you doing for them? What are you protecting them from?" someone else said.

"Does it matter? They could be hiding from anything, a big boss, an ideology. The point is she crossed a line and now she's in trouble. You're not supposed to smudge the lines, not even supposed to go near them. Someone I knew, we used to be close in high school actually, wrote some lyrics and performed them to an audience of thirty people, not even. His father said the cops raided their house, took all of his son's books, and letters, his guitar too. Guess where the musician is now? Dead. Hung himself in jail supposedly. All he did was sing a song."

"Whose side are you on man? We're part of the machine here . . . "

"Not all the parts are loyal to the design, I guess. I'm just doing my job. I don't care if it malfunctions and blows the hell up in my face. Our people are too meek—it's pathetic. You too, with your loud mouth—"

"Watch it, asshole. I can turn you in for this shit."

"You don't have the guts." Bodies shuffled. "Go ahead. Who would you even go to? Report to the wrong authority and it's you with a noose around your neck."

I hugged my knees tighter to my chest.

"Ignore the boy, man. He's in love with an antique vase." The laughter resumed.

I scooted away from the column, my eyes now adjusted to the darkness. When I could see the wooden doors, I stood up, grabbed a candle by someone's knees and ran.

"Hey!" a voice called after me.

I didn't stop. I ran and ran, with the flame pressed to my chest.

As a present for my eighth birthday, Mother allowed me to keep the hen she was supposed to kill for lunch as a pet. The hen was grateful to me, the reason she was spared, so she followed me everywhere. When I went out with the other children and left her behind, she would caw incessantly. And when I sat on a high stool to do my reading, she would flap her wings and shred her feathers all about until I brought her onto my lap. She became quiet then, light, golden, and soft.

Years later, I had to let her go. I remembered when I put her down and watched her strut away to her more genetically similar friends; she bobbed her head and pecked at the smattering of kernels just as energetically as the other chickens. She didn't follow me again after that. Soon, I could no longer pick her out amongst the flock of birds.

On my birthday, the other boys who I hadn't seen again since my first day at the camp suddenly appeared on our building's veranda. The little girl was there too. They must have seen my birthday cake through the opened door because immediately they queued up in a manner not unlike soldiers, arms stiff and pressed against their sides, backs as straight as rulers. My soldier gave them each a slice of cake on paper plates. The little girl ran away, carrying her plate, and the boys swarmed after her like a band of young coyotes. I wondered if they were going to a secret spot the little girl and I had found under the barracks—a gap about one meter tall, one meter wide, and two meters long, used by the French during the war to imprison Vietnamese soldiers whose lives were beneficial enough to keep for ransom. There was no use for it now.

I hesitated at the front door, wishing that they weren't so happy with my birthday cake, wishing all the more that I didn't have one because I knew none of them had ever had a birthday party, let alone a cake. As they pushed past one another out the door, my soldier came in with two other men. One was middle-aged and had on a gray fedora hat, which was similar to my grandfather's, so much so that I started to cry for reasons I had no access to. The other was older, perhaps in his sixties, and had a cane that he didn't use. He leaned it against the wall before sitting down.

"It's a perilous time. Every move is more crucial than ever," he said.

"How much longer?" my mother asked.

"If you leave, there's no guarantee."

"Hold on." My mother interrupted him. She looked at me and pointed her finger toward the front door.

I left to look for the others, curious to know what kind of games I would be joining. I could guess. At that point, we were all fond of war games. The sounds of make-believe machine guns ringing in our ears, the casualties with bright, fresh wounds we smeared on ourselves using hibiscus petals. The sense of being a part of something important excited us to our bones.

That night when the men in hats and coats had gone, the only sound came from behind the cracked open door of my soldier's bedroom, which was to the left of the front entrance. In a few minutes, Mother would call for me to get ready for bed, which meant I could watch her play the game Prince of Persia on her computer. I would not blink as I watched her run yards and yards through the dank tunnels and jump through open-mouthed saws that could hack her body in half, her blood splashed on the stone walls. But I had a little time now to peer inside my soldier's bedroom. He sat on the iron bed, packed with a single straw mat. White, blue, and green light flashed on his face from a small TV. His uniform was neatly folded and placed at the foot of the bed. He wore a thin white t-shirt and striped boxers. His hair looked even darker now that it was wet.

"Hair," I said without meaning to. My mother had dry and coarse hair. I wanted to touch my soldier's. I put the tip of my nose through the crack. "Can I come in?"

He opened the door for me. My hand brushed the seams of his shorts. The fabric was thin. I felt like I could see through him.

"What?" His brows lifted, a smirk flit across his face. "You like soccer?"

I nodded though I didn't really care about soccer and sat down on his bed. I liked the smell of his room, much different than my mother's, which was heavy with a perfume so distilled that made the air taste acidic. The air in here was laced of multiple things, salt, mint soap, one he used to wash his hair, and something else pungent I couldn't identify. I stared at his legs, pale and hairless above the knees.

"Come on!" he shouted and punched the air. The male voice on TV was shouting too. "It's over," my soldier said, and turned off the TV.

"My mom said to get catfish for lunch tomorrow," I said and hated myself for talking about mother. I didn't want my soldier to think about anyone else in that moment.

"Alright. Now get out so I can get some sleep." He lay down on the bed.

"Do you have a girlfriend?" I said.

"Sure. I have lots of girlfriends," he said, his eyes closed.

"You do?" I frowned.

"No, I only have one girlfriend." He blinked drowsily at

me. "Don't ask so many questions or you'll lose your girlfriend's privilege."

I smiled the biggest smile. "Can I sleep here?"

"No," he said, but did not object when I lay down next to him with my shoes still on.

Suddenly, the only sounds left were our breathing. The room throbbed with my heartbeats. I heard him swallow. My back was to him. I stayed like that, my muscles stiff. My elbow itched but I didn't dare move. After a while, the tension exhausted me and I fell asleep.

I felt someone nudging my arm. I opened my eyes.

"Are you alright? Were you having a nightmare?" my soldier said. He looked so full of concern that I started to giggle. "Oh, you were faking it! Enough of this. Go to bed. Your own bed."

"Will you carry me?"

"What did I do to deserve this?" He scooped me up in his arms.

My mother did everything in bed. I would often find her with her back against the wall, her computer on her lap. The TV would be on, a plate of grapes rotting nearby. My mother's skin was pale, paler than people from our part of the world. She was thin, but when I pulled on the skin under her arm, it stretched out long and doughy. When I let go, it would return to before, fit to her small arms. She kept hundreds of books around even though she did not read. I thought it was a tribute to her younger self, a self she believed she still had. Sometimes when her laptop was closed, she'd be reading loose pages that were nothing like the novels or manga I loved. The mere sight of bold headings shrunk my brain to a dot and made me yawn. I crawled onto our bed and pretended the papers spread out everywhere were floating ghosts that would wake, grow bones, skin, and fangs if I as much as grazed their edges.

She was still awake, playing her game. This was my favorite mother, the one who was so focused on bringing the Prince of Persia to his betrothed that she wouldn't look for a reason to yell at me, or worse hit me when her fury called for it. There were thousands of levels in the game, she had told me. She was at an especially difficult part.

"What if we could leave the camp if I won the game?" she said.

I loved what-if games, "What if in real life you could jump through the saws and get home right away. Our before-home. Would you do it?"

"Yes." On the screen, metal spears shot up from the ground.

"What if you had to jump through three of them?"

"I'd do it. I'd do it if we could go home."

"Five?"

"Yes."

We both looked across the room at the windowless wall, or maybe we were really looking at the air in front of us, hoping for some dangers to materialize. A tangible threat we could defeat.

4

Sometimes the little girl and I played in the underground cell. We went there because of the rain. We were walking around the camp when we first heard thunder. I didn't want to go back where I would be yelled at for getting in Mother's way. We ran for a while under the pouring rain, until our clothes glued to our bodies. I saw her small, visible ribs, imagining for a moment that she was only a skeleton. If all her flesh were gone, what would keep her from disappearing?

We lifted the metal door where once long ago a Vietnamese prisoner who was forced to permanently lie on his stomach had a small view of people's feet walking by. On my walks with Mother, we had seen similar cells overgrown with daisies. She'd told me of her uncle who had been kept captive in a similar prison during the French war. When he was released at the end of the war, as he tried to stand, his spine collapsed, unable to hold up the weight of his body.

The little girl and I crawled in side-by-side and lay down on our backs next to each other. I had many things on my mind that I wanted to tell her, but did not have the words for them. I often felt this way and usually hoped that the nameless things would slowly go away. Sometimes they did, but this time I did not want to forget.

"Do you ever dream about something that has already happened?" I asked her.

"No, why should I? That sounds dull," she said. "Dreaming is for what you can't actually do in real life. Last night, a miniature elephant was standing in my palm." She opened her hand so I could see.

"I never had anything like that. No, nothing like that," I said.

"Well, try harder. You can borrow mine to start with. When I go to bed tonight, I'll think really hard of you. You think of me. That way, you can join my dream," she said. "What do you dream about?"

"Always of the same night. Four years before my soldier brought me here." I felt her scoot closer to me, the goose bumps on her skin grazing my own. "That night, I woke up to pee. I saw my mother put on a long green dress. She was in a hurry. She put her fingers on her lips and told me 'shush, go back to sleep,' so I did."

"That's it?"

"When I woke up, she was gone. I'm not sure what actually happened anymore," I said. "I have the same dream so often that—I can't tell. Something changes each time. What she said, how she said it, what she wore."

"You didn't see your mother for four years. That means you were three years old when she left?" She asked. "It's not possible you'd still remember it."

"Does that mean ten years from now I won't remember lying here with you?" I said.

At that moment, I heard the sound of a creature scurrying toward us, probably a mouse. I lifted my head and saw his eyes. Two round, floating beads.

"Stay still." The little girl told me.

We held our breath, our bodies as still as corpses. The mouse ran as far as to almost touch his nose on our toes, but not further. He paused to look at us and went back to the shut-eye darkness.

Someone left a newspaper crossword on the foyer's end table. Upon seeing it, I was immediately seized by the desire to fill in the blanks, to solve the mystery. The questions, though, proved to be enigmatic.

1. What did the Trung sisters die of?
2. The reason princess My Nuong dropped swan feathers and led the enemy to her father, causing the downfall of Vuong dynasty.
3. What is another facet of defeat?

And other similar questions. I tried to recall the history lesson I received at school on the Trung sisters. They were raised in a military town and were the first women warriors in Vietnamese history. I was both fascinated by and anxious about one detail: the elephants they rode to battle. Elephants were slow and cumbersome animals. Even though their appearance was intimidating, getting struck by a single spear was enough to bring them down. Had the sisters always known they were riding to their death? In order to avoid getting captured by Han's army, they drowned themselves in a river.

Legend portrayed these women favorably, from their encouragement of other women to revolt even while pregnant, to their double suicides. The word *suicide* didn't fit the empty grids so I tried to pencil in *honor*, *fear, illness, delusion.* Nothing worked. Then *self-love*, I added at last, which amounted to the right number of squares. But I decided that couldn't be the answer. It was a word I'd seen by chance while flipping through one of Mother's novels. It had jumped out at me amongst the thicket of words. The solutions to two- and three- across also had the same number of empty spaces as one- so I filled in the same answer, partly out of impatience and partly because something else had caught my eye.

On the right column of the page, in small print, was a personal account of an undercover cop who was responsible for tracking down a notorious drug ring. There was little mention of the organization, how he'd infiltrated it, or who would be charged with what crime. Instead, the story focused on three girls, one in particular, who skillfully engaged the cop's attention by accidentally dropping an ice cube between her legs, then opening them to a wide V so he could see her bare skin and nude-colored underwear, damp either from her bodily fluid or the melting ice. A fog-like clarity invaded my mind. I squeezed my legs together and looked around fearfully to make sure I was alone. I scanned the rest of the article, but the words had become a pleasant blur. Leaving the newspaper, I stepped out to the courtyard. The sun was beating down on the building's marble front steps. On the ground several meters away, I spotted the shadow of my soldier approaching. In my mind, he seemed older, but he must have been only in his twenties then.

"I have something for you." He took a ring woven from areca leaves out of his shirt pocket. "I made this," he said and raised it above eye-level, the same way a person would to check the authenticity of a bill. He squinted his eyes as if he expected to see something through the circle.

"Give me your hand," he said.

I spread out my left hand, the one without the chewed up knuckles. He inserted the green band through each finger, but it was too large even for my thumb.

"Hm. Maybe when you're older," he said and put it in his pants' back pocket.

I was going to tell him that he'll probably sit on it and break it but his face had taken on a familiar look, one many others around here also wore, placid and faintly angry. I put my arms around his waist, my nose pressed against his stomach. I felt the heat of the sun burning my scalp and coursing down the rest of my body. My hands, however, remained icy cold. My soldier did nothing, only stood with his arms dangling by his sides. Maybe we both became aware of something then, a small and vague thing, which kept us rooted to our spot, our merged shadows one elongated, shapeless dark.

5

I didn't know how many days, weeks, months, years I'd been at the camp. I'd forgotten to write down a few dates in my notebook and eventually lost track. It felt like two summers had come and gone, but I wasn't sure. Why wasn't I glad? Before coming here I never liked school. You had to memorize equations, poems, whole essays, and recite them in front of the class. For every mistake you made, you would get hit with a wooden rod. I didn't have a precise memory.

"The hypotenuse is the longest side." My soldier pointed to a drawing in my textbook. "The right angle is always ninety degrees."

"How long will we stay here?" I asked, scratching the underside of the table.

"Hmm? You can play after we finish these problems," he said.

"I mean when do I go home? My other home."

"Don't you want to be with your mother?" He looked straight at me. Adults only did this when they were preparing themselves to crush any argument you might come up with.

"Yes, but—"

"Don't you love her?"

"Yes."

"She loves you very much," he said.

"Why are we here? She doesn't have a uniform. Everyone here wears a uniform. My mother doesn't. Why do I do these exercises? I don't get a grade. There are no teachers. I don't have any classmates. When—" My fingers were trembling. I rubbed my knuckles vigorously.

"Your mother is doing important work. You should be proud of her," he said, squatting down so he was at my eye level.

"Do you work with her?" I asked.

"No." He laughed and rubbed my head. "I'm only a soldier. I'm assigned to protect you."

"You wash vegetables. You rent tapes for us to watch."

"I do those things too. I'm here to help."

"To make life easier?" I'd heard this before, maybe from the old man with the cane or the younger one in the fedora hat. Somebody had said to my mother if she needed anything just ask the soldier.

"Exactly." He said.

After the tutoring session, I was afraid to face my mother. I was always afraid to ask too many questions, talk more than I was supposed to. She didn't like talkative people. "Your father was a quiet man," she would tell me with warmth and pride in her voice. I'd been rambling to my soldier. Even though there were many mosquitoes outside, I hid in the sugarcane field until night fell with my chicken clucking softly beside me. My eyelids were swollen with bug bites when I decided to give up.

The smell of fried garlic wafted from the kitchen. My mother was making my favorite dish. Boiled shrimp dipped in a garlic soy sauce.

"Wash your hands," she said.

I put my pet hen on the balcony and gave her a scoop of rice. Maybe my soldier hadn't said anything.

"You need to eat well so you can be strong. You're getting so thin." She made a ring around my wrist with her thumb and forefinger.

"I'm sorry," I said.

"Would you like to go on a trip? There's someone I want

you to meet. A good friend." She peeled a shrimp's head off and gave me the whole shrimp, still juicy.

"Let's see. Maybe we can leave Tuesday. No, I've got to be here then. How about Wednesday? But you need to be healthy. I can't have you getting sick."

I stuffed another shrimp into my already full mouth. My eyes were itching still and now tearing from smoke in the kitchen. A trip! What was a trip like? I pictured being driven in a van with my mother, the wheels rolling on a gravel path and farther away from the electric fence, through which I'd entered on a visit and had stayed.

We watched a boy get bathed in the courtyard. He averted his face from our gaze as his mother ladled water from a bucket and poured it over his head. I wanted to tell the little girl about the trip my mother had promised, but something held me back. It felt as though the more people knew, the more likely the trip would get sabotaged. Even as an adult, I would continue to hold this superstition—the belief that one must never reveal the thing one most hopes for. For the next few days, I suppressed my excitement, even to my mother. I didn't want her to know how much I looked forward to it.

The boy was spitting bubbles and crying because the little girl and I would not stop looking at him. He didn't tell us to go away but only stood there with his hands cupped between his legs while his mother rinsed off his tears with another ladle of cold water. I thought that the little girl needed a wash herself. Recently whenever we met, her face would be streaked with a fine, ashy dust and she would smell like the pond at my before-home where tiny fishes lived with floating plastic bags. She also smelled a little like rust. Her hair was just cut short, while mine was long past my shoulder. I feared she would slowly become a boy and join the other children.

"You're going to leave one day, aren't you?" she said.

"I was just thinking that you were going to leave me." I was surprised.

"I can't ever leave. All I know is how to plant sugarcanes so I'll become a farmer here. My father doesn't teach me words. I don't know if he can read." The browns in her eyes seemed to have lightened. "You—you're special somehow. You'll leave here."

"Don't be stupid." I laughed, but she didn't laugh with me.

"I am stupid," she said.

"I can teach you words. If that's what you want, I'll teach you," I said.

"Can we maybe read those manga you always carry around?"

"Yes, and you can borrow them anytime." I was relieved to see her cheered. Though we had looked at books together, I hadn't noticed I was always the one reading out loud. "What will you do when you grow up?" I asked.

"Tell me yours first," she said.

"A zookeeper," I said. "Or a train conductor. I can check people's tickets and compliment their coats. I'd like to fly an airplane too. Or hunt treasures. Did you know people make shadow puppets for a living? You shine light on the puppets behind a clear screen. I could do that. There are so many things I want to do. What about you?"

"I don't know," she said. Her eyes went dark. "I can't picture anything. I'll be a little girl forever."

6

We got on the ferry, my soldier holding my hand so I would not lose my balance. My mother stood at the other end, leaning over the handrail. The wind and salty air had given her hair more texture, made it wavier. I thought she looked beautiful. She looked the way she'd looked in a photograph she'd taken with my father when they said goodbye on his ship before his month-long journey. Their smiles were lightly touched by sadness, but they still seemed happy. Perhaps, she could feel his touch in the wind. It lifted her hair and stroked her neck.

"Don't ever leave me," I said to my soldier.

He frowned at me without responding. My nose reddened and I could feel warmth rising from my cheeks into my eyes.

"I don't want to lie to you, my little girl, we all must leave each other some day," he said after a while.

"No!"

"As long as you remember me," He pulled me to him and kissed the top of my head.

"I'm going to forget you." I said. "I forget everything. Stupid equations, stupid grammar rules, stupid everything."

"Don't worry." He held my chin and lifted my face. "It's not so easy to forget. Not like you would think."

"What were you like when you were a kid?" I asked.

"When I was your age? Oh, you know, I was the most popular boy in class."

"Really?"

"No." He chuckled, "I didn't like rough games. I was—should I say—sensitive. It's not good for a boy to be too soft." He adjusted the gun on his belt. "I preferred to make things. I would make insects, animals out of leaves, like that ring I made you. It was too big."

"Would we have been friends? Would you have liked me?" I asked.

"Yes, I would. I wish I were much younger or you were older. But then I wouldn't have met you. So things are perfect as they are." He detached my arms from around his waist and leaned on the railing.

We arrived at the island around noon. Women, young and old, were washing clothes, rinsing vegetables on the shore. Naked children ran back and forth between the ocean and sand. Their skin was dark and smooth. I mimicked them and took my shoes off. The islanders looked at us when we passed, but when I looked back, they turned their faces away and resumed emptying buckets of shrimps into shipping containers and rinsing fish blood and guts off the street with a hose. They talked, yelled, and laughed at each other as they worked. Two men on mopeds drove up and asked us where we needed to go.

"The national prison," my soldier said.

"Seventy-five thousand dong. One hundred and fifty round trip," one of the men said.

"Fifty for both mopeds," my soldier said.

The man nodded and pointed his thumb behind him. My mother told me to get on. She got on behind me. My soldier rode with the other man.

The prison's stone wall seemed to have absorbed all natural light. Though the wall was immersed in shadow, it felt warm on my hand. A beggar pushed a wooden stick figure in my palm when I crossed the entrance.

"Anything to help this old body. Please." He fumbled with the hem of my mother's dress. His whole body trembled.

I tried to give back the wooden man, but he waved it away.

"Wouldn't you have better luck at the market? Somewhere with more people?" My mother said as she put a bill in his palm.

"Thank you." He put the money inside his straw hat. "No dear, the market is not such a good place for an old cripple like me. People would walk over me. Don't be offended dear, but visitors here are typically generous. I think it has to do with an exchange of karma. This place reminds them of it."

"I see. How many karma points did I earn?" my mother said.

The old man cleared his throat. I thanked him for the figurine.

At the front desk sat a woman with a bun of silver hair. My soldier told her two names and she flipped open the large book on her table, the only other object there beside a telephone. She scanned the rows of names.

"How are you acquainted with the inmates? Are you family?" she asked, pushing her glasses to the top of her nose bridge. They slid back down to the tip of her nose.

"No." My soldier took a piece of paper from his front pocket. "Here's the permission slip."

The woman eyed the three of us suspiciously. She licked her finger and turned the page. It seemed to pause midair for an eternity.

"Do you have identification?" she said.

My mother gave the woman more papers. Later when I asked my mother why she didn't just give our birth certificates to begin with, she said we should never volunteer information unless asked. If we had given all our cards up front, they might ask for something else we didn't have.

The woman looked back and forth between the documents

and our faces. She frowned, sighed, scratched her arms, and sighed some more. I didn't understand why she found us so irritating. I thought perhaps any company would be better than sitting here alone all day.

"A person like you should be out in the sunshine! This place is depressing," my soldier said to the old woman. I was surprised at his cheerful tone.

The permanent frown on the woman's forehead started to soften. She leaned back in her chair.

"It's a job like any. I help out my daughter-in-law, pay for my grandkids' tuition. It gives me a purpose." She smiled. There were barely any teeth left in her mouth, mostly gums.

"We all need a purpose. It's important what you're doing. Children are our only hope," my soldier said.

"Exactly, exactly. My son is about your age, maybe a little older. He has been here for seven years." Her nose wrinkled. Yellow pus seeped from the corners of her eyes. "He stole from his job. Sold the fish, scallops, shrimp, everything else, at the market. He was so desperate to give us a better life."

"I'm sorry," my soldier said.

"It's alright. I try to see him every other day. I work here after all. There are some benefits. The guards know me."

"You're a good mother. Your son is lucky to have you. So are his wife and kids."

She swatted the air with her hand. "Every mother would do the same. You go on up now. I'll call and tell the guards. Visiting time is limited to thirty minutes, but you take as long as you need."

When we got upstairs, we sat on a bench across from a man in black and white striped pajamas. He had high cheekbones and bluish grey skin, but he did not seem weak or tired. His shoulders were angular and when he moved, the muscles of his arms flexed. His lips were a deep plum color and when he licked them, they became even darker. I did not like the way he smelled but when he smiled at me, I couldn't help but smile back. I wanted him to like me.

"Isn't it my favorite person!" he said to Mother. "Is this your daughter? She's beautiful, just like you."

"Listen to me," my mother squeezed my hand. "This is a very bad man."

"I'm not as bad as all that. I'm only human after all." He winked at me.

"What did you do?" I asked.

"He's ruined thousands of lives. He's the reason our country cannot move forward. There are many more like him. He's part of the reason why you cannot go home," My mother said.

I nodded.

"Your mama thinks she's Mother Theresa." The prisoner laughed. "I lived within the system. I'm not better than it. Sure, I'm corrupt, but at least I'm willing to admit it. Besides, you're essentially committing treason," he added, addressing Mother. "Using military resources to teach your daughter a lesson? Take her somewhere fun. Take her to the beach," he said to Mother, then spat on the floor. I felt a drop on my thigh.

The visiting room smelled damp. Cracks spidered from all four corners of the ceiling. A plastic bucket on the floor collected rain, which dripped from the roof through the ceiling. I imagined the naked children on the beach. They were different from the little girl and I, different from all the children at the camp. They played with the waves, the sun and sand, instead of each other. They had fun together, but didn't need each other.

I listened to the drips of rain as they hit the bucket while my mother and the prisoner talked. I wondered if he found the sounds of falling water comforting or annoying like the tick-tock of a clock. I knew that it was my chance to ask questions of an enemy of Mother's, perhaps my only chance. Mother was too arrested by the man's presence to punish me.

I opened my lips and closed them several times. I wanted to hear him talk more about Mother, to look at his laughing eyes as he mocked her. *I'm a good person*, my mother had often said. *Your mother's a good person*, was what I'd been told repeatedly. A part of me doubted her goodness, thinking only of the blows I'd gotten from her. In front of me was a bad man. What did he think of her?

"Your people are burning car tires at Ban Gioc plant," my mother said. "How creative. Isn't it enough to deprive people of any hope for electricity? You have to poison their air with rubber too." She clasped her hand even tighter around my wrist. My fingers were cold and losing sensation, but I did not dare move.

"Don't make me out to be such pure evil, Mother Theresa. I had nothing to do with that." He combed his long hair back with his fingers. I saw that his nails were long and pointy, like they had been filed. They were milky yellow. "I'm a businessman. We're not so different. Why would I tell anyone to burn car tires? It's not making me any money. Not that it means anything to me. They could be burning corpses for all I care. That would at least be useful. What does the boss say? Why the desperation?" he said.

"For the papers. People were starting to wonder. The turbines were replaced two years ago. You got Mitsubishi the contract. You know it's been ten years," my mother said.

"Yeah, yeah, yeah. They want to know why the factory isn't running, is that it? Car tires. Lots of smoke." He opened his mouth to laugh but little sound came out. I saw dull black molars inside an even darker cave of his mouth.

"Don't you people have any conscience at all?" she shouted. "There are three villages in the surrounding area. You've done enough harm already with that worthless equipment."

"It wasn't my idea."

"Save it." My mother placed a newspaper on the table. She pointed at the date, April 15, 1998. "This was printed one week after the Prime Minister's son came here. Who else would he want to see?"

"That boy is always getting into trouble. He needed some friendly advice." He flicked something from his pinky nail. "I'd do anything to be young again. But please, has your opinion of me sunk so low? I don't work with children. The boy is bored. That's what happens when you have unlimited resources," he winked at me.

My mother crossed and uncrossed her legs.

"I'll put in a word about the tires for old time's sake." He stood up. "I'll keep this meeting between us. You have some nerve coming here," he said, looking from my mother to me. "And please take your girl out. Do something fun. She's paler than a ghost. You've already lost a husband. You don't want to lose your daughter too."

Before my mother could reply, he bent down and said in my ear, "Ask your mother which she would chose: her country or you. She's not doing any of this for you. She does it because power is exhilarating. My old man used to sing the song of sacrifice too." He straightened his back and shook my hand, then he put his arms behind him. One of the guards, who did not look much older than my soldier, around twenty-five years old, came and cuffed the prisoner. After he was behind the closed door, he said loudly so we could all hear, "It's healthy to know the truth. I'm getting more and more fond of it myself."

I waited for Mother to give me a sign, to let me know whether I would be punished for not moving away from the prisoner when he tried to whisper to me. After all, only secrets are whispered, and I didn't pull myself away. I hoped she would slap me so I could cry freely. For a moment, I thought she might when she stood up and stepped away from the bench. She raised her hand, but only to wipe sweat from her brow. I mimicked her and was surprised to find my own temples were damp.

"Have I put your lives at risk? We shouldn't have come—" my soldier said. He'd been standing against the wall behind us all this time.

"He owes me," Mother said. Color was returning to her face. Now that she'd let go of my wrist, I wished she would again hold it.

"There's still someone I need to talk to," she said, looking at the exit. "I'm tired." She took a lipstick from her bag and applied it without a mirror. Magenta.

"We won't be able to come here again for a while," my soldier said, nodding at the guard.

We again took our seats on the bench. After eighty-nine raindrops had collected in the bucket, the guard came back with another man in the same black and white striped pajamas. His face was pockmarked, and he didn't smile when he saw us.

"What are you doing here?" he said.

"This is Minh, a good friend of mine. He's a journalist," Mother said to me.

The man didn't look at me. He wouldn't sit down on the bench opposite us. His body was half turned toward the young guard, his eyes full of reproach as if the guard had plucked him from his comfortable nest for no good reason.

"Don't be so grumpy, " my mother said.

He shrugged his massive shoulders, disproportionate to the rest of his lean body. He sat down.

"Call me Monkey," he said, addressing me for the first time. He was young, nineteen or twenty. His nose bridge was flat and the nostrils flared out. I thought he looked more like a hippo than a monkey.

"Monkey?" I said. "Why?"

My mother laughed a shrill and girlish laugh, one I'd never heard before. She suddenly appeared younger than she was.

"Because he's willing to climb broken branches to get the best fruit. He's one of the bravest writers I've ever known," Mother said.

My head hurt, trying first to picture the man climbing a tree for a fruit, and then trying to understand the meaning of the picture.

"Banana trees aren't very tall. You also can't climb their branches," I said. They laughed. I reddened.

"I just talked to our Prime Minister's right-hand man. He seems relaxed. I'm guessing he won't be here for much longer," Mother said.

"Wish I could say the same," Monkey said.

"I'm working on getting you out of here. Be patient."

"Did you submit my case?"

"Everything in its own time."

"I published that article because you promised they wouldn't go after me. You assured my safety. I'm going to fucking rot in here." He clenched his teeth.

"You're a journalist. I was only asking you to do your job."

"There was plenty of other work. I didn't need that story."

"Don't worry. After you get out, you can go back to pollution and student protests." Mother's eyes twinkled. She knew she'd won the argument.

"If I get out." Monkey's head lowered. He was fingering and pulling on a nail poking out of the wooden table.

"You'll be fine. I just wanted to see you, to let you know we haven't forgotten you. How are you?"

He raised his head. His eyes bulged from his forehead. I'd never seen an adult cry before. I was tapping my foot in excitement.

"I'm dirty all the time," he said. "I can smell my liver, my guts. They stink."

"Minh is dreadfully afraid of germs," Mother said to me. "I'll see what we can do for you. A few mini bottles of shampoos to keep up your personal hygiene? Wouldn't that be nice?"

"Sure . . . "

Mother stood up and pulled on my arms.

"Bye, Monkey," I said as we moved to leave.

It wouldn't be for many years until I understood the lesson Mother wanted me to learn from meeting her friends. Whether or not you were bad or good, you could end up in the same place. Equality is not possible in a one-party government. Unlike what the old beggar believed, nobody was keeping track of karma.

I could see her mood shifting so that by the time we reached the metal gate, she'd lost her birdy voice and her stride was no longer melodic but leaden. When the beggar again pulled on the hem of her dress, she kicked his hand away. For the first time, I noticed the cleanliness of her shoes. Even the heels seemed resistant to dirt. She was angry because she'd told a lie, one she believed was necessary. Monkey would never be free.

Once I breathed the outside air, I realized why I hadn't been afraid inside the prison. Its walls had the same wet and mildewy smell as our house at the camp. Its presence was so full that your lungs grew large with just a shallow breath. Molds are tiny fungi, silent and industrious, working to crumble entire structures no matter how sturdy or looming they may be.

Mother said it was an infinite injustice for a talent like Minh to be kept caged. She spoke passionately about how communism encouraged only mimicry, copies, and how courage wasn't tolerated. Minh was a brave man. I couldn't help but remember that he hadn't been blaming communism for his circumstances; he was blaming my mother. Still I wasn't sorry for him. I liked the bad man better. Minh was an unpleasant person, and it seemed to me, preventing him from being himself was a kind of justice.

After our trip, I never mentioned my before-home to Mother again. The prison had unscrewed my last hold on the memory of a life before the camp. Whenever I tried to recall it, to describe it to myself, it became nothing but a fictionalized place, a haze of words.

7

I found my father's death certificate in between the pages of one of my old manga books, an early issue of *The Queen of Egypt* series. The only reason I had decided to reread it was that the publisher had to delay the translation of the newest issue from Japan that month. Apparently, the government departments of Entertainment and Education were debating the series' ethics. There were many explicit scenes unsuitable for children. The certificate read:

Name: NGUYEN VAN TU

Death: 10 FEBRUARY 1990

Born: 1 OCTOBER 1955

Cause of Death: SHIPWRECK

The certificate was granted eight years later. The paper looked new even with its crease. It couldn't have been there for more than a few days. This was my mother's way of telling me one of our battles was over.

For many years, my father's unacknowledged death had hung over our family. The ship, which was crossing South China Sea on its way to the Philippines, had sunk, taking with it twenty merchants and five hundred tons of cargo. My father, a seasonal worker, was not on the list of those on board. Legally, he had been labeled missing. I took the piece of paper with me and ran out to look for the other children.

One boy was sitting on the veranda in front of quarter B59. I told him to alert the rest of the boys, code 26AD56.

"Woot woot!" He shouted and ran off, his arms pulling on the invisible horn of a train.

I assumed the little girl would be at her apartment. It was lunch break at the camp. It was incredibly hot. Everyone had withdrawn either to the dining area or their own residence. The football field was also empty. I walked under a row of silky oak trees, skipping on shadows of leaves. I made twelve skips consecutively without landing on my heels. By the time I got to her building, I was sweating.

The little girl's place was on the third floor. All the doors to the apartments on the lower floors were open, presumably to let air circulate. I could hear words being exchanged, hushed and unhurried, unlike the boisterous conversations between soldiers. When I reached the little girl's floor, the front door was also cracked slightly open. I pushed it a few centimeters wider and squeezed in. On a metal table by the window were untouched plates of food. They looked different than the things my mother would make. A big fly, the size of the tip of my pinkie, was sitting on the plate of steamed water spinach, cleaning its front legs. I walked to the apartment's bedroom where the door was wide open. The little girl was cradled in her father's lap, his back to the door. Her skinny legs dangled off the bed. Her wide eyes met mine, but for the next few minutes no word was spoken.

"It's alright. You're fine. This is alright," her father said. I wasn't sure whether he was reassuring her or asking a question. His voice sounded sad. His fingers were tracing her inner thigh up and down, then her calves, and her feet. Her toes curled when he touched the bottom of her foot.

Except for her eyes, I couldn't see above her legs. I was suddenly aware of my heart inside my chest. There was that warm sensation again in between my legs. I felt like crying. Since her father hadn't noticed me, I took a few steps backward and stood by the front door.

"Is anyone home?" I said. I didn't know why I hadn't just left. It'd felt too dishonest to pretend I was never there at all. I waited for an acknowledgement.

The little girl's father got up and came out of the room first. She was right behind him. Her cheeks were red and her lower lashes moist. She looked like she'd just woken up.

"She's a little feverish . . . " he said.

"I was just wondering if you want to come with me. Code 26AD56," I murmured to her.

"Can I go now?" She looked up at him.

"Sure. Don't stay out too long," he said.

We met up with the boys under the banyan tree in between building complex A and D, fifty-six steps from a bomb shelter, and twenty-six steps from our other meeting point. The boys were already in a circle. We sat down on a vein of the tree.

"What's the emergency?" the tallest one asked.

I fiddled with the paper, twice folded, now rumpled and sticky with sweat. I could not muster enthusiasm, but was afraid of disappointing them.

"They declared my father dead." I brought out the certificate.

The boys cheered.

The boy who sometimes gave me oranges stood up and pulled my arms. Everyone got up after us, including the little girl.

We jumped up and down in a circle. My father's certificate was passed around and waved in the air like a white flag. It felt special again when it got back to me.

"Yay," the little girl whispered.

"Thanks." I said.

"He looks nice, your father," she said. "Are you mad at me?"

"No. Why would I be?" Not until that moment did I realize I'd been avoiding her eye contact. I smoothed the paper out on the ground and looked at my father's photograph. He was just a stranger. Why did I care what happened to him?

"You should keep this." I handed her the paper.

"Really?"

"Keep it safe for me."

"I'll guard it with my life. I promise," she said.

"No, don't. Do whatever you want with it. Pretend it's yours."

She pinched me hard on the arms.

"Ouch! What was that for?"

"Just making sure you're not dreaming." She smiled. "Look how handsome my father is!" She stared at the photo.

I wasn't sure whether or not she was joking, but it didn't bother me. I was only glad to have made her happy, and from a thing as meaningless as that.

8

During Lunar New Year, the adults were drunk on talk of future successes, defeat of old enemies, increase in financial gains, cosmological happiness. Indoors, the light was turned off. Red lanterns in the shapes of dragons, dogs, pigs, lotus flowers, and heroes from popular Chinese dramas created overlapping pools of shadows. I sat on a stool in the kitchen to be close to my soldier. While I watched him, I cracked open roasted pumpkin seeds between my front teeth and saved them in a pyramid-shaped pile next to me so I could eat them all at once. My soldier was hacking a boiled chicken into various parts. On the counter, there were two full plates of more chopped chicken. Another plate had the chickens' entrails, liver, heart, ovaries. I asked him if I could have some rice wine. He nodded, spooned out a scoop of fermented rice from a plastic container and dripped a little liquid on it. I ate it in one bite. He told me to slow down; fermented rice should be taken slowly. I asked for more. He said he didn't want me to get drunk, but gave me a scoop anyway, even bigger than the first.

"I don't feel drunk," I said after finishing it.

"How would you know if you were?" he said.

I went outside like that, not convinced of drunkenness, with a pleasant tingling on the insides of my cheeks and on my tongue. The little girl was in the sugarcane field spinning in circles. When I was near, she collapsed at my feet. It seemed the clouds themselves were casting a lazy violet on the ground beneath us, rather than merely reflecting the moonlight. It was my second Moon Festival at the camp, and I no longer missed the life I had before. It felt as if I'd always been here and always would be.

"Do you want to hear a story?" the little girl asked.

"Sure." We walked through the field, the thin, long leaves of the sugarcane brushing our hair and faces. I dangled my butterfly lantern in front of us. I pretended we needed it to see the path in front of us, but instead of illuminating our way, light from the candle reflected through the red film of the lanterns sliced our features into geometric fragments. "What's that?" I asked, gesturing to the plastic bag the little girl was carrying.

"Oranges. It's my full moon gift from father."

I have always liked the smell of orange. It was the only fruit my mother would peel and feed me herself. I would rest my head on her lap while she dug her fingernails into one and tore off its skin. The bitter and fragrant liquid would splash on my skin, into my eyes, but I didn't complain. Those were the few times I wasn't nervous around her. I remember one night when my mother was feeding me an orange and watching television. *Gone with the Wind* was at the part when a girl stood barefoot inside a barrel of grapes and a boy was kissing up her calf to her inner thigh. I turned my head away to show I wasn't interested in watching, but it didn't matter because the image had imprinted itself onto my mind. Whenever I had the chance to be alone, I would see the girl again, her ankles inked with grape juice. I would rub myself gently at first and then not without my consciously willing it to, my hand would work on its own, slowing and quickening until my whole body broke away like quicksand, until it no longer belonged to me. The fresh scent of citrus made the space between my legs warm.

The little girl began her story, "Once there was a king who was in love with his daughter."

"I've heard this one before. It's boring," I said.

"No you haven't," she said. "He loved her so much that—"

"Tell me something else." I insisted. For some reason I became agitated.

"Once there was a princess who was in love with her father," the little girl began.

"That's the same thing! I don't want to hear it." I walked on ahead of her. When I looked back, she was spinning in circles again, mumbling to herself, *Once there was a king, once there was a girl, once there was a princess.*

I wasn't ready to hear her story that night, or many more nights after that. It wasn't until a year later when we were lying on an oxcart loaded with green stalks of bananas and looking at the faint, dusty sky that she would again try to tell me. We were ten years old. She no longer pretended that her father was a king and she was a princess. She no longer told herself that he did what he did out of love. Many times I'd seen her gestures, her expressions, both the brief and the permanent, and felt as though she was telling me and not telling me at the same time. Her single act of rebellion was denying his existence, refusing to admit she had a father. When asked if she could come to my previous birthdays, she didn't say "I'll ask dad," but simply "I'll see if I can go," as if she were on her own.

Occasionally, though, he would do something to make her happy. Once he gave her a tube of lipstick that had belonged to her mother, whom he claimed had left right after her birth. She cherished it and stayed home for days without going out to play. As a payment for his gift, I thought.

Her undulating between gross submission and rebellion confused me. Did she love him or hate him? When she finally came back to me, she didn't bring the lipstick.

"It's a whore color," she'd told me.

The flaky skin on her lips still had a maroon stain.

Maybe we just got tired of pretending something wasn't there, even though it shrouded everything we touched, followed us wherever we went, and bound us to a contract of silence. Or perhaps she told me word by word what her father did because I'd earned it. I'd been at the camp long enough for her to believe I wasn't leaving her.

The black shadow that had lurked in so many of our early childhood games suddenly had a name. The child kidnapper, the forest full of bent nails, the little girl's cut. On the oxcart, flies and mosquitos were buzzing around us but we were comfortable. We fantasized about how to take revenge. The best we came up with was that lately, he had been complaining about sharp pains in his chest. Maybe she could climb on top and fuck him until his heart gave out.

I pictured myself in this scene often and relished the face I saw when I looked down at him, fat and filled with blood. I became the little girl, driven with purpose but emptied of feelings. I could not separate myself from her. Her nightmare became my fantasy. Her fury flowed out of me wet and sticky. The spasms that coursed through me were as much mine as they were hers. The only difference between us was that the subject of her inner life was singular, pointed, obsessive, but I did not know who or what I loved and hated with mirrored intensity. My chest contracted painfully from violent emotions and I didn't know why.

These kinds of fantasies occurred more and more frequently, and I resisted them less and less. Never did I picture my own father in these sexual dreams. Only the idea of one.

One Friday, the soldiers didn't have rock climbing practice, instead they were in the adjacent yard striking blocks of bricks with bare hands, so the little girl and I had the space in front of the rock wall to ourselves. I had already started assembling our ship out of bricks when the little girl came.

By then, I had mastered the design, and so did it listlessly. I decided to expand the ship, adding a room for the little girl's imagined elephant, an animal she told me she often dreamed about. Having listened to her describe her dreams in lucid detail so many times, I'd begun dreaming about her elephant too. When I told her this, she said she'd sent him to me. I leaned on the deck of our ship, pretending I was looking out at the ocean. As if she could read my mind, the little girl said, "It's so stormy out there, captain. What if we sink?"

"I'm not captain," I said. Though I wanted to play what-if, that idea didn't rouse me out of my lethargy.

"Yeah, you are. You're your father the captain and I'm your mother."

This suggestion startled and excited me. I said dramatically, "My love, what should I do? I'm afraid to die—"

"Oh, but you're already dead," she said. This made us crack up in hysterical laughter. "It's me who must leave this world behind to join you. Throw me overboard!"

I threw myself toward her, our chests bumping together.

"I'm afraid I can't, dearest. I'm nothing but a—ghost," I said, raising both hands to convince her I was transparent, which was what I assumed ghosts to be.

The little girl sighed, "Must I do this alone?" She climbed on top of the deck, steadying herself as if against a strong wind. "If I must, to be with you again," she muttered and leapt forward, floundering her arms for seconds in the air like a bird with broken wings about to crash. I gasped at her landing on the concrete with a thud, her elbows bleeding. In our what-if games, she would always act as though everything we said and imagined would materialize and threw herself into her role without regard to the consequences. I climbed out of the ship and went over to her.

"Are you okay?" I said.

She grinned and continued at an attempt to lick her elbow with her tongue. When that failed, she lay down on her back.

"Where is the ocean, do you know?" she asked.

"I'm not sure, but when I went to the prison—"

"I wish we could go there together some day."

I nodded and took her elbow up to my lips and licked it. A moment passed. She stood up and began removing the bricks from our structure. She started at the hull, pulling out the blocks one by one. The ship looked wrecked—silently—as though it'd yielded against an invisible boulder. The little girl continued to take away the bricks methodically and so quickly that in seconds the whole thing seemed to have vanished before my eyes.

I was old enough to be at the shooting range. I stood behind my soldier, aiming at a cardboard human with my pointer finger when my underwear suddenly erupted with a thick fluid. I was embarrassed and unsure at first if I'd peed myself.

My soldier had recently started to tell me about an old girlfriend who was studying in New York. She was a brilliant chemistry student. At first, he'd calculated all the ways to join her. They wrote each other letters for a year. Sometimes she would send him postcards with pictures of the city. Like in many long distance relationships, when his life no longer compared to or reflected hers, they stopped talking. She'd faded from his mind, but the picture of glass towers floating on equally glassy water remained.

"Everybody dreams about New York in one way or another," my soldier said while checking the remaining bullets in his gun's chamber. Even if he thinks he's not, he is."

I mimicked his movement with an invisible gun.

"Or maybe it's that everybody dreams about the United States," he continued, and made three continuous shots, two of which landed dead center, and one of which could not be found.

I started to hear about the United States more and more frequently in conversation. It was a place that contained equality, opportunities, dreams, elections. Adults spoke of this country as if it were a temple made of money, money plastered to walls, money floor, money roof. Sacrosanct and exclusive.

"Want to try?" My soldier said. "With a real gun?"

I nodded. The feeling in between my legs was suddenly overwhelming, more than ever before. I was sure I hadn't peed myself because it felt thick, almost solid. I moved behind the yellow tape and squeezed my legs together. Before my soldier could show me what to do, I squeezed the trigger. The bullet left its chamber and I was propelled backward, unprepared for the reverse force. I dropped the gun; it landed on the ground. I crouched down and covered my head with my arms. My soldier bent down next to me.

"Hey," he whispered. "It's okay."

I opened my eyes slightly to peer at him over the nook of my elbow.

"You might not remember, but outside our camp—out there, there is no soldier, no gun, no shooting range."

"What do people do?" I said.

"Go dancing."

When we left the shooting range, I ran into a bush, pulled down my skirt, and squatted. My inner thighs were stained, evenly on both sides, as if someone had dipped a brush in a pinkish red and painted two leaves there. I liked that I'd begun to change colors and liked even more that the color was red. Once I got home, I planned to scoop out some of the substance and put it in a jar so I could show the little girl. I didn't want her to have any reason to call me a liar and I wasn't sure how long red would stay.

"Your bathroom guard needs to go too!" my soldier called.

"Coming!"

When I came out, his face was turned away toward the sun.

"You're getting too old to make me wait like this," he said.

"I'll tell you my color later, but not now," I said. "It's a secret. Not until the little girl knows first."

"Don't worry about me. I've got too many secrets to keep already."

My soldier took me to buy a bra. He said my mother was waiting for an important phone call. I thought Mother was just uncomfortable around me. Ever since I got my period, she wouldn't look at me. The sight of my blood, menstrual or not, had always disgusted her. Once when I fell while running with a ceramic bowl in my hand, a small piece of the broken bowl pierced my knee. I went to Mother for help. She looked at the syrupy liquid streaming down my shin in a single line and grimaced. She ordered me to remove the shard, wash my wound, and cover it with a bandage. While I followed her directions, she stood in the corner of the kitchen with her arms crossed. After that, I took care not to let her see anything that might come out of me.

I'd forgotten to take out the trash one day and I believed she'd found crumpled, stained toilet paper in the wastebasket, though she didn't say anything to me. Soon afterward, my soldier announced we were going on an outing.

"I'm going to miss you," my soldier said. We had been driving for some time.

"Why? Where are you going?"

"I'm not going anywhere, but you'll go far away. Very far away. A place where you can have a future."

"Where?" I said.

"All the women I love leave for New York," he said.

"You'll come with me then. Who's going to protect me?" I said.

"Your mother will arrange it. You'll be safe there; you won't need me. She needs to work and you need to go back to school. It's unrealistic to go on like this."

We got out of the car. Around me, the market bustled with vibrant colors. My vision went blurry. At the camp, everything was gray. Mother too was losing color. Recently, she'd become black and white whenever I looked at her. We went to a stall full of small, lacy things where a woman sat with her legs wide open. A small square of fabric at her crotch was different than the rest of her pants. It looked like it had been recently stitched on. Tall stacks of clothes still wrapped in plastic encircled her.

"What do you need, baby?" She addressed my soldier in the pronoun reserved for older men or a boyfriend, even though she was clearly older than him. I hissed at her under my breath.

"What you need? I've got everything," she said.

"Tell her," my soldier said to me.

"Um. A bra?" I said. My soldier had told me what to ask for in the car.

She laughed, "You little thing? Something without a wire, that's what you need. You don't want a wire at your age. Messes everything up." She stood up and looked around, stuck her hand under a seemingly random tower of things and pulled out a single bra, miraculously the only object not wrapped in plastic. My cheeks were hot. I snatched it from her.

"This is a job for a mother, no? What's a young, handsome lad like you doing here?"

"Just doing my job." My soldier squeezed my shoulder. I didn't like hearing that I was a mere responsibility to him. I swore to myself I wouldn't speak to him on the ride back. "Let's take seven of those. One for each day of the week?" he looked at me and raised his brows.

"She should try it on first." The woman pulled a sheet full of holes from underneath her. "Come on girl. I'll cover you."

I went around the display to her side. I didn't like anything about what was happening. The little girl was older than me and she never wore anything underneath her shirt. What would she say when she saw me with a bra? I was sure she would make fun of me. The woman giggled as I took off my shirt. I could feel her stare on my back.

"Oh my, you young, beautiful brat. How smooth is your skin!"

I struggled to figure out the bra's mechanism. None of it made sense. The woman called my soldier over and ordered him to hold up the curtain. He did so, craning his neck as far as possible in the other direction. She put the bra on me, snapped on something at the back. It poked my skin. I turned around. There was a lot of extra fabric in the front. She pulled on one of the cups and accidentally pinched my nipple. I yelped. My breasts suddenly felt as if hundreds of ants were crawling inside.

"You'll grow into it just fine." She laughed. I decided then that I didn't like people who laughed a lot.

Neither of us said anything as we made our way to the car. Once we were inside, my soldier gave me the bag of seven bras. I put my hand in it and fingered the soft fabric. If the woman was right and I grew into them, maybe I would like them better.

"Can we please stay out longer?" I asked from the backseat.

"We have to go back."

"I know, just not yet."

My soldier looked at me through the rearview mirror.

"You liked trying on new clothes that much?"

"No . . . "

"Since when did you learn to demand things?"

He didn't sound pleased, but I noticed the car decreasing in speed.

We drove past a pond. My eyes followed a line of ducks crossing the water to the other side. When we were farther ahead, they became a blurry, silky sweep of yellow between the sky and muddy earth.

We stopped in front of a shack that was held up by a few bamboo sticks. Inside, where sunlight didn't reach, I saw silhouettes of three or four figures. Out front, a boy who looked my age was sitting on the arm of a plastic chair. His face was dirty, his lips dry and chalky.

"Dropping something off," my soldier said to the boy.

"No kids," the boy said.

My soldier smacked him on the side of his head. The boy half grinned half winced. I was afraid of looking at him in the eye. He seemed to know much more than I about the world of my soldier, the world outside the camp. The boy was also a piece of this world. I'd never felt ashamed of being a kid till then.

Inside, the shack was bigger than I thought. There were bricks everywhere, both whole and broken, as if the shack was raised on top of a home struck by the monsoon. The silhouettes whispered as we approached.

"In your proper attire today, huh?" somebody said.

The shadows giggled. The giggles sounded more tired than cheerful.

My soldier handed one of the silhouettes a bag I hadn't noticed he was carrying. It looked ordinary, a heavy weight at the bottom. I couldn't see the face of the figure, except for her thin legs, scraped and bruised. Her shoes didn't match, though they showed the effort of having had someone force them to. Both were high heels. The woman put her hand into the bag and scooped up a handful of the contents inside. Some fell on the ground.

"Careful!" Someone else said.

I knelt down and picked up the droppings. Rice. Long white grains.

"Thank you," the woman said to my soldier. She glanced at

me and for a split second seemed like she was going to kneel down and help, but changed her mind.

"Can I have a glass of water?" my soldier said.

Nobody answered, so we left.

My eyes took some time to readjust to the sun. I already wanted to go back inside the shack, to look again at the women silently buzzing around my soldier as though he were nectar and they bees. I regretted my earlier restrain from touching one of the women's legs to make sure she was a real person.

"Can you keep a secret?" my soldier asked.

"Who are they?" I said.

"Can you keep a secret?"

I nodded. The only person I would tell was the little girl, who I didn't consider to be outside of myself. I nodded again more vigorously. But my soldier didn't say anymore until I could see the gate to our camp in the distance.

"Keep this between us, will you?" he said.

"Keep what?"

"Never mind," he said.

"Which one of them is your girlfriend?" I asked.

"None of them."

"Which one?"

He turned and looked at me. "All of them. They keep me company when I'm lonely. It gets that way inside the camp. They don't want any money. I just bring gifts."

"Rice?" I said.

"They have nothing."

I tried to picture my soldier holding hands with the silhouettes, forming a circle. I blinked.

"It's adult loneliness. You'll understand when you're older," he said.

9

We started to plan our escape. Exactly what prompted our decision, I wasn't sure, only we didn't like that the old black and blues on our bodies didn't fade completely before new ones were pressed on top of them. We started to fear that if we stayed, our skin would eventually turn a dark purple, an ill-fitting shade for us both. Boyfriends would be nearly impossible then. The beatings, different in the way they were administered and in the reasons why, looked the same on our skin.

After having gone out with my soldier, I confirmed to the little girl that our camp wasn't completely isolated. When we broke out of the camp, we would follow the river upstream to town. There was a market and a shack with a mean boy as a guard. I didn't think he would let us stay there. We would have to beg or sell lottery tickets until we had enough for a bus pass to the city. Unlike in our usual games, we didn't think about the what-ifs, the endless ways we could fail. Failure to make it out of the camp: get caught, get lost, or starve. I feared a great number of things, but voicing them was useless. The little girl was set on leaving.

I didn't tell the little girl what my soldier had said about me moving away, even though it had been on my mind ever since. I had thought myself perfectly content until another option was presented to me. The United States seemed a contradictory place, where a girl my soldier once knew had gone, where he too wanted to go. It was a place that made one person's dream and shattered another's, my soldier had told me. Half of me believed in running away from the camp with the little girl, but the other half wanted to go to New York more than anything.

At the camp, time didn't seem to move forward linearly, instead scattering itself all around us. Everything was horizontal. In the morning, I ate breakfast and studied at my desk. In the evening, I followed the little girl around. At night, I fell asleep next to Mother while she worked on her laptop. I'd forgotten how many birthdays I'd celebrated since I'd been here. I didn't know my age.

All I knew was I didn't want to be a girl forever. I wanted to know the adult loneliness my soldier talked about. There were occasions when he would treat me as an equal, a friend. Unlike Mother, he had never yelled at me or assumed my ignorance. A mutual understanding eclipsed our relationship. I knew he shared with me things he wouldn't talk about to anyone else, even other adults. He valued my intuition. It was a gift, he had said. Though I didn't know what he meant, I promised myself I would nourish and strengthen it.

In New York, I knew from my soldier that there were many tall buildings. One floor added on top of another and the buildings grew vertically until they reached the sky. There would be a sense of time passing.

Though I longed for something new, anything other than the camp, I continued to participate in the little girl's plan. If anything, I was more enthusiastic than before. Usually, it was the little girl who could create anything with her mind. This time it was I who talked wildly about our journey as vagabonds. The knowledge that I didn't have to carry out the plans freed me. It was then that I first became aware of her as an entity outside myself who could be deceived and manipulated.

We were standing in front of the brick wall, where the little girl had waved to me for the first time. We hadn't played this game in a long time—pretend to build our own protected city. That night, we began to stack the bricks in the same way the little girl had shown me when we became friends. I told her the story of the silhouettes again and again, embellishing details and smudging facts. She was captivated. I even suggested that one of these women was her mother.

She bit her lips as she worked. Then she stopped and frowned in a way that made her whole face crumble. When I saw that she was shaking her head, I quickly corrected myself. I didn't want to take it too far.

"Maybe it wasn't her. Could be anyone," I said.

"No, it's her." She shook her head again as if to empty her thoughts.

"What if it's not?" I said.

"I want to see her. I want to go there," she said and sat down on the wall we'd made.

"If that's what you want."

"Will you come with me?" she said, not looking at me.

"Anywhere." I said.

It seemed like the sky could not get any darker, but it did, as if the light was drained out of it. The little girl asked if there were no sun ever again, would I miss it? I told her of course, I would. I would miss anything I couldn't ever have again. We couldn't see well in the sudden blackness so we looked up at the stars. I tried to make out the little girl's face. The sky had wrapped her up in its millions of shimmering lights. I reached out my hand and touched her face. She was as cold as night.

A few months after the shopping trip, Mother showed me a photo of her friend in a newspaper. One side of her face was dented. Where her eye was supposed to be was a smear of skin oozing pus and blood. Her good eye was wide-open, staring right at me. I dropped the newspaper to the ground and ran to the bathroom. I looked in the mirror and pulled on my cheeks. Everything was intact. When I came out, Mother was sitting on the floor, looking at the photo. She tilted her head left and right alternately.

"She used to be my secretary. She was also a talented singer," Mother said. She covered her face. "I hardly recognize her. Come here."

I lay down on the floor and put my head in her lap.

"The article says she was found unconscious on the street. They knew the news would reach me. It's not safe here anymore. I'm making arrangements for you to go to the United States. When it's right, I'll join you."

I started to cry. I was afraid of losing her again. She petted my temple, scratched my back. Her touch felt alien.

"Is she dead?" I asked.

"No. That's the punishment."

On the news, India conducted three atomic tests despite worldwide disapproval. Pakistan responded with five nuclear tests. In the US, Clinton ordered air strikes against Iraq. A gay student was beaten to death. Vietnam dealt with the occasional protests from dissatisfied peasants and non-Party intellectuals. Corruption plagued and inhibited the country's socio-economic advancement. Mother had taught me how to be callused to the tragedies of the world, or at least act as if I was. Nothing seemed important compared to the picture of the young woman, which invaded all aspects of my imagination. Whenever I closed my eyes, everyone I'd ever known had a bloody face, smashed teeth, broken jaw bones that jutted out and then were bent backward by an invisible hand to puncture their throat. Yet danger in my mother's mouth was more like a violent film than anything real. Danger was the idea of running away with the little girl. Danger was the pleasure and shame I felt when my soldier's gaze was on my back the first time I tried on a bra.

Life went on normally while Mother silently searched for ways to send me abroad. I developed an irrepressible rage around animals, who I used to love. I had the urge to grab the necks of stray dogs and squeeze them. I kicked my pet chicken when she tried to get near me so that I wouldn't do worse things to hurt her. I hated anything that was helpless and weaker than myself.

That appetite for physical harm was so strong that I went to the pond one day by myself. It was barely morning. The sun had just broken through the sky. I crept out of bed so that I wouldn't wake Mother. In the foyer, yellow and orange dust pirouetted around in elaborate patterns. I opened the door and left. Overcome by fear and excitement, I'd forgotten to put on shoes. It was better that way. I didn't want anybody to ask where I was going. The pond was north of the community's kitchen and next to the dumpsters. Adults had warned me never to swim there. The water was extremely toxic from years of being the dumpsite for oil and a medley of liquid waste from the kitchen. It was incomprehensible how fish still survived there. Nobody would eat fish from that pond.

I crunched up my pants to above my knees and inched toward the syrupy water. When the water was up to my thigh, I stopped walking. I could feel many fish around my ankles. They were not afraid of me. Maybe if they bit me, I would grow hideous scales on my legs. I reached down to catch them. They were fast, dispersing as soon as my hand shot down into the thick water. I couldn't see anything so I waited until they came back. They always did, circling my legs rapidly. After a while, my whole body was soaked and itchy. Still I didn't catch any fish, but I kept trying, growling to myself. I must have been making noises out loud.

"Hey, kid," someone said.

I didn't know how long he had been standing there by the kitchen's back door. His apron was as ragged as the rest of his clothes. He was smoking a cigarette.

"What are you doing, kid? You won't catch any fish that way." He came toward me and threw his cigarette in the pond.

I'd been caught. I decided that not saying anything would be my best way out.

"I wouldn't recommend eating them either. They'll make you sick. Unless you fry them really well. I mean, you need to fry them down to the bones. Then you can eat them." He bent down and rolled up the cuffs of his pants. "I've been that hungry before. I've been so hungry once I ate a cockroach. I guess these fish can't be any worse."

"You ate cockroaches?" I couldn't help myself.

"Not cockroaches. A cockroach, kid. There's a big difference. Hang on." He scurried off toward the kitchen and came back a few a minutes later with a colander in his hand.

I felt the water beat harder against my waist as he came toward me.

"What did it taste like?"

"Oh, not much really. A bit like licorice." He submerged the metal colander into the water. "Now we wait."

When he pulled the colander out, two little fish were flopping inside. Their bones were visible through their skin.

"What do you want with them?" he said.

"To make them die."

"Kill them you mean. And then cook them?"

"No."

"Listen, I can't take any part in that unless it's for a good cause. If you're not cooking the fish, maybe we can say it's mercy killing, okay? Okay. And it is. God, what a shitty pond. What a shitty life. Let's put them out of their misery."

We dragged ourselves out of the water. I scooped a fish up

inside my palm. It didn't struggle, its heart throbbing lightly against my finger. The man pulled a cigarette from his shirt pocket and lit it. My fingers pressed in slowly against its slippery flesh. I smeared the dead fish on the ground between us. It smelled the way the pond did, but not any different alive than dead.

"Here." He handed me the colander and looked away. I took the other fish and threw it back to the pond.

"One. I only wanted to kill one," I said.

"You only wanted to rescue one," he said.

10

A thin fog had been hanging above us for many days. I raised my finger as high as I could and stirred the air. It felt as though the sky was spinning above me, the tip of my finger at its center. I was wearing a grey dress, one I brought with me to the camp three years ago. It'd risen above my knees, but still fit me otherwise. When it started to rain, I went in the foyer and stood with my nose pressed against the glass door waiting for thunder. Mother had been acting restless and seemed absent. The other day, she had leaned too far out on the balcony, her body draped over it like a blanket. When I asked her what she was doing, she said she was resting.

She was in the kitchen now, a knife in one hand, a white radish in the other. She stood there like a statue, both objects held out in front of her. I moved soundlessly around the kitchen as to not startle her. The clock showed it was past nine and we usually ate at seven. There was already a pan of fried rice and a pot of bone broth on the stove so I served myself. Mother didn't notice. She continued to stare where there was nothing to look at. I had a feeling she was not with me at all. I ate soundlessly and rinsed off my bowl. At the sound of running water, she seemed to come back into her eyes.

"Wash your hands so we can eat," she said.

I did as she told me. I wasn't sure if she would believe me if I told her I'd already eaten. I got out a clean bowl from the cabinet and served myself again.

She sat with me at the table. Her face was pale, blue veins

choked her throat. Seeing her so weakened, I decided to tell the truth. She didn't have the strength to hit me.

"I already ate. Just now, I ate and you were standing at the sink like this," I went over to the sink and imitated her position. It felt strange to say something to my mother instead of reacting to what she said to me.

She looked confused so I acted more dramatically. I slackened my body, grabbed a plate and a spoon at random and held them in front of me. I exaggerated, "You were like this for an hour."

"Does it snow more or rain? You'll need a coat. Dictionary . . . money . . . someone will hold on to it until you turn eighteen," she said absently. "Bandages . . . why you always get hurt, I'll never know. That's silly, I won't pack that since you can buy it at a department store. It's America . . . "

"I already ate. While you were standing—" I continued desperately to get her attention back to the sixty minutes she had lost.

"Your father—if he were alive—wouldn't approve." She put her hands on her knees and stared at her fingernails. "But you're not here, are you? Damn you. I have to take care of everything. I am a mother and a father."

"You were like this." I turned the water on and off. She would not look.

"Last night, I dreamt you found a new young wife. You brought her to me and asked for my approval . . . ridiculous. This girl, this daughter, bound me to you forever, even if you're just a ghost. Send her away, they say, it's for her own good." She paused and looked past me over my shoulders as if addressing someone else in the room, "Will you leave me alone now? I have a lot of work to do."

"Mother—" I said.

"Leave me alone," she said.

I didn't know what to do so I went to bed and switched back and forth from sitting with my back against the wall and lying on my stomach to play with my fingernails. I didn't really want to leave Mother in the kitchen. I was afraid time would slip from her again. If I were not there to catch the seconds that flew past us, they would be lost forever. At the same time I was scared that when she was fully herself again she would yell at me if I didn't go away.

The satin sheets on our bed smelled old, like the armpits of a woman minutes from death. I hated the way the fabric felt on my legs, wrapped around me like giant slithery eels. I kicked and kicked to get it off me, but it clung on, magnetized to the tiny hairs on my legs. I thought about what my soldier had said and what Mother had mumbled incoherently. Maybe I was really going away, but how? With who? Was Mother coming with me? These thoughts overwhelmed me. A small part of me understood that Mother and I were the only unstable elements at the camp. We couldn't stay here forever. We had come from elsewhere and after we came, nothing else had been brought here. We weren't dusty or sand-colored. Water was limited so no one showered every day, but our faces were squeaky clean from frequent scrubbing with soap. While I only studied, the other children at the camp had duties just like adults. They washed dishes, delivered mail, cleaned shoes, and cooked even if they were not tall enough to peer inside the pot they stirred.

The rest of the camp's inhabitants were imbued with a great sense of sacrificial honor, so there was rarely any public complaint. Still, I knew that cries and sufferings hummed on quietly at night. I hadn't seen a smile in a long time. I was always unhappy too, but such sadness had embedded so deeply I didn't see a point in feeling differently. My own smiles would curl awkwardly and writhe like a worm when poked by a dirty stick.

I blamed the weather for my mother's erratic, half-comatose

behavior and my own irritation, along with the malaise of the rest of the camp. Those who remained unchanged by the grey fog were the type who would still mind their dirty underwear if the sky was suddenly bloodied with death. I couldn't sleep. Rolling back and forth in bed didn't help, so I went out.

There were soft murmurs and footsteps heading toward the common hall, where soldiers saluted a photo of Ho Chi Minh every morning. In the thick fog, I couldn't see the people's faces, only their legs, which scrambled forward with more emotions than I could hear from their hushed voices.

"His bunk mate."

"Did he leave . . . "

"No. No note."

"Come on. Let's go."

There was a line of people outside of the common hall, as organized and polite as usual, waiting their turn to see the face of death. Being small, I easily pushed my way to the front. On the walk here, I'd gathered from broken pieces of conversation that a soldier had shot himself that morning. His lieutenant was in the process of determining if it was an accident, but everybody was already sure that it wasn't. Nobody asked why.

There was nothing left to see in the empty hall, except a small hunchback woman carrying a bucket and mopping up the little bit of blood left. People stood by and watched the old lady on her knees push a rag around. Behind me, someone said she must be blind because she kept missing the same spot. I stood there, unable to move, entranced by the silence of the crowd and the squeak squeak sound of the old lady's knees as she crawled round and round. I wondered if she was smelling for blood.

The little girl insisted I had made it all up. She hadn't heard of any soldier who killed himself. If he existed, surely she would have heard of him. It angered me that she couldn't let me have something if she wasn't a part of it. I admitted I had thought of going to get her immediately but I hadn't wanted to miss the scene.

They weren't going to let his body stay like that for long. When she asked if I'd actually seen him, I was compelled to lie and say, yes I saw it, otherwise she would only laugh at me.

"So you saw an old lady clean the floor, she does that every day, so what," she said. I was nearly brought to tears. I didn't know when I was actually leaving, but both Mother and my soldier had made it seem urgent. I didn't want the little girl to think this last thing between us was a lie. I wished that she had been there. I wished she'd heard the whispers, stood in a crowd of people next to me. Of course the adults refused to say anything. They lacked the vocabulary or empathy needed to explain things to children. Adults never wondered how much we knew, only assumed we wouldn't understand. It made sense why they would pretend like it didn't happen. If they acted empathetic, they would reveal that death was in some secret way enticing to them. If they were critical, they would be judged by their neighbors as cold and unfeeling.

I started to doubt myself. The little girl's truth started to become my own. I couldn't dismiss it. If she didn't believe something, I had to question its reality as well. I'd grown dependent on her as a mirror to my happiness and a measure to my suffering. Feelings were not real until she validated them, gave them life. Since she didn't seem interested in the dead soldier, I changed the topic.

"Let's go see your mom soon. I think the sooner the better," I urged.

"Sure." She was unenthusiastic.

"She might not be there forever."

"Where would she go?"

"A different place," I said.

"Where?"

"I don't know, somewhere farther and we won't be able to walk there."

"I can walk anywhere," she said.

"You cannot."

"Yes I can," she said, her face half turned from me.

"Did you already go? You left without me?" I said.

"Don't worry. Even if I get to the tent, she won't be there if you're not," she said.

"What do you mean?"

"Nothing happens in my life if you're not there," she said.

"Would you ever commit suicide?" I asked.

"You're obsessed."

"Would you?" I said.

"I won't, unless you want to. I'm not sure what happens to us after death."

"Nothing. Or maybe we become ghosts. I don't want to be a ghost." I remembered my mother's dream about father.

"Hm."

"Do you think you have to be someone's ghost or can you just be a free ghost?" I said.

"I don't know," she said.

"My father is my mother's ghost, I think. He's always around."

"Then I don't think you can be a free ghost. There's always someone, something you're trying to float around."

"Do you think that soldier's ghost is still here?" I asked. I could feel her glare on me but I couldn't help returning to the same topic. It was so vivid in my mind. I had seen almost nothing, but perhaps that was worse, to see a little instead of all. I imagined the pool of blood growing larger and larger so that eventually the old lady was soaked in it but she wouldn't stop cleaning. She truly believed her cleaning helped. Then I imagined that it was me who was on all fours soaking up blood with a thin rag. I wondered if the old lady had protested when she was told to go clean it up or had she volunteered to? Maybe it made no difference to her.

"I want to be able to haunt people," she said and looked at me. Her facial features were contorted. "If I could have a super power. That's what it would be."

"That's not a super power at all," I said. "Turning invisible, flying—"

She wasn't listening anymore. She spun in small circles around me, pretending to be drifting. "I'll haunt you. I'll haunt you for the rest of your life," she whispered in my ears.

11

Soldiers at the camp started to talk to me. That morning in the bathroom mirror, I noticed for the first time that I was nearly as tall as my mother. I put on the old dress I'd brought to the camp; its hem was high on my upper thighs. I went to the kitchen. On the table was a single slice of cake with yellow candles shaped in the numbers one and two on top. I was twelve and was glad there would be no birthday party.

As I walked around the camp, men called after me. Their words, which I didn't fully understand, were like arrows flying at me from all directions. I felt exposed and ashamed. One soldier waved for me to come closer. He was the only one standing in a group of men sitting with heads huddled together. As I walked toward them, I saw they were playing cards. The standing one fanned out the cards for me look at.

"What should I do next, baby-face?"

I mumbled a non-reply. Among the cards, he had three aces, a good hand if he played it correctly. My heart was beating hard. I was close enough to smell the smoke rising from his pores.

"Blow on it," he put the cards to my mouth.

I shook my head. Fear had clogged my throat.

"Come on, blow for me baby," he nudged my elbow. "I need a virgin's luck. You are, aren't you?"

He looked at the other men. Their eyes met and they roared with laughter. One of the man said, "Girls are monsters these days. Don't underestimate her."

"Not a chance. You know who her mother is, don't you?" someone else said.

"I don't care who her mother is. She can blow me too," the one standing said. This remark was met with thunderous laughter.

"Alright, alright, settle down boys. Leave the girl alone," a man with a cut on his lower lip said.

"You know I'm just teasing. I have great respect for the lieutenant and for your mother," the one standing said. "Now get out of here."

Before I could turn away, he had slipped a hand under my dress and pinched me on the space between my buttock and inner thigh.

I ran until I was out of their sight. Then I walked to the little girl's apartment. I needed to tell her about the blend of guilt, shame, and pleasure that were congested in my chest. Out of habit I pushed the door open without knocking. Her father was sitting naked on a chair facing the door, his legs spread open. He did not seem startled at my presence. He said hello to me while continuing to stroke his large and swollen penis, slightly curved toward his stomach.

"She's not here. She's helping in the kitchen today," he said. His hand went up and down steadily between his legs.

I said nothing. I was not able to open my mouth or move my feet. He stood up and went past me to close the door. I heard the lock click. Then he took my hand and guided me toward the bedroom.

"Are you alright? You seem a little flustered," he said gently. "You want some water? Here, sit down."

I nodded. He went away and brought back a glass of water. He sat down next to me, held the nape of my neck, and put the glass to my lips.

"Drink," he said.

I tried to swallow, but the water poured out too quickly

down my neck. I could feel the front of my dress getting wet, but he did not stop pouring.

"Aw, look at you, you're all wet," he said. "Let me help you." His voice lowered to a whisper. He put a hand on my chest and rubbed the fabric against me. I stared at the apple in his throat as he swallowed. "You were really bad to walk in on me like that. Really bad, you hear me? If your mother knew, she would punish you."

I nodded. He told me to raise my arms so he could remove my dress. He hung the dress over the fan in the corner of the room and told me as soon as it dried I could leave. In one swoop, he picked me up and cradled me inside his arms. I wondered if that was how a baby felt? Then he sat down on the bed and ran his fingers all over my body, from my head to my toes. He kissed my face and licked the tears on my lashes. His hand was inside my underwear.

"Is this alright? Tell me to stop and I will," he said.

No sound would surface from my throat. He rubbed me in circular motion and promised it would soon feel like the best thing that had ever happened to me. I remembered all the dreams I'd had about him. I remembered watching him from behind as he tickled the little girl's toes three years ago. I remembered wishing it would happen to me. Then he placed me on the bed and demanded I lie on my stomach.

"I don't want to hurt you," he said while pulling down my underwear. He put his tongue between my buttocks. Then he stood up and suddenly I felt something hard against me, splitting me in half. I gasped for air and still no sound came out. He breathed heavily.

"Tell me to stop. Just tell me to stop and I will," he said as he pushed into me.

My eyes were wide open but I could not see. In my mind, I looked at the little girl's eyes, wide and rimmed with tears. My own were dry. I bit the knuckle on my thumb to prevent from crying out. I really believed he would stop if I asked. I wanted him to and I didn't, dumbed by a mocking sense of my own power, my ability to stay silent.

Inside me was a shell made out of liquid. The shell opened up when I came near. I climbed into it and as soon as I lay down, the liquid raised itself above me like long branches. They went into my belly button and came out my back, into my eyes, my open mouth. They saturated every open crevice, every pore, until I disappeared, until I was just a pool of water.

When he was done, he dressed himself and gave me my underwear. He looked exhausted and old. White stubble sprinkled his cheeks and throat. I didn't notice before, his ashen skin, his two protruding front teeth, pushing on his bloodless lips, exposing the gum. He was thin, his wrists not much bigger than my own. If my soldier were to fight him, he would die, choking on his own blood. I let myself imagine this for a moment longer. I couldn't control the smirk on my face.

"Liked it, didn't you?" he said, smiling. He played with his fingers like an embarrassed schoolboy. "We could do this again if you want. Anytime you want to."

I didn't move from the bed. I feared that if I stood up, my organs would slip out of me and fall to the floor. He went to the refrigerator, took out a beer.

"Want one?" he asked.

I didn't answer. He brought a can of beer over, opened it, and handed it to me.

"Sorry, I don't have anything better to offer." He sat down on the bed next to me, chugging his beer. I too, sipped on mine, and then spit it back out into the can. He talked about his job, how much he hated cooking, how he couldn't eat when he knew what went on in the kitchen. Cockroaches, mice, rotten meat. He talked about his father, who left him at an orphanage and ran away.

"I knew he was leaving me. I chased him for two blocks," he said. "Then he just turned around and screamed *No.* Was he saying no to me being his son? Or no because it looked so wrong, almost comical, a boy running after his father? I don't know."

He talked till the white sunlight that washed the room glowed a sunset orange.

"You should go before your mom wonders where you are," he said.

It was dry between my legs. I inched myself closer to the edge of the bed and stood up. Nothing came out of me. I pulled my dress off the fan and put it on. He walked me to the door, his hand at the back of my neck.

"Don't worry, I won't tell anyone what you did," he said and gave me a light push out the door.

12

When am I going to America?" I asked Mother. It had been a while since she showed me the photograph of her secretary.

She was sitting on the bed and typing on her laptop. She looked at me as if surprised.

"I didn't know you were so excited to leave," she said and turned her eyes back to the screen.

I stood in the corner of our bedroom trying to find the right words that wouldn't upset her.

"It took time to get your paperwork in order. I just—I wanted to keep you a little longer," she said. "Come here."

I hesitated. Ever since that day with the little girl's father, I had been afraid if I were too close to Mother, she would discover it. She would sense my shame or smell something different on me. I didn't know what she would do if she found out. I thought of the gun under her bed.

"Look at you, you're too grown up to come to me." Like usual, her voice was edged with derision, but this time she also looked hurt. "It'll be a surprise. I know how you like surprises."

My mother was full of half-truths. I thought maybe it wouldn't be long, otherwise she wouldn't have said anything about it at all, yet she refused to give me the exact date. Withholding information was to her a great pleasure.

Just then I heard someone banging on the front door. I went out to the balcony and looked down. As soon as I saw the shoes and cropped boyish hair I knew so well, I ran into the bathroom and shut the door. I could not explain to myself why I didn't want to see the little girl. I sat in the bathtub and allowed my mind to go back to that day at her apartment. It was only a memory now—I could pretend it didn't happen.

Mother didn't move from her bed or ask who it was at the door. She must have seen me out on the balcony and decided I was responsible for the company. For the four years we'd lived at the camp, she had not once asked me about the little girl. She acted as though she didn't see her.

The banging didn't stop. I cupped my hands over my ears and lay flat inside the tub. In my mind, I replayed the moment when I opened the door and saw her father. Small details began to smudge. There were teacups on the table where there were none before. The fan was in the living room instead of the bedroom. The little girl's father was clothed, reading newspapers with legs spread apart. I could see inside his shorts. When I came in, he stood up and asked if I were thirsty.

I fell asleep in the bathtub and woke up to Mother's shadow stretching across my body onto the bathroom's wall. I turned toward the wall to avoid looking at her. Thick strands of black hair were stuck on the ceramic tiles; I twirled the hair around my finger.

"Do you know what time it is? Get up," she said.

I didn't answer her, curling into a ball with my knees to my chin.

"Get up," she repeated and stuck her hand under my forearm to undo me. Though I could feel myself shrinking beneath her shadow, I refused to budge. I wasn't afraid to be yelled at. I didn't care if she hit me. It was the first time I was deliberately defiant toward my mother. This realization made me laugh so hard that I started to hiccup, saliva trickling out the corners of my mouth. This incensed her. She went to the sink, filled a cup with water, and poured it on the side of my head.

As she did everything, she cussed me, herself, our life. Once the cup was empty, she put it down on the rim of the bathtub.

"Stay here all night if you want," she said, turned off the bathroom's light, and left.

I lay motionless in the dark. I was worried that any movement would betray my desire to get out of the tub and obliterated the courage I'd gained. My hair, neck, and shoulders were soaked, but my throat dry. I chewed the knuckles on my fingers and let myself go back inside the little girl's apartment once more. This time, her father didn't acknowledge me when I came in the door. He was asleep on the couch. I took out a razor and stood there waiting until he opened his eyes so he could watch me as I sliced open his stomach. I was still watching his pupils moving from side to side under his eyelids when my soldier came in the bathroom. The warmth of his hand underneath my neck sent a shock through my body. I hadn't realized my teeth were chattering till then. My body slackened, having no urge to resist him and no desire to be anywhere else. He lifted me from the tub and set me down in a sitting position on the damp floor. He wrapped a towel around me and sat down next to me. His own clothes were wet.

"Your mother—"he started to say and then stopped himself as though he could read my mind and knew it wouldn't help me to hear what else Mother had to say. "I can hear the thunder in here. Can you hear it?"

I nodded.

"This is the worst season for soldiers. We still have to practice, still do everything in the pouring rain," he said.

"Did you skip practice to come here?" I asked. I wished we were closer. I wanted to crawl inside my soldier's skin and sleep there.

He shook his head, "I just left early. It's almost eight anyway. Would you like dinner? You must be hungry."

The mention of food made my stomach rumble, but I didn't

want to go outside just yet. I inched closer to my soldier, grabbing the hem of his corduroy jacket.

"Here." He handed me a dense, rectangular block, wrapped in silver. "This will keep you full for days."

The block tasted like a mixture of green beans, soy, and coffee. It was sweet and salty. My teeth ached, trying to bite into it. "Yum," I forced myself to say.

He chuckled, "Soldiers eat these during war time. Imagine being in underground tunnels, listening to the sounds of machine guns firing off, the earth rumbling, and you have been crawling for kilometers—it's very dark underground—just like here. Anything would taste good!"

I finished eating and lay down on his lap. He jerked as though surprised, and then started petting my head, running his fingers though my hair. As I dozed, I heard him say, "Why did you grow up? Why couldn't you stay a child forever."

The next day, the door banging resumed. Like a ghost, the little girl refused to be ignored. I waited for the noise to cease before running downstairs. There was a folded note wedged through the crack under the door. I had been giving her lessons on reading and writing. Still she was more comfortable drawing. The sketch was of two girls, one shorthaired, one longhaired, lying side by side with eyes closed, sharing the same thought bubble. Inside the bubble was an airplane on fire, the only thing colored on the paper. Underneath the picture she'd scribbled *Sorry* the way a blind man might have. Was she apologizing for hijacking my dreams again? She'd always been able to enter my thoughts no matter whether I was awake or sleeping. Perhaps that was how she might have found out I was leaving her, something she'd always told me would happen, and the picture was a warning. Or instead it showed her wish for the plane to crash and for me to never make it to America. I taped the note in my diary where hundreds of her other drawings were. I wrote on the margin of the page, *I don't need you anymore.*

I went out. My hair was caked on one side of my head from sweat and from me chewing on it. I hadn't showered in a few days. A new line was creased on my forehead from frequent frowning. I decided to walk to the pond.

The sun was setting and I expected to be alone. Soldiers were getting ready to go into the common dining area and the higher-ranked officers were with their family.

Two black shadows, one short and the other long, broke the stillness of the land surrounding the pond. Tiny rain drops pricked the surface, forming hundreds of prisms. Paper boats in yellow, green, blue, purple bobbed on the small ripples toward the darker, cooler half of the pond. I walked toward the sound of happy conversation, feeling lonelier than ever.

"I found your friend outside your place. Where were you?" The sound of my soldier's voice rang in my ears. I didn't like seeing him and the little girl together. I'd always thought of them as belonging only to me.

"Sleeping," I said.

The little girl handed me a silver piece of craft paper. "Saved it for you," she said.

"This one is a skilled origamist," my soldier smiled at the little girl.

"You made most of them," she said.

"I helped a little. In my days, we didn't have craft papers. We used banana leaves." My soldier put a paper frog on the pond. In the periphery of my vision, it seemed to hop away and disappear.

"Let's make a mosquito," the little girl said. "What can you make?" She looked at me. I shook my head.

"A pond mosquito? I don't think you need to make a paper one. There are plenty of real ones around here," my soldier said. "How about a square box. I can do that." He picked up a brown piece of paper by his feet and began folding.

They went on talking as though I weren't there, my soldier asking her questions the way he often did me. He always had the ability to make you feel as though nothing stood between you and him, not even air. The little girl was smiling in a way I'd never seen, blushing so that her dark skin looked inflamed.

"Done," my soldier announced. "What do you think?" It was an incredible thing, a box so small he could barely hold it between two fingers. Immediately I wanted to tear it open, to see what it held though I knew better. "Well I have to go now. I'll let you girls be."

Right after my soldier was gone, I started to walk away too. I didn't want to talk to her. My soldier already seemed to like her more than me though he'd never met her before today. The little girl followed behind without speaking. She knew I was angry.

"Stop following me," I said.

"What should I do?" she said.

"Do whatever."

"Do you want to go to the underground jail?" she said.

"No."

"Why not?"

"It's stupid. We don't even fit anymore," I said.

"We fit one at a time. We always have fun there. You can be guard this time and I'll be prisoner," she ran up and walked next to me. Her hair was clean and bouncy, her lips red as if pinched. It was like we'd switched places, me grimy and her glistening. An idea came to me.

"Fine. Let's go," I said.

We didn't hurry our steps though it started to rain harder. The warm water washed away the dirt in my hair, on my face. Streaks of brown ran down my neck. The little girl looked happy. I wondered what reason she had to be so cheerful. We were children of a military camp, we were always going to be. No matter how many places I went to later and how far away, the camp would stay with me. I felt like screaming at her, punching her until she lost the will to play, to invent games for us. That energy was smoldering, stronger than anything I'd ever felt—to shatter the fantasy we'd built together and destroy us both.

A small stream had tunneled its way into the cell. I bent down to look at the floating carcasses of insects, broken pieces of worms, a rat bloated from drowning. I pulled the metal door open.

"Coming?"

The little girl stood a few feet away. There were bags under her eyes, her cheekbones were high, and her lips though thin were sensual. Somehow I didn't notice she'd grown up too. The day we first found the cell four years ago, it'd been raining just like this. That day I saw her ribcage, which looked like toothpicks stacked on top of each other. Her clothes were soaked now just as before, but her ribs were no longer visible. Instead I saw the curves on her body, the nascence of beautiful breasts.

"Can we maybe wait till it stops raining?" she said.

"You're the one who insisted we come here. Get in."

"But—"

I stood up and pretended to walk away.

"Wait." She came toward the opening, sat down with her feet toward the cell and scooted inside. Seeing her half submerged in the filthy drain water made me nauseous. I closed the metal gate, grabbed a tree branch nearby and put it across the space where the bar used to go. She turned around and lay on her stomach. She pushed on the gate.

"Please let me out," she cried. Our game had begun.

"You committed a horrible crime. Do you know what you

did?" I said. There was a sharp, persistent clanging in my ears. I felt as though I could hear the sound of prisoners kicking their feet, dragging their shackles on the concrete.

"I didn't do anything. I swear I'm innocent. Please let me out." She shook the metal bars vigorously. Above us, the sky thundered.

"Why did you let your father do those things to you?" I spoke through the small opening.

"What?"

"Why?" I yelled. I took another branch and hit the metal bars where her fingers were wrapped. She yelped and pulled her hands back.

"My fingers—I think you broke them," she said, the corners of her mouth turning downward.

"Why?" I repeated, unable to control the smirk on my face. I hesitated for a second, told myself that she was lying. I used the branch to hit the metal bars again. She flinched and turned her head sideway.

"I don't know." Were those real tears or game tears? I couldn't tell.

"You wanted him to, didn't you? You seduced him," I said.

"I don't know. Just let me go—"

"Why didn't you tell him to stop? Why didn't you!" I screamed and screamed at her. I told myself I was getting deeper into my role. Then suddenly I saw her, my only friend, my other half, eyes shot red, mouth full of rotten leaves, sunk to her neck in trash and dead animals.

I removed the branch from the lock. "I'm sorry," I barely found enough strength to speak. She crawled out of the cell.

"Look, the fireflies are out," she said as though she hadn't been hurt, as though this was just like any other game. The only sign of her pain was her cupping her one hand in the other. "Let's play something else." She wiped the debris from her face.

"I fucked him too. I don't need you anymore. We're the same now," I said.

She looked at me, grief-stricken. "Do you want to hear a story?" She took my hand. I nodded.

"A long time ago, in the desert of infinite mirrors and shadows," she began, "a pair of twin sisters were on their way to deliver two flames, the purple one for forgetting, and the green one for remembering . . . "

We climbed up the trench as she told the story and walked away from the dark water toward the fluttering lights of fireflies.

A few days later, I saw the little girl with a cast for her right hand. I wanted her to be angry, to trick me into a game in which she could exact revenge, but she seemed to know that not flaunting her broken fingers made me even more ashamed. I followed her around the camp, thinking of ways to make it up to her.

"Do you want candy? I know one of the chefs hides chocolate inside his pillow. I could steal it," I said. I thought of the man who had helped me catch the fish. All I would have to do was ask.

"No, thanks."

"Do you want to get out of here? Let me distract the guards and you can slip under the gate."

She shook her head. "It's not any better out there than it is in here."

"Should we hunt for rabbits?" I asked. I wanted her to know I would break any rule for her.

She looked at me as though she pitied me, then she raised her cast to say that she couldn't catch anything with just one hand.

I was desperate, "Well, do you want to hear a secret?"

At this, she brightened.

"Years ago, I found a case under my mother's bed. It was unlocked so I opened it." I said.

"What was inside?"

"A gun."

"What did you do?"

I scratched my head, "I just put it back. What else can I do?"

"You've got to steal it!" Excitement sprung her up. "You have to."

"For what?"

"Anything! It's a gun—" she floundered for a reason. "For protection."

"But I'm leaving soon. I don't know when exactly, but Mother's been putting things aside—"

"Exactly," she said. "So you can't be punished. You'll already be in America. Give it to me as a gift."

"Alright," I said.

I went home with a slight regret that I'd given away my biggest secret. For all the years at the camp, knowing the location of the gun was a consolation, enough to give me a sense of control, a feeling that I floated above the camp. My mother, my soldier, the little girl, all were impermanent. Destructible.

At the same time, I was relieved that the little girl had asked something of me. I went to the bedroom. Mother wasn't there. All I had to do was grab the case and walk out. I had gone in and out of this bedroom countless times. I convinced myself this wasn't any different.

I knelt beside the bed and looked underneath. The case was there, coated with years of dust. I pulled it out, checked inside; everything was intact. I heard Mother moving around in the kitchen. I snapped the case shut, put it under my arm, sprinted down the stairs, and walked as quickly as I could toward the armory without raising suspicion.

The little girl and I had decided that the utility closet at the armory was the best spot to hide the gun. The arsenal room was always locked and hadn't been cleaned in years. Nobody would need to go into the utility closet. If anyone stopped me on the way there, I could say I'd found the gun somewhere and was bringing it to the armory to return it.

I waited in a nearby bush for the soldier guarding the armory to change shifts, take his lunch, or step away for anything at all. It felt like hours went by as I watched him yawn, scratch, pick his nose, take his gun out of its holster, and put it back. Eventually, he walked behind a copse of trees. I heard him unzip his pants right before I slid through the door. Inside the utility closet, I darted my eyes about to search for the perfect spot. I knew that if I didn't get out soon, I would have to wait a few more hours for another opportunity. In the end, I decided anywhere in the room was good enough, so I put the case on the floor in the corner and stacked a few brooms and mops on top.

The soldier was on his way back as I was leaving.

"Hey!" he shouted.

I ran.

"This is not a place to play hide-and-seek!" He sounded angry but didn't come after me.

I didn't stop running even after I was way out of his sight. Now only the little girl and I knew where the gun was. I was happy, having fulfilled a difficult task. It also helped me look forward to leaving since it was only a matter of time before my mother would discover the case was gone. I didn't wonder what the little girl might do with it, assuming that like me, she only wanted the knowledge of the gun being within reach and that once I was gone, it would be hers alone.

13

The little girl and I decided to burn all the letters we'd written each other, the pictures she drew, the books I read to her. We were happy to have come up with this plan. Since I was leaving the next day, it seemed a monumental gesture that would also protect our secret world. We'd decided to meet at the sugarcane field after dusk to make sure that we would be alone. She had gathered a bundle of branches. I brought matches and gasoline.

We squatted in front of the fire while its shadow danced on our faces. To our left, the sugarcane had grown taller than us, their bundles of long leaves like the hair of a woman rustling in the wind. While the little girl was absorbed in stoking the fire, I secretly tore out a page from my notebook and put it in my pants pocket. It was a drawing she'd given me, a favorite of mine.

Impulsively I threw a match that was almost dead toward the field. Its embers landed on a leaf, glowed briefly, and extinguished. I hurried toward it with a bottle of water just in case. The little girl caught my wrist. She walked toward the field with the gasoline.

"What are you doing?" I asked. She didn't answer. She was consumed by the calmest rage I'd ever seen. She walked methodically down each row, dripping the gasoline alongside her.

"Throw the flame into it," she commanded.

I hurled the lit matches forward with so much energy it

might have been myself burning. Fire, stoked by the wind, licked the field row by row. Smoke rose and formed various black shapes, a large stain in the clear sky above us. The skin on my arms and legs began to warm. For a moment, I couldn't move, spellbound by the blinding blaze, the smell of dying plants filling my nostrils. My leg got caught on an inflamed plant and brought me back to myself. I knew it would hurt much more later, but I couldn't feel the pain yet, my heart and mind racing at the same speed. I brushed my shin where it was burnt and stomped my foot repeatedly.

"Let's go!" I screamed. The little girl was a distance ahead. She turned to look at me, her eyes drilling into me, daring me to stay with her to the end.

Someone screamed *Fire! Fire!* I could hear the footsteps of a crowd approaching. The little girl was still amongst the field and coughing into the inside of her shirt.

"I have to go now," I yelled to her. She said nothing. "I have to go," I yelled again, and turned to run. I ran and ran, as fast as I could, eyes burning with smoke.

As soon as I got back inside my building, I went to the bedroom to change out of my shorts and put on a long skirt to cover my burn, which had already bubbled. In the bathroom, I shakily dabbed cold water on my hot cheeks. I didn't dare check my reflection in the mirror, afraid of any evidence the fire had left on my face, afraid to see the little girl staring back through my own eyes. I tried to tell myself that I had no other choice but to leave her there. In my ears was still the crackling sound of sugarcane stalks.

I left the bathroom to look for Mother in the kitchen. I needed to make sure she wouldn't link me to the commotion going on outside. She was resting her head on the dining table. Beside her was a tape player. Quietly, I pulled out a chair and sat down next to her. Since she didn't react, I assumed she was sleeping. I placed my hand on her back to gently wake her, but she didn't move. Suddenly, I realized that she might be the only person I had left in the world. After tonight, I didn't know what would happen to the little girl.

"Mother, Mother." I shook her more roughly. I was overcome by the dread that I would never see her eyes open again. She stirred and sat up. Her skin under her eyes looked swollen, her lips dry. "I'm sorry, I thought you were dead," I said.

She pulled me into her arms and cried. I couldn't see her face, only felt a slight quiver from her body. Her skin was colder than usual. We stayed like that for a while, the heat from my body passing onto hers and I hoped, stilling her chill.

The smell of beef and spices wafted into my bedroom from the kitchen and woke me up. The bedside clock told me it was two thirty in the morning. At the foot of the bed was a small suitcase and next to it my backpack. I slid off the bed, eyes half open, and walked to the kitchen. There were two pans and two pots on the stove. Mother alternated her stirring between them.

"You're awake," she said. "Good. I was just going to call you. Have some breakfast. You have to leave in two hours."

"In two hours?" I said. I noticed Mother was wearing the same clothes as the night before. She hadn't gone to bed.

"I made your favorite things. There are red beans for dessert—"

"I'm not hungry."

I saw that she was sad so I asked for the sweet beans. Right away, she became lively and added more sugar to the pot. When she gave it to me in a bowl, I stirred it around with a silver spoon. It was still too hot to eat. I put a spoon full in my mouth, scalding my tongue.

"Can I stay?" I asked. I wanted to cry, but no tear would come.

She shook her head. "You need to go to school, have friends and teachers. A normal life."

The camp had erased my memory of my before-home, before-school. I had no concept of normal outside from lessons with my soldier and being with the little girl. America was another abstraction.

"When am I coming back?" I said.

"I'll join you as soon as I can."

"When?"

"Soon."

"Can I say bye to my friend?" I didn't want the little girl to think I'd disappeared during the night to avoid her. I thought about how I'd broken her finger bones from hitting them with a tree branch, how she'd treated me kindly even so. I thought about how she always said I would leave her. The sweet beans tasted like when I'd bite the end of a pen and bitter ink would fill my mouth.

"There's not enough time," Mother said. I heard someone opening the front door. "He's already here."

I got dressed, put a few books in the backpack I came to the camp with. I left the little girl a note on the doorstep with the vague return address of *America*. The black van that had driven me to the camp years ago was parked in front. My soldier was waiting for me in the driver's seat. Mother hustled me into the back of the car. She kissed me before I left.

As soon as the car began to move, I felt a heavy drowsiness and was glad to be lulled to sleep once again.

When I woke up, my soldier told me we weren't far from China's border. Once we got there, someone else would take me to the airport. Years later, I understood that Mother had made sure nobody saw me enter the camp and nobody saw me leave; that the erasure of my records in Vietnam would be complete when I boarded the plane. I didn't answer my soldier. My anger was such that I was afraid if I opened my mouth I would scream. He pretended not to notice my resolved silence and continued to instruct me on what to do at the airport, since I would have to fly alone.

"When you get to New York, someone will be there to pick you up. It's not hard, so don't be scared," he said.

I told myself that once I got to the US, I would turn around, take a different plane back to Vietnam, go get the little girl so we could leave the camp together for good. We'd talked about escaping together so many times that being forced to go without her was unthinkable.

We stopped at a checkpoint. My soldier handed the patrol our passports and some papers. The patrol asked for the back window to be lowered so he could see my face. Afterward, he waved us through. We continued on a stretch of dusty freeway as the only passenger car. Both of the lanes to our left and right were occupied by freight trucks, their surface as gritty as the wind.

After a while, we started down a winding, muddy path. I climbed into the front passenger seat and cracked open the window. The smell of fresh air and water invigorated me. Up ahead in front of a waterfall, I spotted another car. My soldier slowed us down to a halt. He stuck his arm out the window and waved. When we got out, the other man stayed at a distance. My soldier helped me remove my luggage from the backseat. I searched my head for something cruel to say to him for taking me away, but I couldn't hear my own thoughts, only the sound of water cascading down. I was nearly as tall as him, my head where his chin was. There was nothing I could say that would salve how I felt. He opened his arms for a hug. I came close, punched his stomach with all the force I could muster. He stepped back. A gentle look came into his eyes. He held my chin, lifted my face, and pressed his lips on my cheek, the corners of our mouths touching.

"Just in case you forget," he said.

PART 2

1

On a Tuesday at 4:05 P.M. in 2012, I saw him on a subway platform in New York City. I didn't recall his features, but when the stranger looked at me, I turned my head the other way. My soldier, if alive, would be in his late forties or early fifties, I guessed. I could not tell the exact age of the man on the platform. He was heavier than I imagined my soldier might be, his cheeks full and perspiring, yet there was something familiar about him. His skin color was patchy, pale around the jaws and mouth. He'd probably just shaved that morning. When he lifted his chin and looked at the train schedule, he seemed impatiently youthful. On the other hand, his shoulders were relaxed and his legs planted firmly on the ground. He occupied space with the resignation and certitude of a man whose time had passed. I followed him onto the subway car, with the same instinct and privacy of someone recalling a dream. I stood, still with my back to him, and looked at his reflection in the train's window in front of me. I didn't have a lot of time to decide. In a few minutes, we would arrive at the next station. If he got off, what would I do?

Sitting next to him was a young woman with long, slender legs. They reminded me of my own wrists. Her large eyes opened and closed as slowly and gently as the fluttering of insect wings. I thought she and the stranger may make eye contact but they did not. The train pulled to a stop, a shuffle of new bodies came in and replaced those who left. The stranger crossed and uncrossed his arms. He was relaxed and thinking about something more distant than his surroundings in the subway car. The longer I looked at him, the more he began to take the contour of an actual memory. I thought of my soldier and my memory of his face already started to fade—replaced by the stranger's. Two more stations passed. I'd missed my stop, so it felt like something was decided. A voice from the speaker notified the passengers that we were approaching the next station. The stranger had given up his seat and moved to stand in front of the doors. When the subway pulled to a standstill, he got off. I hurried out in front of him and then slowed my steps to let him pass, exit the turnstile, and walk up the stairs to the street.

It was half raining, half snowing outside. My blood had long ago adapted to this cold. The stranger didn't seem comfortable with the weather, bracing himself against the grayness. We walked for a while with a measured pace, and I kept about five feet behind him. When he turned the corner of a bakery, where a Vietnamese couple sometimes gave me French baguettes in exchange for occasional proofreading service, I thought I'd lost him, but the back of his head emerged again in the throng of people coming upstream toward us.

I would have been happy to keep walking behind him, but he eventually stopped in front of a building made of stone slabs, set back into an alleyway. He was looking for the right key on his keychain when I touched him on the elbow.

"Yes?" he said. It was too difficult to detect an accent in so small a sound.

My tongue could not decide what syllables to produce. And in what language? I just stood there, frowning at him.

"Are you okay?" he said.

Too many words.

I walked away. Raindrops had hardened into snowflakes. When did it get all white? I heard him close the door. Perhaps I should have left, but I didn't. From across the street I could see the light switch on in his apartment. He sat down on a sofa and leaned forward, his forearms resting on his knees. He looked like a different man now than the one I saw on the platform. I began to worry whether I'd actually lost him in the crowd and had mistakenly followed another stranger on the street. He looked like any man, tired after a day of work, thinking about what it was he had forgotten to do.

On the wall in my bedroom, hundreds of news articles were pinned—shaped like a reverse S by accident, similar to how Vietnam looked on a map. I laughed at the simplicity of my subconscious. Nobody had ever seen the inside of this room, ribbons of pages torn apart and glued together again, names and phrases highlighted, my own thumbprints smearing the corners of photographs. The thought of someone discovering this wall of haphazard fact-finding about my mother made me feel absurd. It was worse than a shrine a teenager had for his favorite band. Reading about my mother was like getting lost in fiction. It was impossible to tell what was true and what wasn't.

The information consumed me and allowed me momentarily to forget about my own life. Various online news sources gave conflicting information about her. I spent hours looking up words, translating the Vietnamese too sophisticated for my abilities into English and then vice versa, changing the English articles into Vietnamese to see how the words would feel. I tried to cross-check facts, printing them out and adding them to my collection on the wall, but the more I read, the more she became a character in a story, removed from what I remembered of her.

Vietnamese politics were both overly complicated and at the same time banal. People disappeared and, if they were lucky, they might reappear a few years later, hundreds of miles from where they were last seen, with missing fingers, one blind eye, pretending to go on with their lives, or worse—being grateful their country had given them a second chance. I watched video after video of the lucky ones on Vietnam National TV network, men and women apologizing for the lies they had told about the motherland, enunciating every word because their lives depended on it. Their faces were gaunt and sickly, similar to the color of the video's background, which was always the same—white square tiles washed by a bluish light.

For years, I had the habit of keeping up with these videos of the returned and looking at pictures of those who died in mysterious circumstances. I was constantly afraid to find a picture of my mother's face, soft and dented like red clay, her eyes scorched with their last image of violence. I comforted myself with the last word about her from a relative. She had left the camp two years after I did. She was safe. "How?" I'd asked him.

He'd shaken his head, "Sometimes you get lucky and all the people that want you dead are dead."

Mother had not joined me in the US as she said she would when she sent me away when I was thirteen. For five years, before I went to live in a college dorm, I moved from one place to another. I lived with relatives I'd never met as a kid in Vietnam. Once I exhausted their kindness and hospitality, they passed me on to acquaintances of Mother's, including her friends, old teachers, political affiliates, political exiles. Every year, I received a letter from her bearing the same words: *I'll be there soon*. She would not. She was always taken up with a new cause, tangled in a new fight or the same one that shapeshifted into something that looked like her own reflection.

On a Vietnamese newspaper online was a photo of her standing next to the President, his arms around her waist. People gossiped on Internet forums about them having an affair. My heart raced, contemplating the idea that she might have remarried by now and had other children. From oceans away, I watched her rise up the communist ladder. She would chip at the bricks, upset the structure, casually insult the top leaders in government. More people disappeared. Somehow she remained, growing more and more powerful.

A blogger wrote about Mother, "almost mythical . . . an ornament in Parliament." Little by little, she had gone from being in hiding to being in full view on the front pages of most newspapers. She appeared on TV, speaking to the entire country and the forty-five men at the round table whose ties might be too tight, choking them at the throats, leaving them unable to combat my mother's words. Maybe she was merely decorative. Maybe the men were amused. The blogger speculated that my mother was still alive because the country was changing, an optimistic thought, or simply because she was lucky.

A different writer expressed that they didn't think she could survive on luck for long. Something had happened: she'd quoted the American constitution on Lunar New Year during a speech when she was supposed to remind citizens of the Party's legacy. She acted as though she was merely saying it in good spirits, not meaning to offend. But the words were clear, freedom of speech, freedom of the press, freedom of religion, freedom of petition. Those words did not escape even the most insensitive ears. The National Assembly forced her to resign based on charges of dishonesty, citing an incorrect date on the document she'd filed in running for the position of Secretary of Energy. It was small and could have been easily overlooked, except that they were looking for any reason to get rid of her.

She'd taken it too far. Newspapers started to suggest she was an American spy. Family members and friends of hers were brought into the spotlight; their private lives scrutinized and debased. Amongst these lines of journalistic blackmailing, my name was nowhere to be found. When I left Vietnam, my birth certificate was destroyed, my name erased from the record. My mother had no daughter. It was her gift to me.

2

Montauk around January, the beginning of a new year. There were never many people there in winter, and the heavy snow and wind kept the streets of the town even more desolate. I walked from my motel to an Irish bar, the only place open that day. On the window was the sign *Hiring pianist. Must be able to shuck oysters.* There was an older man sitting at the bar, slowly nibbling a fry, his eyes fixed on the TV. The Seahawks against the Redskins. In the back corner, a young couple was drinking soda. I sat down across from them.

"The usual?" The waiter asked.

"Please." I said. I'd only been coming here for three days. In a place where nothing much happened, familiarity was established quickly.

I looked at the woman. Her hair was black and so shiny it was almost reflective, falling over the side of her face and onto the table. She kept pulling it behind her, but it would again curtain her profile as soon as she leaned forward. The more I looked at her, the more it seemed I'd once known her. The man was speaking, periodically putting his whole weight on the edge of the table, or, pressing his back against the chair to lean away as far as possible. He looked as if he was trying both to engage the woman and to distance himself from the things she said, which he seemed to find painful.

The waiter returned with my eggs and sausage gravy. He went over to the couple, nodded to them, and left. The man talked animatedly for a few more minutes while the woman opened and closed her eyes. A small branch hit the window to the man's right. The woman's eyes lingered on the window long after the wind blew the branch away. The man stood up, removed his knit hat, and sat back down. He said something, to which the young woman put her fingers over her lips and started biting them. When he stood up the second time, he put on his hat and walked out.

I put some cash on the table and was getting ready to leave myself. I wanted to get to the harbor before sunset.

"Excuse me," the young woman was standing in front of me. "I'm sorry to bother you. I don't have my wallet. My husband—he just left."

"Are you alright?" I said.

"I'm really sorry," she said. Water pooled into her eyes. "It's a few dollars for the drinks, but I haven't got it."

"Don't worry." I said, taking out a few more bills from my wallet. "Sit down if you like. I was just leaving but we could stay," I offered. I didn't want to see her cry. I wouldn't know what to do with her tears.

She pulled a chair out and fell into it, as if she'd lost control of her weight.

"Where are you going? In this weather?" she asked. Her face was bright again. Had I been imagining a grief-stricken woman?

"Just to the harbor."

"I've never seen the ocean in a snow storm," she said, her eyes searching mine, as if she could see snow falling inside my pupils.

"I don't think I have either."

"Can I come with you?"

"What about your husband?" I asked.

"He's fine. He's watching a movie right now, I'll bet. Our motel has some old VHS tapes: *Dances with Wolves*, *Forrest*

Gump, other stuff. Can you believe it? A tape player . . . " Her voice trailed off. Outside, the wind was blowing harder, rattling the bell of the entrance door. Nobody else came in.

"You're welcome to come if you like, but it's stormy out—it's not so safe," I said.

"I know. But you're going, aren't you?"

I drove to a stretch of beach with no one else around. We parked in front of a rock wall, as close to the shoreline as possible, knowing we couldn't stand outside too long. My companion pulled her hair back and tucked it inside her hood. It stayed there this time. The snow blew against our faces, frosting our eyelids. She walked ahead of me, bending down every now and then to pick up a pebble, a shell, some other discolored and vibrant thing. After she had collected a handful, she crouched down and stacked one on top of another. She continued until there were four miniature pillars.

"Help me," she said.

We connected the pillars with more rocks and seashells until we had a square. I stood up, took a few steps backward, amazed at the little structure we had created. I was so focused on building the walls that I hadn't noticed the baby crab who was now crawling around inside the square.

"Look," I said, pointing the creature out to my companion.

"He'll figure it out." She walked on ahead of me.

"Hey," I called, "You never told me your name."

"Lilah. Lilah."

I smiled at the way she said her name like it was the beginning of a song.

"Who are you?" I asked.

"I'm your new friend, Lilah, who has just helped you build walls around a crab."

I stared at her back, her narrow and boyish hips, and wondered what the little girl might look like as a woman. My body surged with tears that wouldn't fall, pricking behind my eyes. I wondered if it was in that moment that I decided I would imprison any creature my new friend might ask me to, follow her anywhere just for a chance to show her I wouldn't abandon her. To love someone, perhaps, was not about what you could give her, but a way to remedy your loss. A decision both spontaneous and premeditated—to breathe under water and drown together as the rest of the world floated above you.

I chose this part of the beach because I'd sensed somehow that Lilah would prefer not to be disturbed. I realized now that it wasn't necessary to try to find an empty stretch of beach. With the snow falling so thick and the wind bellowing even louder than the ocean, nobody could see or hear us from two or three feet away, even if they somehow desired to be out in this bleary white. Her outline was beginning to disappear when she turned around and waited for me.

"So, what are you doing in Montauk?" she asked.

"Just trying to remember some things. It's my first long stretch of time off from work in two years," I said.

"I get it. I'm so forgetful myself."

My heart was beating faster. I was glad we were now side by side and she couldn't see my face.

"There are things you wish you could forget though. Don't you think?" she said.

"No. I want to remember everything that's ever happened."

"Really?"

"Forgetting is natural. Remembering is much harder," I said.

"My husband has an excellent memory."

"What does he do?" I said, looking out at the waves. We weren't alone after all. I spotted a black dot pushing itself against the waves. When it was further out, the black dot stood up and surfed back in.

"He works at a plant that engineers computer parts. He's a risk manager."

"And you?" I said.

"I make prosthetic eyes, which sounds technical, but the work actually requires a lot of interpretation. I like to think I'm a painter of sorts. Everything is done by hand because every person's eyes are unique, but even within a pair of eyes, there is a subtle difference."

"Because there's more than one self in everyone," I said.

She looked at me, a faint smile on her face, her head slightly tilted to one side. "That's what I think," she said. "So if I do my job right, you wouldn't be able to tell what you're looking at isn't real."

I looked out at the waves and thought if they rolled into me, it would hurt but wouldn't make me bleed the way the little girl had bled when she dove into our imagined ocean. "Can you tell if mine are real or not?" I teased. The cold had made me bolder than normal. She grabbed my shoulders and turned me toward her. Our faces were so close that her breath warmed my nearly frozen nose.

"My clients are forced to remember their trauma every day," she said. "Having an artificial eye helps them forget. Some days, they even feel normal."

We started to head back in the direction of the lighthouse. She fell behind me.

I waited for her to catch up.

"You know," she smiled, stretching her already cracked lips. They bled a little. "My mother hung herself when I was seventeen. Would you want to remember something like that?" She licked away the blood.

"I'm sorry—I don't know. I suppose if you forget everything, you could start over," I said.

"Like a newborn!" She pulled her hood in to cover her chin and it muffled her voice. She walked away toward the car. I didn't try to catch up with her. I thought perhaps she preferred it that way.

Back at my apartment in the city, like thousands of nights since I'd come to the United States as a girl, I sat alone under a softly lit lamp. So many hours had passed in this way—my own silence growing sharp edges while my mother's friends, my host families tried in vain to draw me out, throwing scraps of kindness at me like at a rabid dog. But now I was alone.

During the first few years in the United States, my yearning for Mother and my old life at the camp had morphed from simple aches and tears into sleepless nights full of desperate bargains with the universe and finally—when I realized that there would be no soldier to come collect me for a second time, no reunion with Mother, and no little girl to offer me her rare friendship, that I'd been abandoned—resilient anger.

I'd thought that I could punish Mother by resisting all my host families' attempts to care for me as their own, but I'd only succeeded in punishing myself. I remembered a father, a Vietnamese political dissident, who was especially kind to me, causing resentment in his wife and children. At mealtime, everyone else could use any bowl or plate he pleased but I would always receive the same brown, plastic plate. Even though the father was more attentive than many other hosts I'd been with, he never noticed. One night, he didn't come home for dinner and I found my plate with a mash of food next to the family's dog's dish. I knelt on my knees and lapped it up as the children watched, thrilled and horrified. With every swallow I prayed that this would be enough for them to forgive my intrusion in their life. Encouraged by their laughter, I crawled around and leapt up and down, clicking my knees on the hard wood floor. They laughed and laughed. But I took it too far. When I barked at the daughter, jumping up to scratch her thighs, she burst out in tears. I couldn't help but smile. In order to become real, you have to affect something outside yourself. As she pushed and kicked to get away from my grip, as her mother pulled on my ankles and dragged me off, I knew I was *somewhere,* I was *someone*. I was an agent to a feeling she would not forget—I existed then. The father yelled when he came in and saw me, my forehead, nose, and hair sticky with food and sweat, "What the hell's going on here?"

"We don't know," his wife pleaded, eyes teary. "Something's wrong with her."

One after another, they helped me pack my bags and sent me away with promises of change, of another family more equipped to deal with "children and trauma." I'd heard these words so many times, spoken in hushed voices behind bedroom walls, casually at dinner, and sometimes hurled at me as though they were meant as insults. By the time I understood that America was permanent and became grateful towards my hosts, I was old enough to live without a guardian.

I still wondered, though, why they had found my silence so offensive, as though it was an attack on their generosity. American children seemed to have been born with the innate knowledge of how to be their parents' child. I would see them at the park burying their faces in a sandpit and when it was time to leave, they would kick and scream while their adults carefully brushed sands off their eyelashes, and kissed their gritty lips. I would feel resentment swell in my chest—these children were clumsy and careless. They babbled endlessly. They tortured and attacked their wide-eyed caretakers who seemed more like fanatic admirers than parents. They had done nothing to earn that love. I had been patient and well behaved. I had asked for nothing. And that was exactly what I'd received.

On the Internet, thousands of couples looked for a stranger's baby to call their own. I was fascinated by the idea of surrogacy, disgusted at its promise of fulfillment and completion for these people who did not, would not consider the possibility that they might fail to love the child. And I was hopeful too—if two perfect strangers could devote their life to taking care of a baby they didn't give birth to—then I might be wrong about my mother and how she felt about me.

I looked down at my hands; though I was twenty-four, the skin was wrinkled and stretched thin from being exposed to chemicals at the laundromat. I rubbed the tips of my fingers together, trying to feel for my prints, small swirls that were uniquely mine. There was nothing there. After I took a second job at the coffee shop, I was able to rent a cheap room. I had not wanted more until now. The money my mother had given our relatives to turn over to me if I went to college was gone. I'd registered for the first semester and dropped out after only two weeks. I wasn't ready to commit to a path. I'd rationed the money meant for my tuition and supplemented it with my small income from other jobs. Up until I turned twenty, Mother had continued to send money. It was the only link left between us. I had not heard from her since.

It seemed so simple—loan your body for nine months and get a large sum of money. I would be able to go to the movies, eat a meal in a restaurant without counting my change instead of a diet of leftover stale croissants from the coffee shop. I could even go back to school. In a moment of delirious anger—and hope—I booked an appointment at a fertility clinic.

I called the manager of the granite building where the stranger from the subway lived. He said there were a studio and a one bedroom available. I asked him to send me the application. I told him I intended to move in as soon as possible and no, I didn't need to see it. Then I called my landlord and let him know I wanted to terminate my lease.

I received the keys to apartment 2B in the granite building. The stranger had passed me on the stairs, but showed no sign of remembering our first encounter on his doorstep. I nodded when he greeted me. We exchanged the usual pleasantries. He'd told me he was a lawyer and I responded that I hoped to have a career one day too. Then I busied myself with my moving boxes and excused myself.

A few weeks after I'd moved in, I sat on the steps outside our building to wait for him. My new neighbor had a habit of walking up and down our block in the evening. He came out as expected, wearing a faded green corduroy jacket, which looked threadbare and not warm enough even on this mild winter day. He said hello to me, more welcoming than the usual New York manner that was pleasant but disinterested in further conversation. He was both reserved and welcoming.

"What's a young lady doing, sitting here on a Saturday night?" he said. Up close, I could see the grays on his temples and the crescent wrinkles under his eyes.

"No plans tonight," I said.

"That's not a bad thing. Too many people over schedule, down to when they're going to shit," he said.

"Have you lived here long?" I asked.

"For me, any time is a long time. Yesterday till today. Today till tomorrow. Time passes faster for young people."

"You're not as old as all that," I said.

"No. I'm a newly grown fingernail. A dot in history." He bit off a hangnail on his thumb. He looked like a boy then. "What is it that you do?"

"I make coffee, clean tables. I also launder." I got up and walked beside him.

"Do you enjoy it?"

"I'm good at latte art," I said.

"What's that?" he asked, and then coughed into his palm.

"You make little drawings by pouring milk over the espresso. If I'm not rushing, I can make fantasy creatures, like a jackalope. It's taken me years to perfect—"

He laughed and coughed some more.

"Is that what you care about? You want to draw little hearts and swans on drinks that people will consume in less than ten minutes or put a plastic lid over." The laughter died in his throat.

"If I don't focus on the details, I wouldn't know how to live. Isn't that what life is about? Just a bunch of trivial moments that you hope will accrue some kind of meaning at the end." I looked at a squirrel grooming its tail on a low bush. It was so light that the leaves held it up just fine.

"I want to believe that. I do. But people only remember the general, what history can capture, the records. You told me you were from Vietnam?" I was glad he remembered our brief encounter in the hallway the day I moved in. He took out a cigarette and lit it. "Want one?"

I nodded. I didn't smoke but I wanted to please him. "Vietnam, yeah. Something like that."

He looked at me curiously. "When you told me where you were from last week, you were overly shy. Like you couldn't place the country, or you couldn't place yourself in it. You weren't sure. You remind me of someone." He surprised me by grabbing the ends of my hair and held it in a fist. I felt his aggression and tried not to flinch or move away. He let go.

"Who?" I asked.

"People here still think Vietnam is a jungle—brown savages, an exotic Asian whore who you can't possess, but still satisfies all your sexual demands. It's burnt into the American imagination. You can't change that. As soon as you say something different, you make some old vet defensive or guilty or confused. Try telling them some other tales that don't fit their presumptions. Vietnam—" He dropped his cigarette and crushed it with the toe of his shoe. "Is a war, not a country. Anything besides is irrelevant."

"Where are you from?" I said. I was shaking though not from the cold.

"You're not listening."

"I am."

"It doesn't matter where I'm from. I'll always be the gook from *Apocalypse Now*. And you, your history is irrelevant."

Though I sensed that he wasn't trying to be unkind, I still reddened all the same. "I don't even know your name," I said.

"My English name is D—, but if you spare me the confusion of hearing it, then I'll do the same for you."

If he were my soldier, I should have known, but the sound of his voice wasn't familiar to me. I associated it with nothing. It was a thing on its own, untethered like the way he saw himself.

"Don't you look back sometimes?" I asked.

"Sure, I reminisce. Just about every immigrant does. I have these flashes: standing in a wooden boat, pissing in a river. But it's like stumbling into somebody else's dream. You can't even think of *boat* or *river* in your mother's tongue. Everything you remember is shaped in the new language. All of a sudden, it isn't the same boat anymore and I was never that boy. When you leave the old country at an age not young enough to get adopted into the new and not old enough to know how to reject it, you become this mutant thing: between borders, between languages, between memories." He pressed his temples. "If you ask me, I think it's easier to reinvent than to retrace. You're not the only one, you know. Look at this city and its faces. You're not the only one with an ungraspable history."

3

Lilah and I kept in touch. I had given her my number in Montauk and three weeks after our first meeting, she called me. She asked me where I lived. I told her. She said it would take her less than thirty minutes to get there by train. "Are you busy?" she asked. I couldn't think of any reason not to see her, other than that we didn't know each other at all except for the one time we'd acted like old friends. Few people could make you feel this way—that when you meet, pieces of the cosmos shifted and aligned so that you can look back at your entire history and see how everything had worked out just so you could be there with them. Even now, I realized she was continuing our assumed friendship, something that went beyond Montauk, reaching further back than the first time we'd met.

She didn't apologize for contacting me out of the blue or for nothing, the way people do when they get self-conscious. If I were still a young girl, I would have been smitten, but I decided to be more careful. I was afraid of being too naïve, unguarded, and too willing to let passion drive me. She was dark, attractive, and had a masculine dismissal of her own beauty that was comforting.

I waited by the window, anxious and fearful of seeing her. Since coming to New York, I'd gotten used to being alone. There had been others, people I could have loved if such love didn't demand constant physical intimacy, an act I couldn't engage in without disassociating myself from my own body.

Over time, even the most patient and tender person couldn't stop feeling like they were terrorizing me. No one wanted a victim they didn't create.

Since parting with the little girl, I had not made another friend. The very loyalty of friendships, it seemed, was marked by betrayal. Unconsciously, I placed my hand on my shin. I blinked and there it was again—the charcoaled sky. Smoke-filled nostrils. Closed eyes, a weak defense against the rising heat.

I saw Lilah cross the street. For a split second, I thought I shouldn't come to the door and act as if I wasn't home, or pretend she'd gotten the wrong address. The air wrapped around her had felt dangerous. It had been a long time since I felt the need to run. Which direction I had yet to decide.

In front of my open door, she took off her wet boots and left them outside. Once I invited her in, she put down her handbag at the nearest table, took off her leather jacket and pulled down her sweater that had risen above her stomach. These offhanded modern-woman manners diffused my worries.

"So this is where you live," she said.

"Yeah." I blinked. My anxiety returned, the way it happened when you invited someone home after a first date.

"I brought you something." She fumbled her hand inside her bag and took out a glass case.

An eye—the iris looked liquid. Pale blue spiraled like eddies. My insides were weeping, exposed to its merciless stare.

"Don't be so spooked. I'm not wishing you ill or anything. You understand, don't you?" she said.

"I don't know if I deserve it."

"Well, it's yours. It's not like anyone else can use it now. I made it with you in mind," she said. Then suddenly averting her eyes from my gaze, she asked, "What do you think about me having an affair?"

"What?"

"The man you saw in Montauk wasn't my husband. He asked his assistant to take me because he couldn't. I've wanted to go for a while—"

She sat down on the rug. I was glad she didn't comment on my lack of furniture.

"And that's the man you want to have an affair with?" I breathed.

She nodded and played with her toes. "I know I'm so typical. This is what people do. My father did it to my mother. We're destined to repeat history."

"His assistant?" I said. "Are you looking to get caught? Because you will."

"We'll be careful," she said cheerfully. Her toes wiggled.

"Why not try telling your husband how you feel? Tell him what you're telling me."

She laughed and spread out on the floor. She studied the ceiling as if she could see the impending disasters. "Have you ever been that honest before? Can you seriously be that honest with someone you love?"

"Are you in love with the assistant?"

"My husband is a man who's never experienced true pain. It's sinful to be so naïve."

I wanted to kiss her then if only to startle her out of her insolence, perhaps save one man from having his trust and self-esteem shattered, and from putting others who might love him afterward through unnecessary tests. The cycle could end here.

"Why are you telling me this?" I mumbled.

"I can't do it alone."

"Ever since I saw you, I kept going through a time warp." There. I was being as honest as I could.

"You're just what I need right now," she said. "Someone who'll drive me through the storm."

I smiled, realizing I had already done so in Montauk. That

was why she came here. I sat down on the frayed rug next to her. "So you'll have your affair."

"And you'll have yours," she looked at me with a dare in her eyes. "Nobody's honest, ever. Not if they really know love," she said.

Over the next few weeks, Lilah would show up at my apartment or meet me during my lunch break at work. She asked for my schedule and I gave it to her without believing she would actually look for me wherever I was during the day. Sometimes when the coffee shop was busy, she would come in and sit in a corner to draw, sketches of different colored eyes with reflections of flying objects at their centers, a bird, falling meteorites, a leaf storm. Other times, she would simply stare fixedly at a point in the air. She didn't try to talk to me or even make eye contact. She acted like a regular customer who had found their favorite spot to be alone. I never found her overwhelming, though her frequent visits were noticeable. Matt, my co-worker, nudged my elbow one day, "Check out the hot milf. What's her deal?"

"Leave her alone," I told him.

"Jeez. You know her? You two lovers or something?" he said.

I ignored him and went to join Lilah.

We talked for hours about her husband's assistant. She wouldn't call him by his name, only the assistant. She told me languidly which days of the week they would meet, at which motels or bars with unisex restrooms. She told me about how much he sweated, so different from her husband who never produced a drop even during their most physically intimate moments. I became conscious of the few drops of sweat on the sides of my face. The assistant slathered her with his fluids, both outside and in. He liked to keep her underwear with him so she always brought an extra pair.

"If your wife has an extra pair of panties in her purse, she's cheating!" She squealed, pulling out a lacy, purple thing and dangled it in front of me. "I think he sells my dirty ones on eBay," she said. She was full of energy as she talked. Her hands fluttered between us. At times, I thought she was too animated.

"Do you trust this guy?" I said.

"Of course I do." She shrugged.

"What if he wanted more than just an affair?"

"Oh." She scoffed and swiped the air with her hand once more. "I don't think so. He needs that job. Do you want to hear about how he went down on me or not?"

I soon learned my questions were not welcomed. She was there to tell me stories. They also could not be interrupted or sidetracked. I didn't mind just being in her company, offering little of myself. Visit after visit, I began to sense that something was wrong. Everyone lied when they told a story whether or not they meant to, so I didn't question the details that felt like exaggerations, like his desperate need to be near her, or how he waited for her in the cold for nearly eight hours. It seemed natural that she wanted to be portrayed as the type of woman you would do that for. If she was lying, I was just as willing to participate in her fiction. That was the condition of friendships, the little girl had taught me.

Lilah was always specific about the seduction, how he pampered her, where they went, what they talked about; she rarely offered facts about him outside of their romance, and when she did they weren't consistent. Once, she had said he was a Patriots' fan. Later, she said he hated all sports, anything related to the media. She liked that he wasn't worldly; he didn't read the newspapers and didn't own a TV, unlike her husband Jon who was astute about various topics and could easily contribute to various types of conversation. Once she and the assistant were talking to another couple, the woman was passionately describing how female bodies had been sites for patriarchal abuse and needed to be reclaimed, the assistant had looked into her eyes and yawned. Lilah found it hysterical how he hadn't pretended to be interested.

"He's just outside of conventions, you know. He read me a poem he wrote for me. It made no sense at all. It was a combination of words printed on a meat packet and a Shakespeare sonnet. That's how he feels about me," she said.

Maybe he was truly brilliant, this assistant, or foolish.

"Has anyone ever done that for you?" she asked suddenly.

"What?"

"Given you something that existed absolutely nowhere else in the world?"

My friendship with Lilah filled my days the way a house might suddenly be submerged in water. I was drawn to her because people are drawn to uncertainty, the abyss. Arms of darkness wrenched you from your ordinary life, which had been a long sleep, and pushed you down deeper into comatose, into dreams. And like people you meet in dreams, she was both real and impossible.

I lay down on the couch in my living room. With a simple shut of the eyelids, I was at the camp again. I saw myself holding the little girl's hand, I as a woman and she, still a child. I had loved her as though I were a tree and she a branch that grew from my flesh. The first time we played together, she'd told me her name and I'd quickly buried it at the back of my mind. People used names to distinguish among each other, but in the world of the camp, I had only one little girl. Now I said her name out loud, let the syllables hang alone in the air, separated from myself.

I didn't know where my friendship with Lilah would lead me, but maybe it was enough to want to surrender to it.

It was determined at a young age, the kind of woman that I would let hold me up by a string, the kind of man I would attract because of my fatherless nature, which was less of a fact than a personality trait, the way someone's whole identity centers around the very thing he lacks.

I'd burned a meadow for her, watched tall and lush sugarcane get scorched to the ground. There was no other reason, except that she had asked me to. The little girl—Lilah. Their likeness was impossible, but absolute. My neighbor—my soldier. Time was folding, stretching into infinity, collapsing into a single moment.

Were people who shared similar physical attributes likely to have similar character traits as well? Were they to have similar narratives, the same self-defining memories? Lilah wasn't surprised by my quick loyalty, though she wasn't aware that it'd been tested and retested many times in the past before we ever met. Most people felt the same way about us as we felt about them. I blindly took the role she gave me.

I stopped thinking of her husband, made excuses on Lilah's behalf, and justified my position as just a witness, not an accomplice. She would commit adultery with or without me. It was even a good thing since he would be spared the burden of change. We were used to endings. Endings were parts of our days; programmed in our tired bodies from the moment we closed our eyes. Change on the other hand was difficult to overcome.

Lilah. My neighbor. Me. All in one place again.

Suddenly, I felt like I could breathe.

4

Lilah and I talked to each other as though we were running and suddenly stopped, out of breath. We spent every possible minute together, neglecting responsibilities in other areas of our lives. Our chance for happiness was ruined by our eagerness to share too much and too quickly. After meeting her, I could understand why society condemns certain drugs, which artificially induce a state of being that turn the world into a playground for lovers and reduce all rigid structures to ash. Often we were together alone, indoors, since we didn't need much exterior stimulation. We were absorbed by each other. I had not been to Lilah's home though she came to mine often. At first we always got along because she liked to talk and I liked to listen to her.

One day, she got angry with me. As usual, she was waiting for me when I got off work. As we walked, she told me about a client who had come in earlier that day for an annual exam. The woman asked Lilah if she should tell her fiancé about her fake eye before the wedding. They'd only just met three months prior, but they were both ready.

"She said it's one thing to say you're blind in one eye. It's another to explain how you got to be that way," Lilah said. "I advised against telling him. Marriage needs its secrets, don't you think?"

When we got to my apartment, I carelessly tore open my mail. The heading on one of the letters must have caught her eye.

"What's that?" she said.

"I think I just got approved to be a surrogate mother," I said, staring at the paper.

"You what?" She took the letter from me. "You can't be serious."

"I am. I don't intend to have children of my own so I figure the only way I could know what birthing is like—" I grinned.

"That's fucking stupid."

I was surprised by her hostility. Her reaction was such a stark difference from the receptionist at the clinic.

"I don't know why you think that but—where are you going?"

She didn't hear my question. She was already out the door.

I didn't hear from Lilah for a few days. When she called, she made no mention of our conversation about surrogacy. She asked if I wanted to go spice hunting with her. Lilah had started to enjoy cooking again. She would make a four-course meal for her husband on a Tuesday night. She claimed she didn't do it out of guilt, but a renewed sense of playfulness. She said she had energy she hadn't had in years. Suddenly, their relationship was fulfilling again, she told me. But could she stop seeing the assistant? No. I thought people like Lilah were made to inflict pain, the kind you became dependent on because it was larger than you. The closest her husband could come to being great was by being deceived by her, over and over.

I agreed to go with her, but while we walked down the aisles of the market, she didn't say much. I asked about how it was going with the assistant, though what I really wanted to know was why the idea of me being a surrogate had made her so angry. She just shrugged.

Her husband saw us at the market. Lilah introduced us. His eyes flickered with interest, curiosity, fear, mostly interest. He told us he was going to surprise Lilah with an exotic spice. It was his lunch break. I was touched he thought of her at work, something couples only did in the first few years of their relationship. He was more handsome, taller, and broader than I expected. Her deceit had diminished him in my imagination.

She had called me her good friend, yet he'd never met me before. He seemed perched on his toes, filled with excitement. Here was something about his wife that he didn't know. I imagined it was pleasant for him to learn Lilah would keep something to herself. Something that was merely private. He watched my every blink, smile, gesture toward him and his wife, so I took care to not be overly talkative or reserved. I could tell how much of a relief it was to confront something akin to his worst nightmare and to be reassured of the safety of his marriage. He was right about me, at least about that I wasn't going to wreck his nest of comfort myself.

The three of us left the market without the exotic spice Lilah's husband had come for. Out in the open air, he looked more relaxed like he'd gained back his sense of gravity. He touched Lilah frequently and spontaneously, now affectionately belittling her as his "little woman," then asking me to watch over her since she tended to be passionate, to lose herself in small things. Next to him, her masculine charm was ebbing away, replaced by a practiced humility. He talked about her in the third person as if she wasn't there. He said women knew better how to be there for each other than he ever could.

I felt flattered even though his attention to me was really directed at Lilah. She cast glances at me, a chagrined smile on her face. "Stop it," "Don't tease me," "Oh, don't listen to him," she would say. She was skillful. She knew how to fill the air with words around those who cannot bear silence. For a split second, I was insecure about our friendship, about why she never rushed herself or spoke of mundane things to me.

Maybe it was for my sake. I watched her transform and was fascinated.

He insisted the three of us have lunch together.

"Don't you have to get back to the office?" Lilah asked.

"It's not so busy right now. Plus, you never let me meet your friends."

We decided on a Japanese restaurant nearby. I ordered sake and asked them if they wanted to share a bottle.

"I'll drink with you, but my wife can't. We're trying to get pregnant. Alcohol can inhibit your fertility."

Lilah avoided my gaze so I tried not to look at her. She always drank around me. In fact, I couldn't remember a time we were together without having a glass or two.

"Oh, you didn't know," he said. A little smirk flicked across his face. Perhaps he thought his wife and I weren't so close after all. "This is our second time trying. It's not easy for anybody to go through a thing like that. For Lilah especially." He squeezed her hand. "After our first was stillborn, she didn't sleep for weeks."

Just like that he had minimized all of Lilah's eccentricities. Her infidelities spiraled down to a single grief. Any woman would stray after giving birth to a corpse. I thought that perhaps he was trying to tell her, and maybe me too, that nothing escaped him, that he knew and all was forgiven.

"What about you? Are you seeing anyone? Kids?" he said.

I shook my head.

"Why not? Children are wonderful!"

"Not everybody thinks like you," Lilah interrupted.

"To raise children, you have to know who you are," I said.

"Of course you know who you are. You're you," he exclaimed. "You're overthinking it."

I laughed.

"Please," Lilah said to her husband and turned to me. "You don't have to."

"I wouldn't know how to raise kids. I couldn't decide which to give them: the Vietnamese or American experience." I surprised myself.

"Does it matter? You just choose one and run with it."

"It would be dishonest."

The three of us tensed at the sudden appearance of honesty. I cleared my throat, poured the warm liquid down it.

"Maybe, someday." I said. "For now, I've decided I'm going to be a surrogate mother." I couldn't help myself. I wanted to see how Lilah would react this time, if she would show the same anger as before. She didn't meet my eyes, instead exchanged a look with her husband.

"Ah," Jon said. "I see."

The day after, Lilah was supposed to come to my apartment, but she hadn't contacted me. After lunch with Jon, the three of us each had gone our separate ways. I panicked. It had taken so long to find her. I used to think it was impossible to reconstruct the past, but slabs of memories were stacking up around me like bricks. I was a willing prisoner. Was meeting Lilah a coincidence? No, it couldn't be. I was drawn to her because she was my walking memory, because she radiated an inevitable tragedy, because she made me devoted to her, and because I was going to abandon her.

What I learned over the years—abandonment was love's destiny.

Maybe Lilah could sense what I wanted from her was impossible. In the beginning, my fascination had tilted all the power to her side. Now, she was used to being admired and listened to with wholesome and genuine interest. Everyone needed someone to love him unconditionally. Marriage was, from the beginning, doomed to fail because its contractual stipulation removed love's greatest ambition—for people to be bound together only by their love and nothing else. I was not bound to Lilah by law. I was still able to extend my unconditional loyalty. She needed me and I was going to undo her, pull out the pieces, reshuffle them, and put them back the way I'd found her in Montauk, alone, desperate to bare her grief, in need of a friend. I wanted her to stay weak so we could be strong together.

My phone alerted of a new message. It was from Lilah—a picture of her bare feet on the ground covered in snow. She'd painted one toe red so it peeped out like a cherry. She would sometimes send me snapshots of things. I liked the pictures, glimpses of her private world. Slowly, they formed a map of her mind.

Are you home? The text read. Before I could respond, a second one blinked on the screen.

I'm coming over.

Ten minutes later, the bell rang. Lilah came in, apologizing for not contacting me sooner after our unexpected run-in with her husband.

"Do you want to talk about it?" she stood on the floor mat, brushing snow off her hair.

I didn't answer. I wanted her to feel a little bad.

"I'm sorry about Jon. He isn't usually like that," she said.

"He was fine. He was nice," I said.

"I've never seen him like that with my girl friends. I think he was intimidated," she said. "When he asked me about you, I realized I don't know any of the facts. Isn't that strange?"

"Hm," I said, squirming inside my own skin. "Do you have lots of girl friends?" I tried to find my way out.

"I used to. Of course after my mother died, I became unbearable to be around."

"Is that why you want to stay with Jon? Your mother hung herself and left you so you think love means staying with someone even if you're miserable." I heard myself and it occurred to me that maybe it wasn't Lilah who resembled the little girl but myself. I was bullying my only friend out of a desperate need to see how I affected her. Lilah's facial muscles contorted painfully like she was trying not to bare her teeth and roar at me.

"You've never been married," she murmured so quietly that my shame grew large.

I stared at her, feeling both tender and violent. She looked tiny sitting on the floor and hugging her knees, tears dripping down her cheeks. Crying—one of the few things in life that really stops time. Each sound that escaped her throat was razor sharp against my skin. I offered her no word of comfort. Her always seeming on the verge of tears had attracted me from the first moment we spoke. It was there no matter what she was doing, feeling, thinking. Her tragedy was her single source of power. The more she cried, the more I saw how strength hid behind what was so easily mistaken for weakness. It was comfortable for me to enter that sphere, where our identities ceased to be defined by geographical boundaries and became simpler, truer—our trauma.

I sat down next to her and told her I was sorry.

We learned not to want what we could not have. By some accidental or cosmic determinacy, Lilah's daughter died as soon as she came into the world. In the human brain, such a life-changing event could not stand alone as meaningful or meaningless, but inevitably got rolled in with other autobiographical moments to produce an explanation that was linear, without frays. Lilah told me she didn't want to try getting pregnant again. She failed to imagine a successful outcome. She concluded briskly that she was not meant to be a mother. Actually, it was a relief, like the universe was giving her a chance to step backward in time. She said her mother shouldn't have had children, though Lilah didn't blame her. In her time, women didn't have so many painful choices to make. A woman was not a picture of possibilities, but a vessel to fulfill humanity's deepest anxiety—the desire to be survived by children, to let others know we've been there.

"There are other ways to live now," Lilah said.

I nodded, too aware of my own biological impulse to produce a stranger, to be a continuation of history instead of its outlier. "I don't want children either," I lied.

We were just two friends, holding hands, convinced that we had conviction. At least, it consoled us to pretend we did.

5

Lilah asked me to come with her to Crater Lake for a work trip. A client had insisted that Lilah see the lake before they could continue making his eyes. He had grown up going there and was convinced that its image was burned into his corneas. The man had offered to pay for Lilah's ticket to Oregon. She told me that he was a peculiar man, a musical prodigy who had damaged both his eyes in a performance that included four natural elements: water, lightning, metal, and earth. Since it would only take the weekend, I agreed to go.

On the plane, Lilah told the stewardess that we were on our honeymoon.

"What did you do that for?" I said.

"Free booze." She exaggerated a wink.

She was right. We got one whiskey after another during the long duration of the flight. The stewardess kept glancing our way, her face full of awe. Encouraged, Lilah interlaced her fingers into mine. She whispered, "See? It pays to be two attractive lesbians." I giggled, happy to be drunk.

At the Portland airport, we rented a car. I did all I could to hold myself together; my chest was like fireworks, threatening to burst with laughter. At first, I'd had some doubts about the trip, thinking that it was easy for two people to get sick of each other if they spent uninterrupted time together. Walking to the car, her hand still not letting go of mine, I realized I hadn't had so much fun in a long time. We decided that I was more sober, so I got into the driver's seat.

The drive seemed to calm us both. Lilah preoccupied herself with the radio, changing stations. We listened to pop, country, classic rock, and even Christian songs for a good half-hour. Then Lilah fell asleep. I rolled down the window on my side, let in the fresh snowy air. On both sides of the road, the trees were getting thicker. I imagined that we were inside a looping video with the road, the sky, and trees stretching on forever, religious hymns droning from the car speakers, our destination not a place on the map.

The inn was made up of several adjoining cabins, ornamented with stalactites dripping from the edges of roofs. Our room was simply furnished, a queen bed, a round table with mismatched chairs, a small lamp, and pine cones everywhere, on the windowsill, next to the bathroom sink, in a small basket by the door. On the bed, I picked up a folded handwritten greeting card that said *Congratulations! I hope you enjoy your stay with us.* Apparently Lilah had also used the honeymoon tactic when she booked the place.

"Should we go for a hike?" I was ready to stretch out my legs after the drive.

Lilah took out her phone, looked at it, and then buried it at the bottom of her suitcase. "I turned my phone off. Not going to talk to Jon for the rest of the trip."

I sensed that she wanted me to ask her why, so I did.

"I want him to miss me. He should miss me," she said. She lifted the comforter and slipped under. I went to the window and looked out. It was beautiful here.

"Do you want to walk around? We leave early tomorrow, so maybe we should try to see the lake—" I tried again.

"Do you think I care about seeing some stupid lake?"

"Your client—"

"What kind of a request is that anyway? I seriously don't get it. If I could, I would paint them neon yellow, something bright and self-absorbed, because that's what he is. A self-absorbed asshole. You know what? I should do it. He wouldn't know it himself and I sort of doubt anyone would dare tell him. People don't talk to the blind."

"It's not so strange. I mean, whatever it is he saw here, it probably influenced his music." I didn't understand why I was defending someone I'd never met, knowing it would further irritate Lilah.

"Jesus, you've been in hippie country for five minutes," she said.

I reddened. "Fine. Stay here if you want."

I took a trail map from the information booth and started uphill. After about half a mile, I realized my shoes weren't suited for this kind of hike. The path was rocky, narrow, and made even more difficult by the frozen snow. My feet were soon cold and wet from stepping in snowmelt puddles. Leaving in a hurry, I also forgot to bring water. Even though I was still frustrated with Lilah, I enjoyed the scenery. From up high, I could see the lake, a thin and colorful sheet of ice on its surface. While I walked, I contemplated what I would say to Lilah later.

The sky got dark quickly and suddenly. I hurried back. I was walking too fast and tripped, puncturing my knee on a sharp rock. Blood, bright and thick, oozed from the wound. I cursed, ripped up a piece of my scarf and wrapped it around my knee. The cabins were visible from the distance so I limped on. As I got closer, I saw billows of smoke and—immediately forgetting about my injury—I ran toward it.

I saw the bonfire before I spotted her amongst a group of people, young and old. The women were attractive, their clothes threadbare, their jewelry tarnished. They seemed to draw strength from their physical body, lithe from movement and fresh air. They were completely different from the many women I was used to seeing in New York City, whose pants and coats were pressed and ironed, jewelry always sparkling. The men looked ruddy, their cheeks flushed from being close to the fire. Lilah's hair was braided in two pigtails, which made her look like a girl. Her puffy white jacket with white fur rim also stood out amid more earthy tones. My arms felt redundant by my side. I didn't know if I should pretend not to see her and go straight to our room or head toward the fire. As though she could hear my thoughts, Lilah looked up at the hill where I stood and waved for me to come over.

She introduced me to everyone as if I was late to a party she had thrown. I politely shook a few hands, perfunctorily nodded and smiled. I sat down on the ground. A young woman, blonde, with two nose piercings that somehow looked elegant, sat next to me.

"I'm Carly. Lilah told me you're on your honeymoon. I've always wanted a winter wedding. It's just so romantic."

"We're not really married," I said. "We're just friends."

"Well, the best couples always start as friends," she said.

I sighed, decided it was no use to convince anyone not to believe whatever tale Lilah had spent the last few hours spinning.

"Do you want to dance?" Carly said.

I shook my head. "To what? There's no music." I felt uncomfortable and was planning to make an exit back to my room. "I also cut myself." I pointed to the makeshift bandage.

"Just a slow dance. It won't hurt." She took my hand and we both stood up. Out of the corner of my eye, I saw Lilah watching us.

Carly had soft hands and her features were more handsome than Lilah's. Even striking. Her hair was thin and brittle, but it suited her small face and angular jawline. As we moved awkwardly away from the group, me trying to guess at the silent tunes she was dancing to, Carly told me about herself.

She studied graphic design at University of Portland; she had a Siamese cat; her parents were farmers. For a moment, I let myself be swayed by her brimming youth, her spontaneity of emotions that only those with most of their lives still ahead of them would have.

"I feel like kissing you," she said "Is that okay?" I looked over my shoulder at Lilah and laughed at myself for getting so used to her honeymoon joke that I felt guilty being with Carly.

"Lilah might be upset," I said, half jokingly.

"Aren't you just friends?" She emphasized the last two syllables. It was skillful how women could choose the story that best suited their design. I was sure that if the pursuit was reversed and she hadn't found me attractive, I would seem all the sudden too married for her taste. My silence didn't deter her. "Don't you like me? Do I seem too straight? Not alluring enough? What is it?" she said.

"You're very alluring," I assured her. "I'm just not in the position."

"Are you and Lilah really married?"

"No. I was trying to tell you earlier. She has a husband, actually —"

"And you're still into her. It's so unfair."

"I guess a kiss doesn't hurt." I closed my eyes, but before I could lean forward, I felt a hand on my arm tilting me away. It was Lilah.

"I'm tired. Let's go to bed," Lilah said and dragged me toward the cabin. Carly followed behind us.

In the room, Carly took off her shoes and spread out on the bed. Lilah washed her face at the sink. When she came out, she looked refreshed. It seemed she had reapplied her eye makeup.

"Carly, isn't it your bedtime? Your parents might be looking for you," Lilah said.

"I'm twenty-two," Carly said earnestly.

"You sure seem young," Lilah said. "If you've forgotten, this is our honeymoon and I would like to consummate our marriage." I wasn't sure if she was mocking me, Carly, or the joke.

"She told me you two aren't really married. You're just an old woman having a midlife crisis," Carly said.

"Oh my god, get out. Nobody wants you here," Lilah sneered.

I tried to interject, "It was nice meeting you, Carly. But it's time—" but no one paid attention to me. They were locked in a private battle.

"Why don't you get your own room? You're the third wheel here," she said to Lilah. Then Carly turned to me, "Come with me." Everything escalated after that. In a swift motion, Lilah yanked Carly from the bed with surprising force. When her arm slipped from Lilah's grip, she grabbed her long, blonde hair, pulled and pushed her out the door. On the other side of the door, Carly yelled a few obscenities. Then I heard her stalk away.

"What a maniac. I'm sorry. I should have looked after you. I was having too much fun," Lilah said. Her back was to me.

"She's really pretty though, isn't she?" I said. In the bathroom, I took off my jeans, stood in the bathtub and let water run over my knee. Lilah came in to keep me company.

"Jesus. That looks bad. I really can't leave you alone, can I?"

I limped to bed afterward, a little exaggeratedly. I couldn't help but to find Lilah's attention flattering. In a way, we were both acting. She must have enjoyed her role as the gentle and caring partner too, fluffing my pillow before I lay down, insisting that I should take off my shirt so I could be comfortable. She removed her own shirt, though keeping on her bra, before scooting up against my back.

"I have a cut on my leg. I'm not sick, Lilah," I said, smiling.

"Shush. I don't want my wifey to get a cold too," she said. "What will we do then, huh? What will we do?"

I closed my eyes. I'd always known what-if games were dangerous. Lilah too had gotten caught in its lattice. Fortunately for us, our honeymoon would end the next day.

6

One night, two months after our trip, I came home from work and heard the sound of water sloshing about in the bathtub. The kitchen counter was covered in grocery bags. I suspected Lilah had probably used the emergency key I put under my neighbor's potted plant in the hall. I opened the door to the bathroom and was wrapped in a wet fog. Lilah's black hair laid in swirls on her breasts around two erect, crimson nipples.

She was pinching them when I came in. "I don't get to keep the baby, but I got these mommy nipples. How are they so dark? They've never been nursed on. You should have seen me when I was younger," she said.

"What are the groceries for? Is there something I don't know?" I wiped a circle on the mirror.

"Jon. He's coming over for dinner at eight. I told him you asked us to."

"That's soon and you're going to step out of my bathtub to greet your husband. What ideas are you trying to give him, Lilah?" I said.

"I don't want to keep any more secrets from my husband," she said.

"What about the assistant?" I said. At this point he felt more like an invention than a real person. I'd only seen him once in Montauk, his narrow and birdlike shoulders, a long back, a small waist. According to Lilah, they were still seeing each other occasionally. An affair, by definition, was full-fledged; otherwise it wouldn't be worth the effort. I didn't believe her. She'd been here with me three or four nights out of the week until past midnight. Maybe when she left, she'd go see the assistant, but it didn't seem likely.

"You know that's not what I'm hiding." She stood up inside the tub. She made no effort to get the soap off her body. Tiny soap bubbles encircled her belly button. "Come here."

I didn't move, instead she stepped out of the bathtub to stand behind me. We'd never been this close before. The heat from the bath made it difficult for me to breathe. I turned on the cold tap at the sink and washed my face. I pretended I didn't hear her, which was partly true since my heart was beating so loudly I felt it inside my ears. With one hand, she closed the toilet lid, and with the other she wiggled inside my pants and grabbed my buttocks. She caressed them for a long time, breathing on my neck heavily as if overcome by her own desire, as if she was indifferent to the knowledge that I wanted her too. I felt her fingers slicing up and down my crevice, spreading the slime from my front to back. I steadied myself on the sink.

My body felt ghostly, like it didn't belong to me, and at the same time I felt more ownership than ever of the hair on my skin, the nails on my toes, the saliva in my mouth. I turned around. Welcomed by her open mouth, I took her tongue and sucked on it hungrily. I was excited, in a hurry to explore the rest of her, but also I didn't want to stop kissing her. She sensed my hesitance and made a decision for us both. She sat me down on the toilet lid and knelt down to unlace my shoes, pull my pants down to my ankles. I helped her, using one foot to push the other side of the pant leg off me. I hesitated again. I worried about Jon walking in on us. I worried he would think we'd been deceiving him all this time. It wasn't true, was it? Why wasn't she afraid? I wanted to ask her, but I didn't. I was more scared that *this,* this moment wouldn't happen again. I felt myself entirely at her disposal. I felt lucky.

With her fingers, she traced the scar that ran from my knee to above my foot, her lips parted, full of questions. *Not now.* I shook from my mind the image of red and yellow flames twisting like ribbons around the little girl. *Let me have this*, I begged.

When Lilah's lips enclosed me, her air of expertise fell away. I realized that she'd never been with another woman before either. She tasted me slowly, confused, hurt, satisfied by what she found there. She licked me shyly at first and then angrily. She moaned as if it were she who was being pleasured. She pushed her tongue as far inside me as she could, greedy to touch every bit of me. Just when I thought I wasn't going to come from mere childish exploration, I shuddered and held her head against me. I wanted to suffocate her, drown her in my pleasure. The more my body writhed against my control, the more pleased she seemed. She flicked her tongue speedily, informed by the spasms and shivers on my body. I came again and again.

She guided me to bed. I watched as she undid each button on my shirt. She took off my shirt so that I was fully naked. I searched her eyes for some hint, wanting to know, not to know.

"Will you have my baby? Ours?" she said.

I fell asleep while Lilah cooked. When I woke, I was suddenly conscious of my nakedness. I looked through my closet for pajamas, changed my mind, and put on a pair of burgundy, lacy panties instead. Only an hour or two ago, Lilah had taken off my clothes piece by piece and I didn't think about whether or not she would find me attractive. Her actions in themselves had my full attention. Now I was worried. My right breast seemed outrageously smaller than my left. I felt lopsided. I cupped both breasts in my hands. They were soft, but too small. I stood in front of the mirror and inspected myself. On my right thigh was a mole from which a little black hair grew.

I pulled on the hair a little, decided to leave it alone for now. I turned my back to the mirror to look at my butt. I'd had stretch marks there for as long as I remembered. A man once called me a zebra because of how evenly spaced each line was. I thought that was a nice thing to be so I started to think of my own butt as the behind of a zebra.

"How do you like your steak?" Lilah called from the kitchen.

"Blue," I answered.

I imagined her handling thick, red meat. How much I admired her. We were good friends. I decided to wear a thin, pink cotton shirt without a bra and form-fitting pants. My nipples were lighter colored than Lilah's. I rubbed them gently so they would show through the shirt.

Lilah had made a beautiful dinner for us. She told me Jon was held at work so maybe we could talk, just us two.

"It's better this way," she said. "Can you do it?"

She was referring to the question she'd asked me earlier. I didn't want to talk about it so soon. My head ached. I bit into the bloody meat and drank the wine. Everything was delicious. I had to remind myself not to eat too quickly, to savor it.

"I just think you're the right person. I want a child with your smile and Jon's eyes."

"Jon. He's important to you." I phrased it like a statement, but it really was a question. I had to be careful not to push her away. "Why my smile? What about yours?"

"We've tried so many times. I'm exhausted," she said. "I can't go through another failed pregnancy. I don't think my body wants children. It's what nature intended. I told you about my mother—somebody should have told her not to have kids if she were just going to—I'm not dying to pass on my genes. It's better that the child comes from two people I care most about. How amazing would that be? "

"Suicide isn't genetic—"

She ignored my comment. "But you—you're still young. You were going to be a surrogate for strangers anyway. Why not do it for me?" She cut her steak into little cubes. "Have more of mine. I've made too much food." She pushed some onto my plate.

While listening to Lilah talk, I cleaned up my plate. If I said no to her, nothing would ever taste so good again. I had no desire to have a family, not in the traditional sense. I had every intention to please Lilah. I couldn't afford to lose her. Yet I hated her for asking.

"Obviously Jon and I would compensate you . . . " she said.

"Is this what it's all about? Earlier? And now?" I pointed to the food, to its staged perfection.

She said she was thirty-eight years old. Realistically, she didn't have a lot of time left to try again. Jon wanted a family and their relationship might not survive without children. I laughed at that. I did not overestimate her. She was a woman who wasn't afraid to use her power.

"I didn't think you were one of those women. You know, the sort who uses kids to keep their marriage," I said.

"You think it's pathetic. Just say it."

"It's fucking pathetic."

"What would you do in my place?" she said.

"I don't know."

"You see, unlike you, I'm willing to make mistakes. That's how life is. You can't blame everything on the waves because you got washed up on a shore. You still have some choices."

"Choices!" I shouted and threw my plate in the sink. It broke in three pieces. "If it were up to me, you would leave that hopeless marriage."

"It's not hopeless. Not anymore. Because I have you. Help us."

I wanted to fall asleep, but I found myself walking outside until the streets became unfamiliar, engulfed in a new darkness.

I left Lilah with the broken plate, the aftermath of the dinner she had cooked for us, and an empty bottle of wine. I realized now she'd drunk little and not eaten much. She wasn't the one who was caressed, touched, pleasured, and I had felt justified to demean her all the same because she'd asked me to carry her child, something I might have felt honored by had the circumstances been different.

It humiliated me that I'd lost my temper. Words fell from my tongue as if down a flight of stairs; bruised, foolish, nonsensical. My face burned with shame, my hands ice-cold. Lilah had stared at me as if hearing me for the first time: someone without borders, someone who had been hiding behind a borrowed language.

What I really wanted was to yell a series of insults carefully chosen and at the same time spontaneous groups of words designed to puncture, to gouge a wound. But I was not allowed to get angry in English. For as long as I had lived in the United States, I had not shown myself to be anything but quiet. Subtle. Controlled. When I tried to yell in my mother tongue, my vocabulary fell short. Instead, I screamed incoherently as if possessed, sharp sounds that belonged to neither language. I was furious at her for peeling me away, layer by layer, as if pulling a shroud off a corpse. We had faced each other in the narrow kitchen and dining area, me as my seven-year-old self, she as a woman stunted by the power she'd had all along, the same power she used to make herself a victim. Perhaps she didn't know she was doing it, casting that reckless, girlish spell on everything she touched.

When I got home, Lilah had already left. I walked to the bathroom. The fog had evaporated, but the nutty scent of the coconut shampoo she'd used was still there. On the tiled walls were a few long strands of hair. I thought they looked like Lilah's, darker and thicker than my own gossamer, but I wasn't sure. I pulled at the end of one strand and spun it around my forefinger. My mother's hair, coarse and abundant, was the only other woman's hair I'd pulled off a bathroom wall. As a child, they had been something for me to play with while I showered. Inside the bathtub was also where I'd cried, knowing that the sound of pouring water would drown me out, though I didn't do that so often. After coming to New York, I hadn't been able to produce a tear. In the mirror, my nose and eyes were red, but dry. I smeared water and soap on the mirror, squinted my eyes. If I tried hard, I could blur my face and see Mother in my own reflection. "What do I do? What should I do?" I asked her. My life had nothing for me to boast about, nothing I could tell my mother if we ever spoke again, and yet I still held on to this one fact—my inability to metamorphose my feelings into tears, into a navigable sorrow—as if it were something to be proud of.

I had fallen asleep with Lilah's hair twisted to a nest around my finger. When I woke, most of it had unraveled, lying lifelessly on my chest. The mattress was soaked as though somebody had dumped a gallon of water on it. For a few minutes, I wasn't sure where I was. Then comprehension set in and I gasped, horrified at what I'd done. Was I seven again or was I an adult woman who had just pissed the bed for no good reason? I curled in a ball and laughed into my knees. I couldn't stop from shaking, my own laughter like an ice cube lodged in my throat. Then, a hand touched my shoulder, "Morning." I turned my head, shocked to realize I wasn't alone. Lilah. She'd come back last night. I couldn't look at her; couldn't speak. Her clothes were damp from my urine. She rolled towards me, toward the puddle beneath my body. As she had once done at Crater Lake, she put her arms around my waist and held me tightly against her.

"There's nothing dirty about piss," she said.

We cramped our bodies in the tiny bathtub. Lilah squirted half a bottle of shampoo in the water, nearly drowning us in soap bubbles. How hard it was to really look into someone's eyes without being embarrassed by anything, yet as Lilah stared into mine, I held her gaze, letting her look at me, letting myself be seen without anywhere to hide. Then she asked me the same question I'd asked her when we met in Montauk, the question I would have dreaded had it been any other time.

"Who are you?" she said.

I began with my bedroom wall, tracing in my mind the outline of my mother's country, one that didn't exist in any history book or pictured on any map. I told Lilah of the Vietnam I knew, lost to me forever no matter how many times I might try to return in the future. I talked to her until the water in the tub grew cold; the bubbles dissolved, opened up, and our bodies appeared, naked and submerged. Our skin the same, wrinkled and gray.

It was Saturday; the sun had just come up. I had the morning to myself and decided to go for a walk in the park. Dogwood branches crisscrossed above my path, covering it in a dewy darkness. Needles of sunlight penetrated the thicket, giving me the sensation that I was visible and not alone. I'd walked for nearly a mile when I saw him. He was on a bench, pulling pieces of what looked like a leftover sandwich from a brown bag, crumbling and tossing them at his feet. A few sparrows, a couple of starlings and doves, circled him. Given our situation, he was supposed to be my rival, but it was hard for me to summon such feelings watching him feed the birds.

"Hey, Jon," I said.

Before answering me, he tossed the brown bag into a trash bin. The birds scattered. "Hey," he said.

Suddenly I'd the urge to tell him about what had happened with Lilah. I wanted to hear someone say that it was cold of her to combine adultery with a favor. But what was I going to say—that I wanted my first kiss with Lilah to be pure and not ridden with consequences—I could not. She was never mine to begin with.

I sat down next to him. He took a joint from his shirt pocket, lit it, and handed it to me. I inhaled and leaned back on the bench, cold morning dew tingling my arms.

"Sorry I couldn't come to dinner the other night," he said.

"It's alright."

"No. It's not."

We passed the joint back and forth a few more times, then Jon put it out on the rim of a trash can and tossed it. We exchanged a few more words about the sky, the temperature—warm for late November; a one-footed pigeon on the opposite bench, which we both expressed pity for, then Jon stood up.

"Lilah hasn't been home much lately," he said.

"I'm sorry—"

"Why, is it your fault?" he asked, but didn't wait for an answer. "Thanks for—it was nice."

I nodded.

"Can we—is it okay if we keep this between us?"

"Sure," I said, though I wasn't sure if he meant our chance meeting, us sharing a smoke, or me finding him in the first precious morning hours alone, not a husband or a could-have-been father, just a man feeding wild birds.

7

Another light bulb in the coffee shop broke. It was past eleven at night and I'd finished putting away the chairs. I checked the bathroom walls for chewing gum and pried it off. I'd worked here since I'd dropped out of college a few years ago because it was easy and I could talk to hundreds of people every day and still preserve my solitude. Now I was still in my twenties, but felt that it wouldn't be long until I was replaced with a fresher face and a less sullen manner. With the money from Lilah and Jon I could finish college. I'd gone to the fertility clinic with a simple desire to make money and to be able to live near my neighbor, yet Lilah's need had collided with my own. In the corner, my coworker Matt was sweeping.

"Hey, Matt," I called.

"What?" He looked up. His boyish face contrasted with his deep voice.

"When you realize you have feelings for someone, do you tell them right away or do you wait?"

"It depends," he said.

"On what? Timing?"

"I think it depends on whether or not you want anything to change." He shook his head. "I don't know—people like to confess their feelings, but afterward they're not ready to face the fact that nothing changes."

"You alright? Rough talk with the girlfriend last night?" I asked.

"She wants different things. I'm amazed anyone in this world can find love at all. I'll probably end up alone." He swept a dust pile into a corner. "Anyway, you're probably asking for a reason. So who is it?"

"Someone I can't have," I said.

"Well there, that's your answer."

There was a game I used to play as a girl. One person would ask "what if" and the other would answer. Nobody ever explained the rules of the game. It was the kind of game that was not possible if the participants didn't automatically know the rules. On my phone, I sent Lilah a message.

What if I were walking down an alley alone with a hundred dollar bill pinned to my chest?

I had taken the long route home though I was tired.

I would think you're a huge idiot, but would wait to see what happens next.

She understood. I took a decorative pin off the breast of my sweater, pierced a bill through, and pinned it on my outer jacket.

Only have a twenty. I pressed send. In front of me was an elusive orange tabby cat. Repeatedly it waited for me to catch up with it and then ran further ahead. It was looking back at me now from under the bridge.

What if tonight was the last night of humanity and you were walking alone in the dark with money pinned to your chest, and I were drinking water even though I'd rather have vodka?

I would tell you to have as much vodka as you like. I continued to follow the cat. Behind me there was the sound of shoes crunching on dry leaves.

Having one now. All better.

That was how the game worked. In small increments, it changed the state of the world.

Someone's following me. What if he's a murderer?

Tell him you'll give him twenty dollars to kill you.

I smiled. My heart was beating rapidly inside my chest. Under the bridge, the cat lay down on its back and rolled around on the concrete. Part of me wanted to keep walking so that I wouldn't lose it, but I turned around and faced my shadow. He was a man, small in stature, eyes like a hawk. His lips disappeared into his mouth.

"If you kill me, you can have this." I pointed to the bill on my jacket.

"What?" He walked up to meet me. "Kill you?"

"You can have it," I said "If you kill me."

He squinted his hawk eyes. "How?"

"That's not for me to figure out." We both looked at the water.

"I could give you a push over there. It would look like you committed suicide?" he said.

Going to jump off the bridge. With help of course.

Jon is on his way to rescue you.

The man and I walked side by side. We reached the underbelly of the bridge. I didn't see the cat. We climbed a short flight of stairs up the bridge.

"Why do you want me to kill you?" he asked.

I shrugged.

"Why did you think I would accept? There's something about me, isn't there? People are always asking this kind of thing from me."

"Honestly I didn't think you would accept. I was playing a game with someone. It's my bad luck that you agreed," I said.

"A game?"

I nodded. I leaned over the railing and looked down. The water looked like jelly. I believed that I would not die if I fell. I would slowly sink into the jelly.

"What if I really pushed you?" he asked. He seemed to be full of questions.

"It was your idea," I said. "I would either die or survive."

I stepped onto the railing. His entire face was scrunched up, only his eyes remained wide and unblinking.

"Damn you. Damn you all," he said. "I'm not going to do anyone anymore favors. You can wait your turn just like everyone else, alright?" he growled and walked away. The back flap of his jacket fluttered behind him. He seemed to be flying away.

I checked my phone and saw a missed call and a text message from Jon.

Free for a drink?

I gave him the address of a bar nearby.

"There's no one else, is there?" Jon said and drank from his high ball. "For a while she made me feel like there was another man."

I shook my head. For a while, I'd believed so too. "You're the one she chooses. You're who she wants to have children with."

The music was loud so we huddled our heads together to talk.

"But it's really you I'm having children with," he winked.

I smiled. I understood flirting with me was his way of being kind. Even though I hadn't told Lilah I would accept, I already felt myself leaning toward Jon. Perhaps it was the alcohol, or perhaps it was standing on that bridge and feeling that it didn't matter if I fell. "I'm the conduit. If you feel uncomfortable, we can just inject your—"

"What's the difference?" He leaned in and kissed me. I could taste Lilah on him, or maybe I had been tasting him on her. I opened my mouth to let his tongue reach as far to the back of my throat as he wanted. Then he sat back.

"There's nothing difficult about it. I love my wife, so I'll do whatever to make her happy. But why are you doing it?" he said. I thought he didn't only love Lilah, he also trusted her. Trust was more dangerous.

"Tonight I met a man who others ask impossible things of," I said, "He's so used to it that he didn't blink when I asked him to kill me. I want to be someone too."

"You're the type of person who'll do anything, be anybody."

"That was true before tonight. Now I want to be the one to give you and Lilah something that doesn't exist anywhere else in the world. Please let me. I'm tired of being just anything."

We were drunk and ecstatic. The sky opened up above us and though our sense of a physical reality was distorted, habit helped me guide him and I safely back to my apartment. At my front door, Jon stopped and said, "I've been here before. I followed her a few times. I'm not a fool—"

I pulled him inside and locked the door behind us. In my bedroom, a flood of light from the ceiling fixture sobered us a little. Jon covered his mouth. Perhaps like me, he too was shocked by the intense uncertainty of our future.

"Are you sure? I know Lilah said—I feel like the three of us should have discussed it together." He shivered and looked at my open window. He seemed a different man than the one I met at the market and the one I ate with at the restaurant. He was humbled by the plan Lilah had for him, me, us.

"Close it if you want," I said.

He closed the window and let down the curtains.

"Come here," I said and suddenly felt choked up by the spontaneity of my words, the same words Lilah had spoken to me only few weeks ago.

He undressed away from me and kicked his clothes and shoes under my bed, I believed, as an attempt to show me he respected me, he wouldn't intrude on my space. It had been a while since I was intimate with a man. For the first time, I really looked at him, the plump lips, perhaps too plump for a man, the narrow eyes concealing bluish-grey irises underneath—the color deeper now than when we were at the bar—the straight brows that revealed the balance of his world.

When he came under the covers, he got hard, growing impressively between my thighs. I was glad of Jon, even if our freedom to choose was only an illusion, even if being together now was part of Lilah's plan. I consoled myself with the thought that the baby would be conceived out of love, even though the loved person was absent.

I took his penis in my hand, fondled his balls. When he entered me, he seemed surprised by my readied wetness. He kissed my mouth, grateful for the emotional truths our bodies contained that we had no control over. I squatted on top of him, went up and down. He let me decide how deeply I wanted him inside me, but grabbed my butt to control the speed. We sped up, slowed down, and sped up again until we were both blanketed by pleasure, until it was too late to define what it was we were to face.

Just when he was about to climax, Jon pulled out. His cum dripped between our legs onto the sheets. I looked at him, surprised.

"This has nothing to do with Lilah," he said. "Not that time anyway."

I dropped onto my back and lay down next to him.

"What does it mean?" I asked.

"A man and a woman." He pulled me on top of him and held me there, my nose snug in the cave of his collarbone. We melted into each other as if we'd been there together since the beginning of time.

The second time that night, Jon stayed in me when he came.

Lilah and I. We weren't little girls anymore.

8

My neighbor said he was going away for a while and asked if I could water his plants while he was gone. If I received anything from St. Ann Hospital. I should open it, scan the letters using my phone, and e-mail them to him. He was waiting to find out if he was a match for his twenty-three year old stepson, who needed a marrow transplant. My neighbor said even though his son was from his ex-wife's previous marriage and not connected to him by blood, he had taken care of him for eighteen years. If that didn't make him a father, he didn't know what would. It was the closest he would come to being one, he said, and then corrected himself—he was one.

"You'll judge me when I tell you this, but when my boy called and told me he was sick, I was devastated. Of course, I was. But it was like a little spark of happiness too." He blinked slowly, leaned back on the couch, inhaled from his cigarette and let out smoke that thinned out into strands, whirled around each other on the yellowed ceiling. It looked like a ritual he knew well, a position he'd been at for many years, sitting under this cloud of smoke. "I felt happy he called because he needed me. How shitty is that?"

I looked around his aged apartment, thoroughly soaked with tobacco, the brownish and lumpy wallpaper looked like the skin of its occupant. A cheap, short shelf made out of pinewood and metal sat on the right side of the door and served as both a shoe rack and bookshelf. There were a few books on aircrafts, one on the history of trains in the United States, and one that caught my eye, on hotels. It had none of the sparkles and relaxing blues of typical travel guides. It was a paperback and the spine was well creased. I pulled it out. I always felt entitled to books in other people's homes.

"Let me show you where the plants are."

I followed him to his bedroom. As soon as the door opened, a familiar heat and humidity sunk into my skin. I gasped. The whole room had been converted into an indoor green house of tropical plants, dusty pink and yellow hibiscus, red flamingos, white orchids, and a multitude of other plants of various shapes, sizes, and colors. Five heat lamps gave off bright light from different angles. I knelt down and fingered the petals of a hibiscus flower. It was in full bloom.

"Take it," he said. "It's a crime nobody ever gets to look at them. I'm all they've got and I'm not much company."

I plucked the flower, put it to my lips, and sipped on its stem. The sweat nectar sat on my tongue like a ghost.

My neighbor zigzagged around the plants like a wise gnome in a garden that went on forever.

"This used to bring me joy," he said. "When I found out I wasn't invited to my son's wedding, I thought that's it, you know. If I'm not a part of his life, I have nothing here to hold me back. I was always figuring out some new places to go to. Now I'm finally going."

"It's so," I struggled to speak, "real." I looked up. Several butterflies were feeding on sugar trays that hung on nickel wires from the dome-shaped enclosure. "Are they?" I asked.

"The butterflies? Of course, but don't tell anyone."

"Where are you traveling to now?" I said.

"Vietnam, my mother's country," he said. "There will be flowers like this. Just outside."

"That should be nice, right?" I said distractedly. I was on my tippy toes, trying to brush at a butterfly's wings.

"For a little while. I don't know. I've gotten used to the second-best thing." He looked around the simulated garden. "This will be my last trip."

My neighbor handed me a list with what at first seemed like detailed information on each plant. As I read it, I realized the list didn't tell me how to care for the plants, but was a compilation of their mythical facts and meaning, like the jasmine, which has a fragrance so powerful that it could bridge our world with the spirit world. The garden was so well-orchestrated that it would survive without my interference. I just had to remember to refill the sponge in the sugar trays. I was so absorbed by the bedroom garden that I'd failed to notice there was no bed anywhere.

"Where do you sleep?" I said.

"On the couch." He winked conspiratorially, as if expecting me to understand everything about him in those three syllables.

I lay down on the ground in the bedroom garden and imagined myself a girl again. Now that he'd shown me his secret, I felt safe to show mine too.

"I'm having a baby," I said. It was the first time I'd admitted it to myself. Saying it out loud didn't make it feel more real like I'd hoped. "It won't be mine. It belongs to someone else."

My neighbor laughed a kind laugh. "May I?" He showed me his palm.

He sat down next to me. I lifted my shirt so he could feel. It had only been a few weeks since Jon and I slept together so naturally there was no visible change in my belly, yet I imagined that the organs inside my body had already begun to shift shape to accommodate the idea of a child. My neighbor's rough and creased hand was warm. I relaxed under his touch.

"Everybody makes this mistake. You're young, so you do too. But a baby belongs to no one. An adult doesn't, so why would you expect a child to? Just because you give birth to her doesn't make her yours. Just because you didn't doesn't mean she's not yours either. It's not up to us asshole adults to decide, is it?" He was cheerful, exuberant. My news had livened him. Seeing him this way made me laugh too.

"I guess it's not the worst deal in the world. I'll be that favorite person. Children always have that one person, don't they? An aunt, an uncle, a grandfather," I said.

"Having a child will change you. The question of belonging—I think it's not who your baby belongs to, but that even before he's born, you already belong to him," he said.

I placed my hands on my stomach. I had spent years telling myself I didn't want a home, but like dealing with all things unobtainable, it was easier to pretend it wasn't important than admit you couldn't have it. Now I asked myself, what if the child growing inside me was the home I most needed.

After my neighbor left, I stopped by his apartment often, more frequently than I needed to. I walked from wall to wall and dragged my hand across the surface. Though my neighbor wouldn't admit it, I believed he was happy. Here, enclosed by four walls, he was contained. My neighbor would visit the world of his mother and of his adopted son, but he would not stay long in either one. Geography wouldn't fracture him, but the people would because they expected him to be one thing and one thing only. A Vietnamese son. An American father. My neighbor wouldn't admit he was more himself inside these gray walls and the wooden floor that had memorized the pattern of his footsteps day in and out than anywhere else. Time and aging had given him the peace they hadn't yet given me.

I sat down on the springy couch, stood up and went to his bedroom. I checked the temperature and humidity. I made sure to inject the sponge with more sugar water so the butterflies had enough to feed on. When it got too hot and humid, I went back to the living room and read the book on hotels. I'd skipped this part in my travel as a child, moving from my before-home to the camp, then as a teenager, leaving Vietnam for the United States. I hadn't stopped at any in-between lodgings, yet every new place I moved into had felt liminal, impermanent, no matter how long I would find myself there. I had heard of others like me who found home by constantly moving. In trains, cars, airplanes, the rhythms of their heart would start to sync with their surrounding. Between destinations, resistance fell away. Yet traveling didn't put me at ease. Being nowhere was not a state I could embrace.

I hadn't told Lilah that Jon had succeeded in impregnating me. I was paralyzed by difficult choices. How much would I be involved in the baby's life? How much would I want to be? What about Lilah and I? Lilah and Jon? Jon and I?

I didn't want to talk to them before I could resolve these questions myself. I recalled the time I'd found Lilah in the bathtub. Her beauty had incapacitated me. Yet not all desire was sensual. In that moment, I believed I'd always been attracted to her. But did I want her beyond those moments of passion? I didn't know. I was afraid of anything I couldn't walk away from. Remembering how the night had turned out, I couldn't help but nurse a suspicion that I was being used. Did she think that if she had asked me to carry their child before we made love, I might have refused her? I pictured the two of them talking, Lilah telling Jon that I would accept whatever she might ask of me. Perhaps while I was sleeping, she had called Jon and told him not to come to dinner, that she would be able to convince me on her own. I was debating whether her calculations were selfish or an expression of trust. What I didn't want to and wouldn't admit to myself was that it felt natural to yield to the role Lilah gave me. I was relieved the same way someone who had been on the run for a long time might feel when he was finally caught. There's a kind of freedom in letting others make our most significant life choices for us.

On my neighbor's couch, I put my elbows on my knees and my face into my palms. I wept and wept. I was living my life the only way it made sense to me and I could feel its palpable weight. I was sinking. I was being erased by someone I hadn't met, but felt I already knew and loved. I tried to stand up to find my phone and call Lilah, but I couldn't. Beneath my feet was nothing but air.

9

I decided to meet Jon in person to tell him the news. Having sex with him made it easier for us to talk. Deep inside Jon's skin I'd felt Lilah's presence. I'd wanted to expel him from me and so be free of her, but while we were having sex I clung onto him. Even afterward. I hadn't realized how much they resembled each other. I'd focused only on their differences when I first saw Jon, partly out of insecurity, partly out of jealousy. I couldn't admit to myself that in some ways they were right for each other. Together they formed an enviable feminine and masculine whole. Just as when Lilah was without him, she grew sturdier and more handsome, when he was without her, Jon became softer, more fragile. His skin seemed more alert to caress, his gaze spanned beyond the present moment, full of dreams. The night we were together, he had sat at the foot of the bed, deliberately silent. I could tell he wanted to talk about himself, tell me something private because the moment deserved it. He'd put his fingers to his lips and bit them. I didn't want to hear him. I was afraid his words would complicate everything.

"I'm a man. I have feelings. I need feelings to make love to someone," he'd said.

"You didn't have feelings for me before. If you do now, it will pass," I'd said.

He nodded and stared at the hangnail on his thumb.

When I finally told him we needed to talk, Jon invited me

over to their house for dinner. Lilah was visiting her father in Connecticut for the weekend. Without me asking, he assured me it would be okay with her. She understood that I wasn't ready to see her yet.

I refused his offer to come to their house and suggested we meet at a coffee shop near his home instead.

When I saw him sitting in the corner of the café, I decided for our next meeting I would let him choose the location. He looked painfully out of place, his limbs too large and strong. His legs shook constantly as though craving movement. He was ready to leap up and go somewhere else when he saw me.

"Thanks for coming here," I said. "What are you drinking?"

"Not much of a coffee drinker. I'll take an iced tea. Thanks," he said.

I ordered and brought back a black iced tea and a small coffee.

"How are you?" He looked at me and then at my stomach, as if I would begin to show immediately. I hadn't yet said anything, but he might already suspect what I was about to tell him. I'd chosen a café instead of a bar to meet at at eight o'clock at night.

"I think I'm pregnant," I said.

"So soon? I mean, what am I saying?" He scratched his temple. "That's great."

"Are you happy?"

"Lilah will be ecstatic," he said.

"So should we talk legal stuff?"

"Jesus. It's all happening so fast." He leaned back in his chair and wiped his forehead though there was no sweat there.

"Don't tell me you're not ready to be a father, Jon."

"No, it's not that. It's just that when our daughter was born—all your life, you've been told you'll get this gift. It's the most precious thing, more beautiful than anything you ever imagine. So you anticipate it, you know, the same way you couldn't wait to open your Christmas present. When you finally unwrap the box and look inside, it's not just that it's empty. It's much worse than that. You're staring at yourself, newborn and without breath. She was gone before she could open her eyes to see us, her parents. Our daughter had so much of us in her that seeing her so cold made me feel like I was already dead. There's not much difference it seems, you know, being dead or alive. Being in a cradle or a casket." He took the straw in his mouth and drained half the glass. "How can I be a father?"

"You don't have a choice, now," I said.

He chuckled, took my hand to his lips and kissed it, "Thank you."

Over iced tea, the old-fashioned way, the same way my Vietnamese ancestors had invited guests into their homes and talked about their troubles, Jon told me how badly he wanted to surrender to something, anything, to not have to question it. At first, I turned away from his confessions. I didn't want to integrate his loss and longing into my own; I didn't want to care about him. It felt as though I was betraying Lilah. He continued talking anyway, maybe because some things were too private to share with people who loved us most. It would change the way Lilah saw him. I, on the other hand, was just close enough, yet still a stranger.

He told me about his family. Jon's grandfather was a pale-skinned German, so blond his hair looked white, eyes so blue they made him seem blind. His grandmother was Jewish, olive-skinned, with thick, wavy black hair. They spent their lives loving each other and feeling full of guilt. When his grandmother talked about Stockholm syndrome, something she'd read in the newspaper, his grandfather got defensive, angry, sometimes violent. His daughter, Jon's mother, got the occasional slap, nothing more. But the old man would get depressed every time after he'd touched his wife or daughter, as if each blow carried the weight of a thousand whips, of the inescapable cruelty of their generation. He died, Jon said. His self-hatred was so deep he'd passed it down to Jon's mother.

"I think I have a lot of my grandfather in me," he said. When he saw me flinch, he shifted uneasily in his seat. "Don't worry. I would never act on it. I just get these flares of hate. Why can't you ever get away from history?"

"Maybe the three of us are writing a new kind of history. An untraceable one." I put my palms on my stomach. At the same time, I fought the urge to get as far away from him as possible. As Jon talked, I fantasized about going back to Vietnam and raising the baby alone. Then I forced myself to stop this train of thought and said, "Hey, let's figure out this paperwork. Make sure you two get your baby."

Jon smiled. This time he looked genuinely happy.

10

On most days, I liked to pretend I had no family, no one to answer to, disappoint, or live for. It was an almost truth, by geographical, social, cultural, psychological distance. It was Christmas Eve, already almost a year since Lilah and I met. Small white flecks fell from an equally white sky. I remembered something I'd once said to the little girl. I made a wish: one day, let me show her the snow. Why did I remember such a promise?

I was three months pregnant and battling the thought that someone like me shouldn't have a child. It was one of the few times that I wished I could talk to Mother. Did she not know of her lack of interest in being a parent until after I was born, or did she only realize there were other pursuits, other desires having a child could not fulfill? I was afraid I was using my own life to understand hers. Was I destined to do the same as she had, to bear a child only to send her away?

For the first time in a long time I wanted to see my mother if only to tell her about the baby I was carrying. Would she feel any kinship with it, or would it be so far removed from the drama of her life that she couldn't conjure up any feeling even if she wanted to? I imagined that was how she thought of me too. Between us, love had become more like a fact, something you knew existed outside of yourself, and less like a feeling.

Lilah and I started to see each other again. I went to her house one day. Unlike before, she didn't pretend Jon didn't exist. We were surrounded by his things. She talked about him sarcastically, lovingly, sometimes indifferently. In the span of a few minutes, she showed herself both to be a woman full of desires and one who fell asleep contentedly at bus or train stations and missed her ride. How she fluctuated between complete passion and utter boredom. She would upset me by making jokes about the future of our daughter.

"You and Jon should move in together. I'll come visit twice a week." She would laugh. Or if she was feeling cruel she would say, "It's not too late for you to get an abortion," or "I don't know if Jon is ready for this. He's such a boy, you know? Why don't you and I just run away together?"

All the scenarios she suggested made my heart throb. It reminded me of the what-if games I used to play as a child. Everything was truly possible and impossible at the same time. I felt as though there was no safe moment, no tangible outcome to my pregnancy. I was in a dream and the baby would stay inside me forever.

"Can you please stop being so horrible?" I said to Lilah.

"I'm only messing with you," she said, seeming apologetic. "But would it be so awful if it were true?"

"If what were true?" I said.

"I have a headache," she said, and walked to the bathroom.

I followed and stood behind her while she looked searchingly at her own reflection. She had been doing this a lot lately, staring at mirrors. Once while we were walking, she had stopped abruptly, blocking a line of cars. While people honked their horns and cussed at us, she calmly took out a compact mirror and held it at a strange angle from her chin.

"Come on. Let's get to the sidewalk," I'd said, but she didn't react, not to me and not to all the anger directed at us.

Now in her bathroom, her concentration once again dissolved all the objects around her, including me.

"Come on, Lilah," I said. "What are you looking at?"

She shook her head.

"What are you looking for?"

"I thought something in me would change. I want a sign." She pulled her hair from her face and opened the vanity's drawer. She took out a pair of scissors and started to snip the ends of her hair.

I wanted badly to stop her, but I knew it would only fuel her to be even more determined about the task, so I said nothing.

"Do you not want a child anymore?" I said.

"You still don't understand that it doesn't matter what I want. The baby is yours. Not Jon's, not mine. Yours."

"That's ridiculous. I didn't want this."

"Are you sure? You agreed after all. You're going to protect it with everything you've got. You will not get rid of it no matter what the circumstance."

"I agreed because it was what you wanted," I said weakly.

"Don't try to tell me you're doing it for me," she said. "Look at you. Your cheeks are rosy. God, your hair is thick and full. Do you know what I looked like while I was pregnant? You're made for it."

"Is that what you want? For me to get rid of it?" I said.

"It doesn't matter what I think." Tiny pieces of hair fell rapidly down the sink.

I put my arms on her shoulders and turned her toward me. I took the scissors from her. I gripped her wrists and looked into her eyes, "You're going to be a mother."

"You're so lonely, you know. There are consequences to that kind of loneliness," she said. She bent down and kissed my stomach.

11

Three weeks after my neighbor left, his letter from St. Ann Hospital came. I took a picture of it and e-mailed him. *I'm sorry,* I wrote. He wasn't a match for his son. A few days later, boxes started to show up every day. I would come home from work to find another package on my neighbor's front door mat or a paper stuck to his door to let me know when to expect a second delivery. All of the boxes were light except one. I stacked them next to his small shelf of shoes and books by the entrance.

On Christmas morning, I went upstairs to his apartment to open them. I told myself I would take a photo of each item just in case he needed to know what he received. As I began to open the boxes, I realized the sender was the same person. The items were small and seemingly useless. In the first box was a metal hair clip. Next was a piece of wood with a burnt end. I put it to my nose and inhaled. It had an earthy fragrance, a mixture of cinnamon and dirt. Next was a candy with a picture of a mangosteen printed on the wrapper, and then a stick of incense, a square of cloth. I went on to open all of the packages with equal excitement. Each item on its own created confusion if I handled or looked at it for too long, but all together they washed me with the most satisfying pleasure, like all my senses were nourished. I almost got to the heaviest box when my phone alerted me to an incoming e-mail.

I had the feeling I wouldn't be a match for him, but it didn't stop me from hoping. I'll be back in two days. Thanks for watching after everything and sorry about the impolite amount of stuff I sent there. Have the candy if you like. It's a rare flavor you won't find anywhere else, not even in a world market like New York.

I put the candy in the pocket of my sweater and took the heavy package downstairs to my apartment. I'd asked my neighbor to look for the little girl and wanted to ask if he'd found her, but refrained. I would wait till he got back to New York.

Outside my window, the plants inside my window box were paralyzed by the cold. The leaves that were still young a few days ago now looked stiff and eternal. My neighbor's words soothed a loneliness I hadn't known was there. A thought came to me: maybe he intended for me receive all those boxes. Maybe they weren't just for my neighbor's own use. I smiled at this possibility and eagerly cut open the last package.

The moment my hands cupped its cold and serene surface, I knew what it was. I had held a similar object many years ago, my father's urn. His body was never found after the shipwreck so instead Mother filled the urn with the ashes of objects he had used. I released the brown urn from its wrappings of paper and plastic and held it inches from my face. It was heavy. I could barely hold it up even with both hands. A black and white photograph of a young woman was glazed on the ceramic. Though the picture was faded, her facial features were sharp and clear. She was too beautiful, as if she had pulled all the vitality of living things into herself. Looking at her the light in my room seemed to dim, my own outline diminished. Underneath the picture engraved the date of her birth and death. She had lived twenty-five years.

I traced her face with my fingers. Who was she to my neighbor? There was no doubt he couldn't forget her. She was the type of girl to whom one yielded all defenses, the type that it would be a tragedy not to love because you would have missed the only experience in life that mattered. But loving her would be even worse because your life would be reduced to nothing afterward. With such a girl, you always saw the end moving toward you like an incoming train as you stood on the tracks and waited for it to crash into you so that your body ceased to be whole, splattered into smithereens. You gave up your right to a physical form so everything you felt would never betray you, would last forever.

I lifted the top of the urn. The leg of an insect-like creature stuck out from under the powdery ash. I picked it up and shook it. An origami praying mantis. Puffs of dust scattered and dissolved into the air. I breathed in slowly, aware that the ash of her burnt body was binding to my lungs. I closed my eyes and saw a field of charred lumps, what was left of the sugarcane field. The little girl's face smoldering. I turned the mantis around, trying to make out the script on its head, its under belly, and wings. Broken up into parts of the paper insect, the words didn't make much sense. I hadn't seen Vietnamese written longhand in over ten years, since after my first five years in the United States, Mother stopped writing. Holding these familiar words in my hand, fear stopped me from breathing. Flashes of the soldier who committed suicide inside the camp's common hall many years ago suddenly hit me. Those who were left behind always expected an explanation from the departed. I thought that death neither scorned nor praised and preferred silence, yet no matter how overdue an explanation, it always came.

I began to pull the praying mantis apart, starting at the wings. Two, three, four words unfolded, a sentence. Soon I had a square piece of paper flat in front of me. I read the note, surprised by how easily understanding came to me, as if the written symbols awoke a portion of my brain that had been asleep. The paper gave spirits detailed direction on how to cross the river of forgetting in order to move on to the other side of the world.

No matter how long you have to wait, wait for the small wooden boat with a single rower. Give him a coin and he will take you to the other side. Do not look back. Do not get impatient and wander away from the river. Do not set foot in the water even if it looks shallow. Behind you will echo the voices of your friends, your family, even strangers you've long forgotten. They will sing your praises. They will ask for your forgiveness. They will make promises they won't keep. Ignore them. Your only task left is to forget everything.

The note should have been burned up with everything else the dead needed to begin their process of rebirth, but here it was in a cold apartment a continent away. Many other things were probably burned: a paper house with gold-colored walls cut out in intricate patterns of birds and flowers, paper shoes, paper clothes, paper jewelry, paper money. These things were still waiting for her across the river, but where was she?

Holding the note in my hand made me aware of an unbearable loneliness. Lilah had said she and Jon were going to be in Montauk for Christmas. They had decided not to go to either family this year. She told me this kindly. I wondered if she had meant, "you don't have to be alone, unless you want to." Had they done this for me? Alone with my thoughts, there were many possibilities. I got dressed hurriedly, ran upstairs to grab my neighbor's car keys and headed out.

The streets were empty, except for a few stubborn cars driving against the blizzard. On the sidewalk, a man and a woman stood still smiling as snow peppered the fur on their jackets and fell into their open eyes. In extreme weather, I often felt reckless, as if in one sweep the wind could obliterate everything and in doing so would give me what I truly wanted. I was used to solitude, not only from it being my constant condition as a child but also because it was a component as essential as breath to migration. Someone on the move must be ready to lose everything that is important to him. They must accept that being alone is not a state that can be overcome by making friends, learning their friends' language, mastering their expressions of love, fear, anger. Solitude is the result of cutting themselves free from the umbilical cord that connects them to the womb of their motherland.

I scrolled through text messages to find the name of the motel and the room number Lilah said she and Jon would be at. I didn't write or call to let her know I was coming. I was afraid she might deter me from traveling. *It's too dangerous for you to drive, we are coming back tonight anyway, there are no more vacant rooms at our motel,* I imagined her responding. I asked myself, who was I really going there to see?

The motel parking lot was narrow and mostly empty.

I walked past the icebox to the first window. Half of the curtain was drawn. A boy sat on the bed reading something out loud. By the stove at the far corner of the room, a woman was brushing her teeth. I realized it was before noon. Maybe Lilah and Jon were still asleep. I approached their window. The blinds were closed, except for a thin gap. I looked in. They were laying with their backs to the window, Jon's back and buttocks pressed against Lilah's chest and stomach. He was deep inside her embrace.

Their room was suffused in a soft green, probably from the reflection of the carpet. They looked like any ordinary couple, so distracted by each other's faults and selfish afflictions that they forgot how easily and naturally they were in a shared sleep.

I put my hands underneath my coat and sweater. Seeing them on the bed forced me to admit that at times I had wanted Lilah to myself and that at times in her absence I'd desired Jon. Agreeing to be a surrogate mother came from an unbearable need to belong. It was not apparent to anyone else but myself that there was another life inside me. The little girl from my childhood would not accept being an outsider. Through her and only through her would Jon and Lilah be able to express their feelings for each other. She would be both a recipient and a transmitter of their separate life.

Outside of their motel windows, my feet gripped the soles of my shoes.

I could get in my neighbor's car and go back to being alone again.

I knocked. It was Jon who met me at the door. He had put on shorts and cracked the door only slightly.

"Hm." It was hard for me to speak. Our breath fogged the air between us.

Jon scratched his head and opened the door wide enough so I could slip in, not so wide so that the arctic wind could fill their room. Lilah rubbed her eyes and sat up when she saw me.

"I have a present for you. Do you want it now?" she said, still sounding of sleep.

"I'll make us tea. We all want tea right?" Jon said while buttoning his shirt. "It wasn't safe for you to travel—" He glanced at my stomach and quickly looked away.

"Sure, Jon, please make some tea," Lilah said. We both watched him walk over to the burner. He was a good man. He was always going to be.

Lilah got off the bed, went over to her duffle bag, and removed various items. She pulled out a small, clear blue bag.

"Merry Christmas." She handed it to me.

"It took her a really long time to—" Jon said.

"Jon, she hasn't opened it."

"Sorry."

It was cream-colored baby overalls with patterns of wild animals, bears, rabbits. A typical baby item. I turned it around to look at the front and my eyes froze on the beautiful stitching in butter yellow and mossy green threads that had been done by hand, apparently after the overalls were purchased.

Quoc-Anh.

"It's a very difficult name to pronounce," I said. I was smiling.

"Yes, we know," Lilah said. "*Kwok-Ann*, that's how you say it. Right?"

I nodded. "It's a boy's name."

"We don't know its gender," She breathed in slowly. "We just wanted—I think our baby should have a Vietnamese name. Jon picked it. We listened to Google pronunciation for hours. He said this one sounds beautiful and I agree. We can always change it."

"I like it. I like it very much," I said, squeezing the overalls between my fingers and burying my nose in it. I closed my eyes and saw the baby's face. She would have a boy's name and that was perfectly fine. Did Jon and Lilah look far enough into names to know *Quoc* was the root for *country*? I looked at Jon, who was pulling tea bags from the pot and squeezing the bags so the dark, potent liquid dripped out. Lilah was getting into her jeans. Looking at her, I hoped the baby would have such beautiful long legs too. I was filled with tenderness for them both, together as a couple and separately.

Maybe it was possible to love in this way.

Outside, the snow was falling heavily. Large mounds of dense snow were accumulating on top of pavement, sidewalks, cars.

"What will we do?" I said and turned from the window.

"We've got everything we need here. Food and water," Jon said.

"Come sit with me," Lilah said. She took the remote from her bedside and switched on the TV.

I got underneath the blanket, already forgetting about Jon,

at the same time feeling glad he was there. Lilah and I had spent many hours this way before, with a blanket pulled up to our chins, hours and hours of confessions. It was impossible not to love another when she had revealed so much to you. Jon brought our teas to us. He sat down on the bed next to me. We were silent, watching whatever was on TV. No one changed the channel. Hours passed in this way, fusing us into one unit. We found pleasure in watching one car commercial after another, the end of a movie, more commercials, the beginning of a cooking show. Cold air grazed the skin on my neck; warm tea soothed my throat.

"It's crazy to think six months from now the three of us will have created a brand new person," Jon said.

Lilah and I looked at him. An absolute silence overtook the room. Then we burst out laughing and laughing. Tears swelled from the corners of our eyes. Jon smiled, a little embarrassed at first, then joined us in our helpless laughter.

I stayed for a night and drove back the next day. My neighbor was on his flight back to New York and asked me to pick him up the airport. Lilah wanted to ride back with me, but I told her I had to go right back to work so it would be better if I left alone. We embraced each other. Jon kissed the top of my head.

In the car, I laid the baby overalls on the passenger seat. It took all my concentration not to keep looking at them and focus on the road. The wind hissed past my car and the world ahead looked vast and directionless. White flurries rained down with such speed on the windshield that I couldn't see well. I didn't care. I was happy and knew I couldn't explain that happiness to anyone else, yet I desired to talk, to share my new joy with others. Up until then I had been preparing myself to be rejected. I had been waiting for them to tell me they no longer wanted to be parents, or that they regretted involving a stranger in their quest for a family. I imagined they talked to each other warmly, reassuring the other of how wonderful it would be and then in private, I imagined they prayed for the baby to die in my womb. Instead they had quietly pulled me in. Without words. In facing me, an uncontrolled variable, they eased back into their own safety, their love. Perhaps they didn't mind that I floated around them because I never showed I wanted more. I hoped their feelings for me would not soon go away and that mine for them would not grow too quickly.

I waited for my neighbor at the arrival gate, head bowed the way I'd once waited for my soldier. These untraceable manners were perhaps all that made a person. From outside, I spotted his head by the conveyor belt. It suddenly seemed strange to me that he was waiting for his luggage, a thing too cumbersome for a man who always carried in him the desire to leave. When he came out, he gathered me in for a hug and pinned my head against his chest. My neighbor, what history he had, what language he hid beneath his unaccented and faultless English—it was too late to distinguish between the man he was and the man I saw him to be.

We didn't speak at first, instead communicated by busying ourselves with our hands. I gave him the car keys since it was his car to drive. He took them, lifted his luggage into the trunk, shut it.

It was soothing to be with him. We shared a silence only people who had witnessed how a large piece of time affected each other would. Behind the steering wheel, he sighed. The skin on his cheeks was sun-beat, white stubble grew there. He looked as if he had gone somewhere for the purpose of aging gracefully. He looked much older than I remembered, and more handsome.

"Were you—were you able to find her?" I turned my head to the window so he wouldn't see my face.

"Yes," he said.

No other words were exchanged until we nearly reached home. I didn't know what I wanted to know about the little girl, except that she was still alive and I hoped, rooted in the same field she'd farmed, entangled in a deep sea of green, her eyes bleached white from a blinding sun.

"Did you talk to her?" I asked.

My neighbor nodded. "She wasn't curious about who I was," he inhaled sharply. "I didn't think I would miss this cold. You know, I don't think she was curious about much. I remember she didn't ask a single question. She looked ill."

Illness. What did he mean by this? Thoughts whirled in my head. Was it something he observed or was it a fact? I frowned and shifted in my seat.

"She's very poor. That shouldn't surprise you though because almost everyone there is. And everyone who is poor is also sick. I gave her some money."

"Money."

"Are you going to visit her?"

"Eventually," I said though up until that point I hadn't considered it.

"Good," he said.

After he parked, my neighbor stretched in his seat.

"I could go for a long sleep," he said, and looked at the baby overalls in my hands. I was not conscious that I'd been squeezing them, rubbing the fabric between my fingers this whole time. I opened my palm so he could see the threaded name.

"A hidden talent?" my neighbor asked.

"I didn't make it—" I hesitated, not knowing why I didn't want to tell him the truth. Even though he didn't know their names, he knew about them. "It's a Christmas gift from Lilah." It was the first time I'd spoken her name to someone else.

"What does her husband think of it?"

"The name was his idea. He likes the way it sounds."

"It's either a wonderful or dangerous thing," he said.

"I'm happy. I haven't been so happy—and I don't feel cold. I've been feeling this chill in my chest and my stomach, like an iceberg, for years. They make it go away," I stumbled my words. I felt protective of Lilah and Jon, sensing a harsh judgment about to come from my neighbor.

He simply nodded. We left the car and walked the block toward our apartment building. Suddenly, I looked forward to being surrounded by my white walls, the empty space filled with possibilities.

"You said you won't travel again, right?" I asked him.

"No, I don't ever need to leave again," he said.

In that moment, I felt like I had everything.

As I got heavier every day, I started to feel desperate for the mother I never understood, the country I never knew. All the time I thought of the little girl, of the woman she'd become. I wished badly to be seen by her, to be remembered, and reflect on our mutual memory—places, circumstances, and feelings that only existed for us and no one else. I wondered if she remembered my mother.

I heard my neighbor's footsteps coming down the stairs. He came in and told me he would make us dinner. I nodded. I easily accepted help during those days and was grateful for his company. Watching him hunch over the cutting board, carefully chopping up the lemongrass and mincing it on the stove, I wasn't sure what it was that brought a sharp pain to my chest. Was it because we were two strangers whose displacement from ourselves was so great that we found comfort in seeing our reflection in each other? Or was it because the smell of lemongrass had so acutely penetrated my senses and took me back to my mother's kitchen inside our house at the camp? Or was it my soldier who refused to be found but was everywhere?

The dish my neighbor was making was traditionally eaten by the poor. Pork fat fried in shrimp paste. The war against the United States had turned it into an essential dish for many families due to food shortage. It was popular because its saltiness meant it could be rationed into many meals to trick the brain into thinking it was eating meat. Meat didn't last very long so usually fat was preferred. In peaceful time, other vegetables became available, and it was often eaten with cucumbers.

"Who do I remind you of?" my neighbor said as he pushed the pork around on the frying pan. He must have felt my gaze on him.

"Nobody. It's a great effort for me to remember anything," I said.

"Everyone remembers their childhood. Those first memories," he said.

"Who do I remind you of?" I asked.

"All the women I've ever loved."

I chuckled, "Are we so alike?"

"No. We're just doomed to love the same person over and over again, whether or not they wear a different face."

"I don't know—" I said.

My neighbor turned off the stove.

"What was she like?" I looked at the urn he had sent from abroad, still sitting at the highest shelf on my bookcase. "You have to lose in order to love. You always lose at the end."

"You only lose if you let go, but you haven't. You've made me him, whoever he was." He gave me a plate. It smelled sweet and salty. It smelled like empty seashells, fish skeletons, a sinking boat.

"I never meant to. Why do you go along with it?"

"I don't have a choice. People accept the role assigned to them so they can be in each other's life," he said. "This is delicious." My neighbor looked at the meat clasped between his chopsticks as though he couldn't quite believe he'd managed to conjure these flavors again after so long. He continued, "Don't you think that when we tire of someone, we're really just tired of who we are when we're with them? So we leave and try on new cloaks. The first step to remaking yourself is to get away from the person who knows you best."

I nodded. The crunchy freshness of the cucumber was perfect with the savory pork.

"Tell me about her and I'll tell you about him," I said. Perhaps tonight would be the needle through a mirage, the beginning of a tear through the fabric of our imagined friendship, an assumption that we'd met long ago and would continue to meet again.

"The last thing she said to me was she knew how much I loved her," my neighbor said. "You're just about her age when she was at her most beautiful, even while she was dying."

Unconsciously I touched my hair and realized I'd been wearing the hair clip my neighbor had sent. It must have belonged to her. In the living room the wood, too, was burning, giving the apartment a warm fragrance of cinnamon and dirt. The candy was still in the jacket of my sweater. I wondered with panic whether it'd been her favorite flavor. Since I met my neighbor on the train, I'd drawn comfort in his familiarity and not realized I'd also given him the freedom to mold me. I again fingered the cool metal of the hair clip, uncertain of what to do. My neighbor's hands were on the dining table. He reached out and touched the tips of his fingers to mine.

We sat there, silent, inside an impossible memory in which I was the girl he loved and he was my soldier, my father, my mother, my country.

12

The baby moved inside me as I let rain pour down my shoulders, my stomach. My mother had once told me Vietnamese children were strong because they were exposed to the elements early on. Motherhood would be brief for me so I tried to give her as much as I could. I sang fragments of Vietnamese nursery rhymes to her. Lines I couldn't remember I would either hum the tune or fill in my own words. The baby seemed pleased with my effort. I talked to her daily as I moved about my apartment, visited my neighbor upstairs, went outside. I always told her about what I was doing, not omitting even the smallest detail.

As I washed the dishes, I told her of the soap I used which smelled of lavender and basil. I described the pattern on the plates, elephants entwined in vines of leaves and flowers. And for the white ceramic bowls, I tried to tell her about the color white, like a sun-filled sky, a spirit wishing to be seen. As much as I could, I told her the truth, my truth. She was the first person I'd ever been completely honest with. I promised her that after she was born, I would go to Vietnam. Even though I hadn't met her, I sensed she was already a sociable child.

During the last trimester, I got used to having company all the time. Sometimes Lilah would come alone, sometimes Jon would. Often they visited me together. Against my repeated refusals, they brought over baby toys, bottles, and even a bassinet. When Jon began assembling it in the living room, I became frustrated.

"What are you doing?" I said.

"Making a crib. We'll need one."

"Why don't you make it at your place?"

"We did. We'll have one over there and one here," he said.

I stared at Lilah, pleading with my eyes for her to intervene. She avoided my gaze and continued to sit on the couch with her knees pulled in to her chest, flipping through a magazine.

"I'm not raising the baby. You two are," I said.

Jon smiled as if the idea of having only two parents was extremely humorous. I grabbed the hammer from him.

"A baby needs its mother's milk. It's the healthiest thing for our child. I thought you might want to spend some time with it too."

"Well, I don't," I said. "I'll put the milk in bottles and bring them to you."

Jon went to the couch and sat down with his arms around Lilah.

"So you think after you give us the baby, you'll just avoid us forever?" Lilah said.

"No—" I said.

"So you'll be in our life and act as if you're like any other friends of ours with no relationship to the baby whatsoever?" she said.

"We don't have to tell her anything," I said.

"Children ask questions," Jon said.

"I'm not going to lie to my kid. You're the birth mother. What we have—the three of us have—is nothing to hide." Lilah went back to flipping her magazines. "Jon will stop building the crib if you like. The point is we can share some of the responsibility if you want to. I know you do."

Inwardly I was hopeful and grateful for the prospect of spending more time with the baby, but the arrangement worried me. Lilah seemed to resist anything that could be named. She drifted toward ambiguities like an object in perpetual free fall, never touching the ground. Jon and I were figures in the dream she'd created. Who was I outside of her fantasy? There would be no baby, no joy that resembled grief, no sob that sounded like laughter, nothing at all.

"I don't want the crib here," I said.

They didn't insist further. Jon gathered the remaining parts and pushed them in the corner of my living room together with the unfinished crib. These minor disagreements between us didn't bother me. I was glad they happened; glad to have one foot on the deck of a drowning ship. Otherwise, I was too happy to play the role of a member of the family.

Because it was spring, I sometimes left my front door open for fresh air. My neighbor needed to walk by my door to go upstairs to his apartment. He saw Lilah and Jon but never acknowledged them. One day Jon sensed this and said hello. It was one of his weaknesses—his discomfort at the idea of anyone not liking him. My neighbor glanced at Jon as though he didn't understand. It was a pretense and also a self-defense tactic all immigrants had taken part in at times to avoid conflict—act as if they didn't know English. Seeing this, Jon waved his hand dramatically, but my neighbor had already disappeared up the stairwell.

"What's with him?" Jon said.

I shook my head and pretended I didn't understand the question.

"Let's take a vacation," Lilah said. I wondered if she was unaware of what just happened or simply didn't think it involved her.

"What?" Jon said. "It's not a good time, Lilah."

"After the baby is born, we'll be too busy. The three of us could go to the beach or the mountains. Whatever you want," she said.

"I don't think I should travel." I touched my round belly, imagining a sweaty hike up hills.

"It'll be good for you," she said to me. "Fresh air, peace and quiet. We'll get back way before your due date."

"Alright," I said.

Upon hearing my plan to go with Jon and Lilah to Martha's Vineyard, my neighbor immediately expressed disapproval.

"You are too big to travel." He shook his head.

"It's not far. They will drive, but I'm flying there," I said.

"You should be looking at colleges. I thought that's what you wanted."

I was hurt. "I will after the baby's born."

"They're paying for a service, for you to give them a child. No matter how much you think they may care about you, they'll forget about you once they're busy being parents. They're not your family," he said. We were standing under a mini palm tree in his indoor greenhouse. "Focus on the life you actually have."

"And be like you?" I said.

He ignored this remark. "You can work at my firm part time as a paralegal while you go to school. If you want to, you can take the bar exam. I'll make sure my firm hires you. It'll take a while, but—"

"Being a lawyer isn't going to help me."

"No, but it's a solid position in society. Nobody questions a doctor and a lawyer. All people want is for you to wear a nametag. They'll leave you alone once they've identified what you are. Don't you want this?"

I nodded.

He became quiet. His butterflies had surrounded him. One with crimson red and orange wings perched firmly on his arm as he moved about and watered the plants. They were used to his presence, he was just another tree in the garden. "You can be as disjointed as you like, but it's important to look predictable if you want society to accept you. The older you get, the less forgiving people will be. Pick up a nametag. Doesn't matter what it is."

On my way to the airport, the baby kicked violently. I cupped my hand over my mouth. The cab driver asked me twice if he should take me to a hospital instead. I shook my head and told him I was going to spend a few days by the sea. Lilah and Jon had opted to take the scenic route instead of flying, so I would get there before them. As soon as I got on the plane, a sharp pain rippled across my stomach. I pressed my teeth together in order not to scream out. I'd heard of women giving birth before their due dates, but I'd hoped my baby would stay inside me as long as possible. I was not ready to let her go.

As soon as the plane landed, I went to the restroom and vomited. Nothing came up but water, since I'd taken care not to eat that morning. Sweat soaked through the front of my shirt. Immediately I felt better.

"Your first?" A woman with streaks of gray hair and a youthful face asked me.

I nodded, smiling.

"The first one is so special. They all are, but nothing is like the first," she said.

"How many kids do you have?" I said.

"Three. Two of them work in the city. One lives here on the vineyard," she said. She was radiant with pride. "Good luck to you."

As soon as she turned her back, I leaned on the sink and heaved heavily. The tears behind my eyes had dried up and felt like thorns pushing through. My eyes burned but I could not cry. I had nobody but myself to blame.

The house we stayed at belonged to Jon's grandfather. The back porch opened up to a morass of bright green. An egret stood against a softly lit sky, diffused by spontaneous sweeping brushes of orange, purple, aquamarine. Two deer trotted on the edge of the marshland and disappeared behind the trees. Jon came out to join me on the porch. He handed me a cup of cinnamon tea.

"I came here every summer as a kid. When I met Lilah in college, I took her here. We come back every summer," he said.

Lilah was inside running up and downstairs, grabbing and distributing towels and bed sheets. The house was as familiar to her as it was to Jon. I wondered if as a college girl she had treaded lightly on the wooden floor, careful not to let it register her awkward and confused footsteps. I didn't know what to do except stand as still as I could and disappear into the picture that surrounded me. Was marriage like this, a continuous folding of memory and longing for the past that every sigh, every breath, a glance over the shoulder only happened once and every attempt thereafter only served to strengthen or dilute the original. Standing next to me, Jon was simultaneously the man of ten, fifteen, twenty, thirty years ago. No matter who he was or who he may become, the house would hold him there spellbound, energized by the promise of a new love.

"Our kid will have this too, just as I did," he said.

"It will be a perfect childhood," I said. I thought only a man who'd had such a happy youth would be able to love so simply, fearlessly.

I went into one of the bedrooms. Lilah was sleeping on top of the blankets with a book over her face. I lay down next to her, put her hand to my lips. The sunlight coming in through the bedroom windows warmed my closed eyelids. Though I was nearly twenty years late, I still hoped we would share the same dream.

When I woke, it was half past ten at night. Lilah seemed to just wake as well. She yawned lengthily.

"That was the best nap." Her face was rosy.

"Hm." I smiled.

After eating an elaborate dinner Jon had made, clam chowder, seafood risotto, fresh berries and cream, we sat on the couch in the living room with a cool breeze on our back and the sound of mating frogs all around us. We talked only of the future. They asked what I would study if I went back to school. I told them that I wanted to be a journalist and cover the ordinary life of citizens in places assumed to be broken and violent. I realized that I had something resembling a dream only as I said it. I also hoped to find the camp where I grew up though I would need to walk there blindfolded, guided entirely by intuition since I was never told where it was. They said that I should go as far as I wanted and do as much as I was able. They would raise the baby to know me and love my name no matter where I was. I felt they had sensed my panic as the day approached. They assured me that they weren't afraid of the baby loving someone else beside them. They reminded me of the deer I'd seen from the porch, so remote and unburdened that you didn't want to get too close so as not to startle them from a beautiful dream. I decided that my neighbor was wrong about them.

The next day I woke up early and walked alone to the beach. A boy with blond curls ran with the waves, squealing in excitement. His father stood close by, typing on his cellphone. I put down my towel and joined the others who were mesmerized by the rhythm of the sea. The boy's father acknowledged me right away. We were the only people on the beach unaccompanied by other adults. Soon he came to introduce himself. I knew he'd taken noticed I wasn't wearing a wedding ring.

"Is your husband with you?" he said.

"I'm not married," I told him.

He looked thoughtful, typed something on his phone, then put it away in his shorts' pocket.

"Your son is beautiful. Not just in the way that all children are either," I said.

The father tilted his head slightly as if he was observing his son as a person for the first time rather than an extension of himself.

"He takes after his mother."

"Is she not fond of water?" I said.

"She passed away many years ago." He sat down next to me. "It was perfect with her here."

"Perfect," I said.

"Don't get me wrong. I'm happy now too," he said. "The lucky ones get to know that feeling once in their life, the feeling of home. I wanted nothing more than what I had." He took his phone out of his pocket, looked at the screen. "Sorry, got to take this." He got up, brushed off the sand and walked away.

"Want to go for a drive?" Lilah asked.

"Where's Jon?" I said.

"Catching up with his friends. Don't forget he grew up coming here."

"Right, let's go."

Lilah drove us off the main road, down a bumpy and dusty path. Sometimes, she closed her eyes briefly as though she didn't care where we might end up. I refrained from telling her to pay attention, though I was scared when she kept her eyes close for too long. I looked at our surrounding carefully like I was the person behind the steering wheel and not her. The landscape was featureless, only a few shrubs and mossy boulders. Nausea rolled through me and I yelled at Lilah to stop the car.

"We're almost there!" she said, making no attempt to slow down.

Bitter saliva filled my mouth. "Please stop the car," I said again, only to feel it pick up speed. I checked the speedometer and swallowed. Fear had temporarily suppressed my nausea. "Slow down," I begged her. Over the hill, I could begin to make out the shape of a tree. Lilah pressed on the gas pedal and the car shot forward toward the tree trunk.

"We're almost there!" Lilah cheered. Moments before we would crash into the tree, I grabbed the steering wheel and hard turned it to the right.

"What the hell is wrong with you?" The car stopped. I stumbled out the passenger seat. "Can't you hold off your games for one second? I'm fucking pregnant. With your baby!"

"I'm sorry." She came toward me, knelt down and hugged my stomach. "I wasn't going to let anything hurt you. I just wanted to feel close to her, for you to feel close to her too."

"Who?" I unclasped her arms around my body, not wanting her to discover how fast my heart was beating.

"My daughter—the baby—we buried her here." She stood up and walked to the other side of the tree. I followed. There was no marker of a grave, just damp grass and a few wild flowers. The smell of wood rot. I noticed for the first time that Lilah was barefoot, her heels smeared with mud. "I'm really sorry. This is how I've always driven here—those last few minutes of near-death. It makes me feel like I have a choice to be with her. Like I could, if I really wanted to."

"You'll just have to wait, Lilah," I said, not withholding the sarcasm in my voice and turned to begin my walk back. I didn't want to get in the car again.

"Hey," she called. "Doesn't it feel good though?" The sun had begun to set, saturating half of Lilah's face with its liquid gold.

"What could possibly feel good about what just happened?"

"Now you know how much you wanted to live."

I didn't answer her, didn't want to give her the satisfaction of being right. The walk was long, but I was glad of it, glad of the dry weeds pricking at my ankles, of the sweat on my neck. I cradled the underside of my belly, glad too of the life inside me.

The weekend trip with Lilah and Jon had energized me. As soon as I got home, I searched online for information about academic programs. At first I was overwhelmed by the amount of specialties, concentrations I didn't know existed. After reading further, I became excited by the different possibilities. I asked myself if it would be better to study journalism or another subject in order to be the kind of journalist I wanted to be. Perhaps it would be more crippling than helpful to become adept in the history of journalism and the rules of news writing that provided concise and impartial information yet left the readers so unengaged and bored that they'd be pulled into the latest celebrity gossip. I thought political science and public policy would give me a better understanding of the system I was a part of and how to work with it while still carving my own path.

Over the next few days, I moved only between the library and my apartment, forgetting about the world. Almost a week had passed. I realized I hadn't talked to either Lilah or Jon since we said our goodbye at the vineyard. They'd dropped me off at the airport and drove back to the city shortly after. I called Lilah to tell her I'd started my college application but she didn't pick up. Then I tried Jon's number. The phone rang a few times when a strange female voice answered. I introduced myself and asked to speak to Jon.

"Oh . . . it's you. I'm sorry we haven't talked before. I'm Jon's mother," her voice was warm. "I was just going to call you. It's just been—I'm in New York for a few more days. Can we meet?"

"What happened?" I said.

"Where are you? I'll come to you."

I looked around my apartment, the unfinished crib, the plastic bags full of baby products I hadn't taken out because I'd planned to return them to Jon, spider webs that had thickened during my absence. I told her I would meet her at Jon and Lilah's place instead.

"That's fine. I'm already here," she said.

When I got there, I noticed another car parked in Jon's usual spot. It wasn't out of the ordinary that he might have parked somewhere else, so I looked down the street to see if his car was in sight. Everything else about the front of their house looked the same, an empty bottle of iced tea on the lawn, young daffodils starting to bloom.

His mother opened the door. Her blond hair, despite her age, was thick and glossy. She had it loosely pulled back in a low bun. Her cheeks were smooth, her teeth looked white and strong. The small wrinkles under her eyes were the only betrayal of her age. Jon had inherited much from her. I realized I'd not spoken since she greeted me nor opened my arms when she hugged me. I was looking at the shoe rack inside the living room for Lilah's black boots, the only thing I'd seen her wear. They weren't there.

"How long until you're due?" she asked once we were inside.

"Next week. Where are they?"

"Jon told me that they'd found a surrogate. Everything—everything was just getting so much better for them." She looked down at her hands folded on her thighs. "April 17, they were between route—and—a truck swerved into them. The truck driver was not drinking, or using his cellphone, or on drugs, the police had confirmed. He said he didn't know what caused him to momentarily lose his concentration. They died on impact. It was an accident, that was all they told me." She spoke without pause. She'd had to say the same exact words to many others before me. She looked at me now, seemingly apologetic that she hadn't thought to call me until now.

She didn't cry or even appear as though she wanted to. Her eyes looked past me vacantly as though she were waiting for someone to suddenly appear through the windows.

"I'm sorry, dear. Did you know Jon well? His wife?"

"I knew them," I said.

She looked at my belly and leapt up suddenly, saying, "My grandchild. My grandchild!" Then as if abashed from losing her composure, she sat down again with her elbows on her knees and cupped her face with her hands.

"I'm keeping the baby. You can't take it from me," I said. My neck felt hot. I realized how angry I was getting.

"Oh no, dear. That's not what I meant. I'm just happy that at least—but are you sure? This isn't what you signed up for, but we don't have to talk about it now."

I put my hands on my stomach. It was all I had.

"We're having their funeral in Connecticut next week. Both of our families are there. I'm here to pack up the rest of their things." She looked over her shoulder. "Will you be able to come?"

"I can't travel when I'm due so soon," I said.

"Right, I understand." She stood up, smoothed her skirt, and went into the bedroom. She came out with a box of Chilmark chocolates. "This was all that was left from the back of the car." I looked at the dented box. She let out a small, bitter laugh. "I can't eat chocolate. I feel like they would have wanted you to have it."

As I was leaving, she gave me a card with her phone number. "Please call me when the baby's born. Call me for anything," she said.

When I went out, the empty iced tea bottle was still at the base of the potted plant. The entire lawn was motionless as if even the soaked spring leaves had turned to stone. I could not take another step forward, my own feet cemented to the ground. I tried to twist my upper torso to look back because I felt Jon's mother eyes on me but failed. A moment later, bony fingers pressed my lower spine, turned me around, and guided me back inside.

Cynthia, Jon's mother, shifted in and out of the bedroom as I dozed. Through the slits of my eyes, I watched her move soundlessly, listened to the sound of her pouring hot water into a washbowl. The steam rose as she repeatedly dipped the hand towel into the bowl. She wrung it with the strength of a young man, muscles swelling on her arms as she twisted and twisted the towel dry. She cleaned my feet with it, holding each toe in her long, thin fingers. She seemed like a spirit and I a body she was preparing for burial.

I recalled the last expression on Jon's face when he dropped me off at the airport. *See you tomorrow*, he had said like asking a question as if some parts of him knew. I felt as though it was me who had died in a plane crash and they had made it safely back from the vineyard. Our planes of existence were only different—they were in the same world where I was, except I wasn't there anymore. I wondered if it was I who had died instead.

"Cynthia," I said.

"What is it dear?"

"What are you doing?" She had positioned herself behind me on the bed so that my head rested on her chest. She applied a balm on my temple, behind my ears, my jaw and massaged my face in circular motions.

"Don't you feel better?"

I nodded. I fell asleep. When I woke, my lashes and cheeks were wet. My lips tasted salty. Cynthia was still behind me, supporting my neck and head with her stomach.

"You were crying in your sleep," she said. "Did you have a nightmare?"

I shook my head, "It was a good dream. I climbed up a mountain—there were large bunnies there, the size of elephants. From far away, I could see them nibbling on grass. When I got closer, I saw they were just statues."

"They're with God now," she said.

My neighbor was right after all. Lilah and Jon were now in a permanent state of forgetfulness. I and the child I was carrying no longer existed to them. The acme of all love was abandonment, the only point at which we would fulfill the promise of immortality, to persist in our love for those who are absent, into oblivion.

Evening came, then night, and morning again. Cynthia emptied the basin, refilled it, wiped away my sweat and stilled my shivers. On the third day, I could walk into the living room. The orderliness of when I first came was gone. Various cans of instant food were left open on the sink, fruit flies circling above them. Prescription bottles were everywhere in the house, on windowsills, on the floor, between seat cushions, either empty or on their side with only one or two pills left. Cynthia was still in the same skirt she wore the first day we met, now with brown stains on its front. Her hair had loosened almost completely from the hairpin; visible gray strands curtained her profile. She was looking out the window while eating the Chilmark chocolates she'd given me.

"They're with God," she said.

I took a trash bag from under the sink and swept the cans into it.

"Leave it," she said.

I continued to move around, picking up pieces of balled up paper, plastic spoons and forks off the floor.

"Leave it," she said more loudly and forcefully. "If you feel better dear, you can leave."

I was grateful to her and so I let her be, her only chance to grieve for her son before the funeral, where she would be forced to organize, greet the guests, and politely accept their condolences. When I came near, I noticed she was gripping a pack of cigarettes in her fist. I asked for one. She explained she wasn't normally a smoker. We both looked at the bump on my stomach. It seemed that between us an understanding was reached silently. She lit one for herself. We sat and smoked together, looking out the window for a hint, a sign.

13

That night, I couldn't sleep and rummaged through my old things. I found one of the tapes Mother had given me on my first day at the camp. It was at the back of my closet, wrapped in a white cloth that had turned yellow. She had put it in my backpack when we said goodbye before I left the camp for the last time. I had wanted to listen to it many times, but the families I lived with either didn't have a cassette player or I never found the time and privacy to play the tape. Over the years, I came up with more rules and circumstances to delay listening to it. I gave myself temporal landmarks and told myself I would find out why she had included only this one tape on my sixteenth, eighteenth, twentieth birthday. More years went by and the idea of what the tape held grew in my mind. It was a small thing, like the butterfly that changed the history of the world. In my hand now, it weighed almost nothing.

I remembered that my neighbor had brought a portable cassette player back from Vietnam. I went upstairs to borrow it. He was asleep on the living room couch so I grabbed it from his book and shoe shelf. Then I went back to my own bed, got under the covers, inserted the tape, and pressed play. My mother's voice—it was different, gentler, slower than I remembered. It was the voice she only used when speaking about my father.

I'm taping over the one I made for you before you were able to move to the camp to live with me. When you're listening to this, we're already separated. I heard her sniffle, a small tremor in her voice. I balled my hand into a fist and bit my knuckles.

Since I won't be there to wake you up when you have nightmares, I'll tell you a few stories you can listen to before bed. You'll have good dreams then. Think of it as your own a Thousand and One Arabian Nights.

She cleared her throat and began. She told the story of the fisherman lost at sea and returned a hundred years later to a changed world; a rabbit who changed his name and went on an adventure; a mummy who was buried deep inside an ancient Egyptian tomb; when he woke up, and unable to get out, spent the next thousand years grieving for the woman he had loved and lost when he left her to go conquer other cities. Once in a while, she interrupted the stories to let me know which one had been my father's favorite, which one her own. I listened to the tape, cradled in the warmth of her voice, both known and unfamiliar. Through the night, I listened.

At about three in the morning, I felt a sharp pain in my stomach. I was having my first contraction. I called my neighbor and he came down to meet me carrying a stack of towels.

"Do you want to be taken to a hospital?" he said. He could see the bewildered expression on my face, since I'd never considered another option. "Some women prefer to deliver at home. Do you have a midwife?"

I shook my head. "Let's go. I feel like it's coming."

At the hospital, we were quickly ushered in. My neighbor nodded when a nurse asked if he was the father. I was grateful for this gesture. Neither of us felt like explaining.

When the baby came, my neighbor sat next to the obstetrician and was allowed to catch my daughter's head. My daughter seemed to have sensed my pain and exhaustion from the previous days; she arrived without too much effort on my part. The nurse cleaned and handed her to me. I searched her face for something of Lilah's, an illogical but hopeful thought. I found only her soft brown hair and her eyes, a tint of grayish blue, much like Jon's.

I looked at the ceiling of the hospital room and felt the strength of my own determination. Sitting there under the fluorescent light, I could finally admit to myself that for weeks I'd wrestled with guilt, thinking about what Cynthia had said, that I hadn't signed up for this. In Connecticut, Jon and Lilah had been laid underneath upturned earth for several days. Jon was right after all. There was little difference between being in a cradle or a casket.

I touched my daughter's fingertips to my own, the impossibility of her skin, her nails, her palm. The utter impossibility of her—and there she was. *I'm so sorry, Lilah*, my tears fell on my daughter's closed eyelids. It looked as though we were both crying. For the first time, I realized that a mother could never move on from the death of her child. Lilah had been whom I thought of as the woman I loved and yet I'd understood nothing. She was—beyond everything—a mother without a child.

My neighbor held the baby during the cab ride back to our apartments. Cradled in his arms, she was silent and docile. I leaned my head against the car window, remembering the snowstorm in Montauk that had led me here.

"Have you thought of a name?" my neighbor said.

"Quoc-Anh, Jon picked it."

"What about an English name?"

"No. She only needs one name." I could tell by my neighbor's expression that he was concerned. I understood it too because so often a name could determine the way a person is perceived. Names that are difficult to pronounce are passed over in favor of common names. Those with sonically beautiful names tend to be more successful in life. I also used two names, neither of which I was particularly attached to. A name could make you whole or fracture you.

"It sounds too foreign. Makes it harder for her to fit in," my neighbor said.

"I haven't accomplished anything by trying to fit in," I said. "I may have gotten a few gigs because of my English names but the surprise on people's face when they meet me—they look as if I'd lied to them."

Once we were inside my apartment, I was struck by how well Jon and Lilah had prepared me to bring my daughter home. While I nursed her, my neighbor went through the plastic bags full of baby items I wouldn't use for several more months. He held up a two-layered container, one of which would be filled with hot water to keep the baby's food warm.

"What the hell is this?" he said.

"It's for when she can eat solids."

"Can't they keep it simple? All you need is a bowl and a spoon."

I laughed. "It's okay if they just eat dirt too, right?"

"Yes!" he exclaimed. "As much dirt as possible. It's good for them." He smiled. "Get some rest. Tomorrow I'll work on that." He gestured the wood planks of the unfinished crib lying haphazardly in the corner. Then spontaneously he leaned down, kissed my daughter's nose, and went upstairs.

That night I climbed up the same mountain and found the same field of giant bunnies. As I came close to one, I called out my daughter's name. The bunny looked at me before hardening into rock. I'd forgotten to let down the curtain and woke up to a blue moon light surging in the window. Bathed in it, my daughter's skin seemed lit from underneath. She was like a translucent fish whose visible skeleton made it look both frail and magical. I sat up in bed to feed her. For the first time I truly felt the loss of Lilah.

The fiber of the dream she'd hoped for us disintegrated like quicksand around me. Alone with my daughter in the cool illumination of the moon, I wondered if this moment was meant to last forever—and wished for us both to turn to stone.

14

The afternoon was filled with the sound of drilling and splitting of wood. My neighbor had brought his work home so that he would have some time to finish putting together the crib Jon had started. He handed me a stack of documents and asked me to look for errors and any incorrect word choice. I glanced at the loose papers and knew that I didn't have the legal knowledge required to copy edit it, but to make my neighbor happy, I took a pencil and started reading. I hadn't set aside my goal of becoming a journalist completely, though I knew it would be on hold for a while. In the meantime, I thought I could learn something by working as a paralegal, so I accepted my neighbor's offer and began to practice more sincerely with the work he brought from his office.

As I read the files, I was moved. My neighbor represented undocumented youths mostly from Mexico, Honduras, Cuba. He continued to feel responsible for the kids whom he'd helped secure a longer stay, putting them in sports academies or finding them temporary homes. If they didn't have a future as athletes, they still risked being deported. It was a job, my neighbor felt, that was never finished. The only success he could claim, he told me, was a boy who crossed the border to come to the United States when he was thirteen. He was now studying chemical engineering in Portland, Oregon. Other than him, most of the children's lives were a series of obstacles and dangers that even adults couldn't overcome. I thought, with a wistful sadness, that maybe I was to my neighbor another immigrant to be saved.

"All done." He stood up and tapped his pants several times to shake off the sawdust. "Jon really thought of everything. This is a good design too . . . "

"Thank you," I said.

With a gentle paternal instinct, he lifted Quoc-Anh from my arms.

"Am I still much like him?" he said.

"Not anymore," I said. I thought of the person I'd chased from the subway station more than two years ago and how my neighbor was no longer that man, a placeholder of memory. "Am I still like her?"

He shook his head. "I wish she and I could have had this, but it would have been a lot different."

"Could you watch her for a while? I want to lie down," I said.

In the bedroom I closed my eyes, but sleep didn't come. It would be at least five or six more years before my daughter would begin to sense her difference, to articulate the difficult questions. Yet I already found myself trying to weave together a narrative to tell her when the time came. I didn't want to hide anything from her, though now I understood why so many parents lied to their children, because they too wished desperately for that alternative version, the one in which their children came to the world simply, unhesitatingly and not through an adult game, a twist of fate.

I went to Lilah and Jon's place often, watching their front door from across the street without blinking as though my concentration and yearning were enough to will them back into existence. My soldier had once said that anything you wanted badly enough, you would get. As a child, I'd blamed Mother for not bringing back father. Against all physical laws, I mumbled prayers, bargained with God.

One time I took my daughter with me, carrying her in a sling tied to my chest. Together we looked at the knee-high gate, the lawn, and the door Lilah had painted green. The window blinds were drawn, but I could see the shape of someone moving inside. It seemed a great trick, a hole in the fabric of the universe, that a structure could go on standing there after the fact. Death had diminished my world, making me wish only for decay, for my surroundings to match my inner state, and at the same time, my body could barely contain the fact of them being gone, exploding with too much color and meaning. Everything was finely woven into a cosmic arabesque. Then—with a sweep—nothing.

My heart stopped when the curtains were pulled and I saw her standing there, her eyes narrowed against the glare of the sun. A nearly exact image. She shaded her face with her hand, turned her head left and right, and closed the curtain. A few minutes later, she came out the front door. She walked out of the gate, paused, looked at me directly across the street.

"My sister had that exact same dress," she said. "Where did you get it?"

"Who are you?" I said.

"I bought her a similar dress from a vintage shop. To think of it—the one you're wearing even has the same tear at the neckline. Where—"

"You must be Lilah's sister," I said, steadying myself. "She gave me this." I pinched the fabric together where the tear was.

She straightened her posture. "Ah," she said. "I know who you are."

I said nothing.

She continued, "Lilah's mentioned she had met someone. Over the years, she'd made up so many affairs that I didn't think you were real. I just felt bad for Jon."

"Do you have a minute? I—"

"Do you want to get some food? There's a diner nearby."

Elijah was younger than Lilah, closer to my age. At the restaurant, she got a coffee and I got blueberry pancakes. She said that she had traveled from Connecticut and gone to Lilah's home out of a longing similar to mine, to be in the same air Lilah had breathed, to feel what was left of her presence. Elijah asked many questions about my background: what time was I born, at what age I started to walk, who was my best friend, when did I lose my virginity, how I ended up in New York. Her easy yet slightly aggressive manner made me reveal more about myself than I'd intended. The waitress came over to pour more coffee in Elijah's cup.

"So you lost your only friend when you left Vietnam as a kid, and now you did it again?" she said.

"I didn't intentionally lose Lilah," I said.

"I didn't mean to lose my mom either, but she killed herself anyway. Don't you think incrementally, we somehow failed to save them?"

"It was an accident, Elijah."

"What about your little friend? She got burnt too, didn't she, when you scorched the sugarcane field?" she said.

"She was saved."

"Right after our mother died, I was always on my toes. I thought Lilah might follow her. They were very similar. It sounds crazy, but for years I'd been preparing to lose her. I've imagined the scene over and over in my mind. Cynthia told me Lilah was in the driver's seat when they found them."

"Don't," I said.

"You don't think it's bizarre that the truck driver just suddenly swerved and there was no time for Lilah to have seen him coming?" Her eyes brimmed with tears.

"We were on our way back from a vacation. We were

happy," I said, less convinced in my own words. "There was so much to look forward to."

After the meeting with Elijah, I went home and slumped down on the floor.

It was the first time I allowed myself to relive the night before I left Vietnam, to recreate in my mind the details I'd willed myself to forget. Her tightly pinched lips had looked like a smirk, like they were mocking my cowardice. Pulling Lilah's dress up slightly, I touched the shin of my right leg. The burnt mark ran from my ankle to below my knee, a long and narrow shape. It'd had a long time to heal and was smoothed out enough to feel like the rest of my leg. The fire had been a way out for the little girl and I, an escape from the camp for good. I'd had the choice of being with her till the end, until we would both be reduced to ashes, our spirits soaring up and away from our bodies. Instead, I'd turned my back on her and trapped us there forever.

I didn't want to believe what Elijah said about Lilah. Yet the more I contemplated Elijah's implication, the stranger the vacation seemed. Perhaps it was more for Lilah's sake than mine, visiting a good memory for the last time. Lilah was right in choosing Jon. I wouldn't have had the courage to join her.

Part 3

1

When my daughter walked, she looked like a confused tornado. She spun slowly until she fell on her knees, then stood up and continued spinning. After she picked up speed, she ran toward me and dove her head into my lap, lifting herself to sneak a look at my face before burrowing down again.

"Where did QQ go? Did the storm take my baby away?" I said, looking around.

In response she squealed with great joy. She also liked to be invisible, transform into animals, pretend our apartment was a desert or battlefield. Though she wasn't talkative and often communicated using only monosyllables, she had a powerful roar. She leapt up from my lap, crawled on all fours, and shook her head so that her hair was a tangled net in front of her face.

"Lion," she said after a fifteen-second roar.

"Maybe more like a dinosaur?" I said.

"Linaur?"

"Sure." I picked her up and kissed her. Her feet kicked in protest. "My linosaur." When I released her, she spun away again, making the whooshing sound of wind.

Having QQ helped me slip into a routine. In the morning, I dropped her off at daycare and went to work. I'd started to work full time as a paralegal. At night, I cherished the little time we had together. There were few chances for Lilah to enter my thoughts. When she did, she took the essential and left me standing in the street, wondering if the shadow of a woman on the brick wall might be her, the colorless fallen feather of a heron. I found her always in nature, especially in things closer to the sky.

Some nights I woke up, startled from a dream, turned over and wept into my daughter's hair. *Thank you, thank you, thank you,* I would say. Loss, I thought, was a fuller experience than love. You couldn't always feel that you were loved, but loss asserted its presence, demanded a bodily response as it carved its way through, leaving you with enough to feel the emptiness. I kept the prosthetic eye Lilah painted on the nightstand. Had she known then she wasn't painting my eye, but QQ's? For a moment I wished she could have lived a little longer to meet the daughter she'd so longed for, but these types of thoughts led nowhere, so I stopped myself.

Now that QQ was old enough to travel, my neighbor and I argued over whether or not I should bring her to Vietnam with me. All of his earlier philosophy about leaving children to the elements so they could toughen had vanished when it came to her. He thought she was too young to follow me on such a trip, especially because I didn't have a clue of what my exact destinations would be once I got to Vietnam.

"Wait till she's six or seven," my neighbor said.

"That's too late. I want her to have Vietnam as part of her childhood memories," I said.

"What is she going to eat there? You haven't been back in ages. You won't know what's safe."

"I'll be careful," I said.

"Leave her with me. I'll bring her to my office every day."

"I know you can take good care of her. It isn't about that," I said.

"Fine. Then let me give you the contact info of an old high school friend. He'll be happy to show you around or at least take you to the house of your childhood friend." He sat down on the floor and QQ crawled over and sat stoically next to him. QQ was serious and calm with him. My neighbor didn't talk to her like she was a child or participate like I did in her imagined world. When she pulled a book off the shelf and asked him what it was, he explained thoroughly, using the same words he would with adults.

"This is a scientific journal. It gives us new studies about things we care about like chronic illnesses, music, money, and art. The study could pair one of these topics with another, for example, the effect of music on patients with brain cancer or how architecture can facilitate learning," my neighbor said while my daughter turned the pages of the magazine. When she found a picture of a gorilla, she slapped it repeatedly.

"We watched a video of gorillas yesterday," I explained to my neighbor. Later she fell asleep with her cheek on the page and her drool smearing the ink of the words.

I wanted to let my mother know I was coming. On my computer, I typed and retyped my e-mail. I worried she would find my Vietnamese wretched, lacking style and grace. I wasn't sure how much to say about my own life and about why I had decided to come back. I hesitated and eventually decided not to tell her about QQ because I didn't want that to influence her decision whether or not to see me. After several deliberations, I sent her a brief e-mail, making sure that I didn't express any particular need to see her. *I know you are busy*, I added. It was in part to incite some sort of reassurance from her, to hear her say that she wanted to see me.

At around 5 P.M. in New York, which is about 3 A.M. in Vietnam, I received her response. It was polite and brief: she was glad I was coming. She was very busy and would do her best to see me. She reminded me to use my American passport, forgetting that she'd directed me to get rid of my Vietnamese one years ago, and to speak English past the arrival checkpoint. Though she didn't offer an explanation, I understood that if anyone found out she had a daughter, it would inconvenience her plan to run for office again. Vietnam still expected its women to put motherhood above all else. My mother's success and ambitions had been accepted because people thought she was a barren widow. Her misfortunes afforded her the right to devote her life entirely to public work. I understood that to maintain success, it was more important to show others what was to be pitied, rather than envied.

2

Ho Chi Minh International airport was a place where newcomers felt like celebrities. Right outside the international arrival gate, people who had been waiting waved and cheered. Many people were waiting for a relative from abroad, someone they hadn't seen for five, or thirty years. People hugged each other and tried to hide their tears. Children ran here and there while their parents yelled, the elderly sat on the floor fanning their sweaty faces. My daughter clung to me as we walked past a line of curious faces. Around us, people laughed and cried. Because Vietnamese people were not of a hugging culture, arms were patted, hair pet, cheeks pulled.

"Are we in Vietnam?" my daughter asked. She pronounced the country's name in a curiously precise accent.

"This is where I lived until I was twelve," I said.

"How old am I?" she said.

"You're almost four."

We got in the cab and I handed the driver the address my neighbor had written down. After we passed two traffic lights, the driver asked in Vietnamese how long had I been abroad. I told him. He complimented my Vietnamese, impressed that I had not forgotten it. His praises felt more painful than flattering so I was silent.

"I know kids who only live abroad for a few years and come back speaking Vietnamese with an accent. It's trendy to be foreign here. Anyway, Vietnamese is a language easy to erase." He shared that his nephew lived in California and asked if he could give me his nephew's number. "He just moved there last month for college. He doesn't know anybody," the driver said.

"I'm sure he'll make friends at school," I said.

"Yeah but it's not the same, it's not family."

I wrote down the number that the driver recited from memory.

"After he finishes his studies, he'll come back," the driver said. "His father needs him here. I know life is better over there, but he should come back."

I nodded. His was a common sentiment amongst people with children abroad. In reality, Vietnamese children rarely ever came back.

"I haven't seen my mother in twelve years," I said.

"Better late than never," he said.

"I don't know. I'm not sure she wants to see me. What will we even say to each other?"

"She wants to see you. She might be scared, so you should take the initiative if she doesn't."

"Scared of what?"

"It's hard to go on denying all the years she's missed if you're right in front of her. My son lives in Hanoi and he rarely visits me. To you kids, time simply passes, but not to us aging parents. Every day we don't see you is another day we lost."

"My mother is different," I said. "But I'll think more about what you said."

"Good," he said.

He dropped us off before the street became too narrow. When we got out, my daughter immediately pointed to a street vendor with a colorful display.

"Mama."

"Hermit crabs. Their shells are painted to make them look pretty." I could tell she wanted one badly so I added, "We won't stay here long enough to keep one. How about I get you cotton candy instead?"

My neighbor had told me that once I got to the right neighborhood, I should ask around for Minh's house. People nearby would know who he was. I asked the man working inside a shoe store for directions. He directed us to go down the narrow street until it split in three directions.

"Take the one to the left all the way to the end and you should be at the right place," he said. As I was leaving, he asked, "Are you a relative?"

"A friend of a friend," I said.

Minh's house was hidden behind a weeping willow, which looked older and more morose than their type usually did because of its sparseness. The thick branches that swept the ground had twisted into braids of white hair. Minh and his wife lived with Minh's father, who had not gotten out of bed since a heart attack last summer. Minh said at this stage in life, the only thing that kept his father alive was a strong will and a sense of humor. When I came in, Minh's wife was setting lunch on a wooden daybed so we could eat together. I watched her glossy black hair, small breasts, lithe body move as if the daybed was a stage and she an actress. She divided the chopsticks and put white rice into four small bowls. She talked to my daughter in Vietnamese without hesitation, as though it was the only language that existed. Quoc-Anh listened attentively and figured out what she meant using a child's intuition.

"Does she know Vietnamese?" Minh asked.

"A few words," I said.

"You should teach her while she's young. It'll only get harder."

I nodded. "I'm not qualified. My vocabulary is less than a fifth grader's."

"That's a lot of words," he said. "And I understand you fine. While you're here, my wife could teach her some basics. She's a kindergarten teacher."

I thanked him and took out a few bottles of vitamins I'd brought from New York, "We're grateful you're letting us stay."

Minh's wife picked up and looked at the labels of each bottle, "Thank you. So you know how hard it is to get good medicine here. We never know what else they might put in it." There was a mumble of agreement from the bed in the corner where Minh's father lay.

"He said nobody else can touch them. They're his," Minh explained. "All yours, dad."

After the food was cleared, Minh's wife, my daughter and I lay together on the daybed.

"I'm glad you came on a Saturday so I have a chance to greet you properly," she said to me while dozing off.

Minh sat at the foot of his father's bed and answered my questions about the general welfare of the Vietnamese people. He said for the past ten years the country had remained a great place to vacation, but not to live. Work was fine as long as you followed the rules and didn't do anything subversive. He thought that in all fields, be it the arts, science, or business, in order to be great, you inevitably had to step outside of the boundary. There was no room for a breakthrough, a great discovery. Talented men and women reached the top of a mountain and camped there instead of taking up in flight.

"Everything's fine. Everything's good enough. That's the problem," he concluded. "How do you know our mutual friend? He and I met at an underground Party meeting. We were so young then."

"So you didn't go to school together?" I said.

He chuckled, "Is that what he told you? We were boys, but we already worked for the Party. All of us had nicknames. In fact, nobody has called me Minh for a long time. I don't even know his real name. In 1970, he heard that room for two more people had opened up on a boat to the United States. He tried to convince me to go. It was after his adopted sister died."

Minh swallowed and rubbed his father's leg absently. "It was a huge betrayal to our Party, our country, our friendship. At least I used to think so. I didn't think he would have the guts to go alone. We haven't spoken in almost forty years and he still told you to come here as if nothing has changed. That's just like him." He looked around at the wooden daybed, his father's metal bed cramped in the corner, his wife murmuring in her sleep beside me. "I met her after my first wife died. At first, I avoided her because I feared she would soon end up being my nurse. But—how is he?"

"I can see why he considers you a close friend. He's helped my daughter and me so much—I don't know what we would do without him," I said.

"He did the right thing in leaving."

I said nothing. How could I begin to tell Minh that though my neighbor had escaped war and poverty, he still couldn't let go of the guilt of having left? His life was a battle of contradictions. He fought for those he believed have the right to stay in the United States, to find there the opportunities their birthplace didn't give them. He also didn't want them to become like him, to work hard for the sake of the family while the idea of family waned away in the noise of their new life. He didn't want them to not be able to go home again.

In the evening, I told them that I needed to go attend to some personal matters.

"Of course," Minh said. "You've been away for so long. I imagine you have many people to visit."

Minh's wife took out a variety of loose pages from a large binder. They had hand drawn pictures of animals and objects on one side and the words on the other.

"You can leave Quoc-Anh here. By the time you get back, she'll be fluent in Vietnamese," she said.

"I hope I'm not gone for that long. Thanks for looking after her."

In that moment, I imagined I saw a gleam of her regret. She was a mother without a child, possibly because Minh thought himself too old to raise one. I told my daughter I would be back in time to put her to bed.

A torrent of rain flooded the street. I paid a moped rider to take me across the river.

"Hang on tight," he said. I gripped his shoulders as he slid through lines of traffic, our bodies always at a slant from the ground. We rode onto a ferry and waited as it carried us to district two. Behind me grey sheets of rain fell mercilessly. The paper my neighbor had given me with the little girl's address had soaked thin. Rivulets of ink flowered from the letters.

"I can only take you as far as the twin temple," he said.

"I don't know my way around here. Is it possible to go to the address I've given you?" I said.

"I suggest we go back then. You can try again another day when it isn't pouring."

"Isn't it the monsoon season? I'm only here for a few days. I can't wait till it dries up."

"I'm sorry, miss," he said.

Once the ferry parked, we rode down a slated chrome ramp and entered the red country. The moped wheels dove deeper and deeper into the soft, red mud as we pushed forward. Despite the water being over our ankles, many cafés and shops stayed open. The waiters held metal tins, which they used to scoop up water off the floor and pour it back out to the street. Here the road was open and empty except for a few naked boys playing in the rain, their chests, necks, faces smeared with mud.

"I can't go any further. I need to push the moped back," the rider said.

"Where is the temple?"

"Keep walking straight on the main road. It'll be up there to the left."

I gave him more money than the amount he'd asked for at the beginning of the trip. He refused. "Good luck," he said, and turned his moped around, pushing it toward the river.

I went into a makeshift shop, propped up by three wooden planks and covered with a large plastic tarp. The shop sold various paraphernalia, seemingly only one of each item, including a sewing kit, chewing gum, an energy drink, a mousetrap. Though my clothes were already wet, I asked for a raincoat and a map. The shop owner was a middle-aged woman wearing old pajamas with a pattern of daisies. Her stomach protruded through the thin fabric.

"A map?" she said. "Like a world map?"

"A map of this area."

"There's no such thing. Where are you going?"

"The twin temple for now. I heard they have lodging there. I don't think I'll make it to where I want to go tonight." I unfolded the sticky address paper to show her.

She shook her head. "I'm not sure where that is. The folks at the temple will help you out."

"Do you have a phone I can use?"

She took a phone from her back pocket, which unlike the makeshift tent, was shiny and of the latest mobile technology. I told her Minh's telephone number and she dialed it. When he picked up, I told him my predicament and that I wasn't able to go back tonight. He said that if I took too long I might not get my daughter back because his wife adored her. Since their house had flooded, she was teaching my daughter to fold swans and put them out to float. In the background, I heard my daughter yell *swim, swim* in Vietnamese.

I plodded in the mud. My legs were wooden. Fatigue crept in, making me question the reason for my return, the aimlessness of my direction. I thought about my last conversation with Lilah and Jon. It had been windy that night. Jon'd had to shut the door to the back porch because tree branches were hitting the glass windows. I'd not noticed the beginning of a storm that night, just as I'd ignored the darkening sky when I set out to look for my childhood friend. For thousands of years, it seemed, the natural world had curated men's sorrow—warning us of our fates, linking us—the material world—to the immaterial. I looked around me for signs that I wasn't alone, that Jon and Lilah were still with me if in some other form. But if they were in the earth beneath and the sky above, I couldn't decipher their message. I asked myself if this might be how you go mad—by looking so desperately that you would eventually see what wasn't there.

I came to a sea almond tree and stood underneath it for a while. Its leaves, a bright glistening green, stood out against the maroon mire, brown clay roofs on houses, the inflamed sky. I looked behind me and saw I'd arrived at the temple, which was a small, two-tiered building with cement walls. There was nothing that indicated it was a Buddhist sanctuary except for a necklace made out of jasmine flowers hanging on the stakes of the gate. I went inside. Off to the side of the main building, another much smaller one seemed to be in progress; stacks of bricks were unevenly lined up to each other. As I got closer, I realized it was probably the work of a child's game. I walked up a flight of stairs. The doors were open as pagodas were expected to be. Two straw mats covered the cement floor. On a wooden table sat a ceramic Buddha, cracked from age. He wore many jasmine necklaces. The whole room smelled of the floral fragrance. On either side of him were candles and incense. I sat down on the mat. For a long time, nobody disturbed me. With my eyes closed, I listened to the static sound of rain and the hollow wind hissing its way through fissures on the walls. A novice monk in gray robe came out to greet me and lead me to a back room where there were baskets of fruits and a stove. He gave me tea and asked whom I wanted to dedicate my prayer to.

"I wasn't praying," I told him.

"Your eyes were closed for a long time in front of Buddha."

"I was only resting," I lied. I'd been talking to Jon and Lilah in my mind.

"Would you like me to pray for someone?" he said

"They're gone now. They don't need prayers," I said.

"Everything comes back. Like a circle."

I asked him if I could spend the night. I was shivering.

"We could provide food, but no lodging. You're a woman," he said.

"Should I go back out there and pray for you to let me stay?" I said, more bitterly than I'd intended. The young monk's face grew pink. "I'm sorry. I'm just tired," I added.

"You can sit in our library. If they ask, I will say you fell asleep reading books," he said.

"You came up with that rather quickly."

"We have to read many scriptures," he said.

As the sun came up, I was woken by the chants of monks. I went out to the courtyard. The air smelled fresh from the rain. Doves and tiny quail covered the ground and pecked at the rice someone had left there for them. An older monk in a mustard-colored robe was sweeping leaves on the ground. I came up to him. I described the novice monk I'd met last night and asked where he was so I could thank him. A beguiling smile swept across the monk's face.

"It's been a while since the brothers have visited us, but it seems they are back," he said. "Are you by any chance a twin?"

I told him I wasn't.

"Curious. Our temple is named after the twin brothers. After one died at war, the other shaved his head and joined the monastery," he said.

"Which war?" I said, suspicious that I was being lured into a trap.

"He died here at this temple with the same bullet wound through his chest that his brother got. At first it looked as if he had committed suicide, but the weapon wasn't found. Murder didn't seem likely either since he was a simple novice monk at a modest sanctuary. Who would look for him here?"

"The person I saw last night was alive. He wore a gray robe," I said.

"Look around you. There is no gray robe anywhere. Our garments are either brown or yellow," he said. "In the past, one or both of the brothers had appeared in the uniform they died in. The people who've seen them before were also twins. You're the first one who isn't."

I walked away from the monastery as the satiny light of the morning sun gushed through the invisible and gaping hole in my chest. For the first time since I came back to Vietnam, I felt welcomed and wanted—my twin, my little girl was still waiting for me.

3

The monk told me it was best to go on foot because the path was muddy, bumpy, and too narrow for vehicles to pass. I tried to walk in a straight line through the outdoor market, but was frequently diverted by salesmen and women offering me their merchandise. When I got to the end of the market on the other side, I came up to a bridge that fit the monk's descriptions: it was locally known as a monkey bridge because it was built out of rope and only a few worn out wooden boards. You had to sway with the bridge as you walked across it. On one side of the bridge, houses were propped up only a few inches above the river by wooden planks. Children swimming in the river screeched with laughter as they watched me inch across. Several times, my foot missed the board when I tried to focus on steadying my upper body. I thought of how my neighbor had made this journey before based on a single address he found in the district archive. Though he hadn't said it specifically, I now knew it couldn't have been easy. I was suddenly overwhelmed with gratitude.

How fortunate that she was really there. As soon as I set foot on firm ground, I saw all around me young green shoots of rice and felt as though she was near. Water buffalos stood around, wagging away flies with their tails. I walked the seemingly endless field and arrived at a village.

She was sitting on the ground near a banyan tree, her body partly covered by shadows of leaves. Immediately I recognized her features, though half of her body was marred by fire. Or perhaps it was from her burns that I knew. I bought a bag of sugarcane juice and watched her from afar. Her palm was faced up in her lap and her lips trembled. A woman who was walking by dropped a few coins and something wrapped in banana leaves, probably rice pudding into her hand. My friend did not move or acknowledge this gesture of kindness, but continued to stare ahead. I asked the owner of the juice cart about her.

"That woman there? The poor thing lost her mind after her husband had a stroke and died. The women around here love her. They bring her and her little girl something every day," he said.

"She has a child?"

"The brightest thing you've ever met. Too bad she's cooped up inside all day. What about you? Where are you from? How did you end up in our little village?"

"Far away. It took me years to get here."

He gave me another bag of sugarcane juice. "Take it to her for me. She'll know who it's from. I've been asking her to marry me for years. You might wonder why, since she is crazy and some might say she's not even half good," he gestured to his own face. "But when I look into her eyes, I feel like she understands me but chooses not to answer. Maybe I'm the crazy one."

I thanked him, went under the banyan's shade, and sat down next to her. I handed her the bag of juice. We drank our juices together.

"You have an admirer," I said.

She didn't respond or look at me.

"When I saw the rice paddies, I thought it must be you who planted them. It had to be. How foolish I am not to know you would never work in any kind of field again," I said. She stopped drinking the juice. I couldn't read her facial expression since there was none. I watched her breathing for any change. Perhaps I'd imagined it but it seemed her breath became more shallow and rapid. I said nothing and sat next to her until the sun retreated out of sight and a pale moon cast a bluish light on my friend's face. I took a piece of paper from my bag and put it in her open palm. It was the only drawing of hers I'd ripped out of my notebook before we burned everything. She had drawn a giant hand, the palm an ocean, holding two miniature elephants. It was a dream she'd insisted I could join when I would go to sleep. She didn't look at it.

"Your admirer was right. You're not crazy," I said. "Say something please."

She looked at me, her face blank, "I don't know you. I have no idea who you are."

Her words grated me. I felt at once invisible and vulnerable to shards of pain. My neighbor had said she was ill. I had not known it was an illness so acute and isolating it could not be cured.

We sat together until night fell. The whole time my lips were pressed together. I was worried I would say the wrong thing. She seemed oblivious to my struggle, and maybe my existence. The sky started to sprinkle again. She stood up and walked away from the banyan tree. I followed behind.

We reached a low bamboo fence. She went in and left it open behind her. I continued to follow silently. Her house was simple and orderly, a straw mat in the corner for sleeping, an oil lamp, and a few manga books. Everything had its own place on the floor. There was no indication of a mad woman living there. A little girl was sleeping shirtless on the floor. When she heard us, she woke up and crawled toward her mother. The girl had round and large pupils, which stared at me.

I bent down to talk to her, "I have a daughter about your age. Would you like to meet her?"

The girl nodded fiercely.

"I'll bring her tomorrow. What's your name?"

"Kem," she said. "Like ice cream!"

"You are just as lovely as an ice cream," I said.

"Mama, do you have ice cream?" Kem said to her mother.

My friend sat down on the straw mat and took the things people had given her that day out of a plastic bag. She gave the rice pudding to her daughter and ate the ball of sticky rice herself. The girl ate the pudding ravenously. She consumed every bit of it with delicious pleasure, the ground beef and pork, the mushrooms. She gave me the quail egg inside the pudding.

"Thank you. When I was a little girl, I always saved the egg for last so I know how special it is." I asked my friend how old her daughter was.

"Five," she said.

The girl smiled a mouthful of crooked teeth. "Are you going to live here?" she said.

"I have to go tonight, but I'll be back tomorrow. I promise." I said. "What are the books over there? Are you reading them?"

"I look at pictures," the girl said. "I love the pictures!" she crawled to the stack of books and took one out to show me. I noticed she preferred crawling rather than walking. Her knees and palms were calloused and black from dirt. She showed me *The Queen of Egypt* manga, the same series I'd loved as a girl except these covers were different, a new edition. She opened to a dog-eared page and pointed to a word bubble.

"The queen is saying to this man take a bath, you're so dirty!" she said. I smiled at her made-up version.

"He does look filthy, doesn't he?" I said.

My friend snatched the book from her daughter's hand and threw it in the corner. In one swift motion, she pulled down the girl's underwear and slapped her behind repeatedly. "How many times have I told you not to make shit up anymore!" She pushed and the girl fell over. She rolled onto her side, pulled her knees up to her chest and mumbled pained sounds, though she didn't cry.

"If you want to come back, come here and teach her to read. Otherwise, don't bother," my friend said.

I agreed and left.

That night at Minh's house, my daughter told me she could count to twenty in Vietnamese and learned twenty animal names in Vietnamese as well. I fell asleep to her reciting rabbit, bear, horse, monkey, rabbit, snake, dog, cat . . .

In the morning, I placed an international phone call to my neighbor. It was about eight o'clock at night in New York. He picked up, hungry for information about QQ. He expressed his concern about her getting stomach flu because neither of us got antiviral shots before going. I told him we were in Ho Chi Minh City where life was urban and we lacked nothing. I said that considering this was our birth country, he sure worried a lot. He apologized, saying that he'd been back and knew things had changed, but continued to think about it the way it was when he was a young boy. I updated him on Minh: that he wasn't well off and felt regretful of the opportunities he'd passed up, but was happy.

"His wife is kind to us. She's teaching QQ to read Vietnamese," I said.

"That's something we should have done, but it's difficult—" he said

"I know."

"It is easier for me than for you. I'll make an effort to talk to her in Vietnamese from now on," he said.

"We don't even talk to each other in Vietnamese."

"Little by little."

"I don't know," I said.

"We'll try."

My daughter got a cold so we couldn't go back to my friend's village as I'd promised. I didn't have a way to let her know so I had to accept waiting until QQ got better. Two days later, we took a taxi to the market near the Twin Temple in district two. From there we walked our way back to the village. QQ was good for most of the trip, only complaining a few times and scratching at the mosquito bites on her ankles. Her legs were not long enough to step from one board to the next on the monkey bridge so I carried her on my back. When we got to the rice field, she tried to press her head to my hip. I realized she was afraid of the water buffaloes.

"That's *con trau*—one of the words you learned. They are nice animals. They won't hurt you," I said.

She became excited and pointed at one buffalo and then the next, repeating *con trau, con trau, con trau.* We arrived at the village. I looked for my friend right away at the banyan tree, but she wasn't there. The juice cart's owner told me he hadn't seen her for two days. I held my daughter's hand and we half-walked, half-ran to the little house with bamboo gates.

In the candid sunlight, the walls looked greyer, the front door splintered at the corners. Inside, an unnatural heat emanated from where my friend and her daughter lay. On the floor, the bamboo wrap from the rice pudding was spread out. The leaves looked chewed on.

"Mama's sick," Kem said.

"Come here, Kem. You and QQ go play outside." I handed them a bag that I'd brought, full of fruits, sticky rice, and mango cakes.

My friend's breath was strenuous and raspy. "You said you would come two days ago," she said.

"QQ got sick. I'm sorry."

She scoffed. "You could have come anyway. Is she dying? It's so like you to run away."

I sat down next to her and put my hand on her forehead. "I think you have a fever. Have you seen a doctor?"

"Who has the money for that? What doctor would treat a crazy woman?"

"Why do you do that?"

"What?" she said.

"Pretend to be crazy."

"How do you know I'm not?"

I peeled a banana and gave it to her. To my surprise, she ate it without protest. As soon as she finished, her complexion improved, colors returned to her lips and cheeks. I gave her another. She ate it and sat up with her back against the wall.

"I thought you were a ghost," she said. "When you gave me the drawing, I thought I'd really gone mad."

"What happened?" I said, not knowing where to start.

"When?"

"I don't know."

We sat in silence for a while, standing on that edge between too little and too much. I opened my mouth several times only to gulp air and hoped my wordlessness could chase away the years between us.

"What if you could go back to that last day at the camp?" she said.

"I wouldn't have left you in the burning field." I looked at the ruined map of her face, the scar, its multiple raised ridges ran down her arms like mountains seen from above, then smoothed out into soft craters. "I wouldn't have helped you burn it down."

"God, I thought unlike everyone else you would understand and not pity me. So what if I got a little hurt in the fire? Can you not see it was a blessing for me? My father never touched me again afterward," she said.

"What happened that night?" I said, sensing there was something else she wasn't saying.

"You ran," she said.

I nodded, taking refuge in my wordlessness.

"I'd taken the gun from the armory before that day," she continued. "After we burnt down the field, I went home. I shot him."

I swallowed, surprised by a pang of pleasure. "You killed him?"

"No—the bullet hit his leg. It only crippled him. He never told on me, made up some story." She clenched her jaws. "I want to tell you I enjoyed watching him suffer, but I got nothing out of it. He just grinned at me like he'd lost his mind. He said he understood."

I laughed. I wasn't sure why. A thin smirk also appeared on my friend's face, "Because of what you and I did, he lost his job at the camp and we had to leave. The years following that were the most peaceful I'd ever had. He wouldn't even look at me, as if I had something contagious. I left home at sixteen."

"I wonder sometimes if the whole thing was a nightmare," I said.

"Yeah, but it was our nightmare. My worst and best memories are there."

"Mine too."

She asked me about my life in the United States. I told her at first it'd been difficult. I learned how to lie about my background using existing assumptions and stereotypes. I thought I could make friends if I made myself predictable, so I told them my mother was a seamstress in Vietnam and my father an electrician. I never mentioned the camp. People doubted what they hadn't experienced themselves and I didn't want to be questioned, pitied or seen as an exotic object. I protected the true story zealously. After high school ended, I was tangled up in too many lies, so I cut off contact with everyone. I kept to myself for a long time until I met Lilah, and then afterward, Jon. My neighbor was helping me raise QQ. As I spoke,

I realized how unfair I'd been to Lilah, how little I'd revealed of myself even when she'd opened doors for me. My affection for her couldn't defeat the memory of my childhood. Happiness, even love, paled compared to the forces of desolation, of misery.

"Maybe a person is lucky enough to have just one true friend in life," I said.

She listened to me, her gaze dreamy and far off. Then she said, "I married your soldier."

I was surprised by this sudden confession and said nothing.

She continued, "I thought it was something you might have done had you stayed."

"I might have. I would have," I said.

I went out to the front yard to check on the girls. My daughter was crawling around wildly in the dirt. She and Kem were talking in codes. Not normally a talkative child, QQ seemed to delight in their invented language that was neither English nor Vietnamese. They shushed each other when they saw me. I went back inside the damp darkness of the house.

"Will you stay here tonight? I know it's not what you're used to," she said, suddenly putting a distance between us.

I nodded. "I'll go get us food. Where's the nearest place?"

"You'll have to go back to the market on the other side of the bridge."

QQ was thrilled that she didn't have to leave Kem when I announced I was going to the market. I opened the splintered door so my friend could look out at our children.

"I'm leaving Quoc-Anh here," I said and left.

At the market, I stopped at a stand that sold herbal medicine and asked for something that would help my friend. The herbalist asked what her symptoms were, then took a few twigs, rubbed them between his fingers, sniffed them and put them into a brown paper bag. To the bag he also added other types of tree barks, an assortment of dried flowers, and a bird's nest.

"Cook this mixture over night and give her the broth first thing in the morning," he instructed.

At the other stands, I bought fish, tamarind paste, okra, and spices. Buying these things calmed me, making me feel more Vietnamese than I had since I'd arrived at the airport. I felt happy imagining the meal I was going to make for my friend and her health improving. Then I remembered she had neither stove nor pot nor pan so I bought some wood and an iron pot. I nearly dropped the bag of medicinal herbs when I crossed the river.

From a distance, I could see that Kem and QQ were no longer playing outside. Without them, the yard looked overgrown, the grass tall but brown and dead. Against a background of three-dimensional, bulbous clouds, the house looked like paper, something you would burn for the dead. I went inside. I looked from corner to corner, as if my eyes could miss my daughter in that small space. I called her name uselessly. Not a trace of her. I touched the straw mat and wasn't sure if the warmth I felt was from the mat or my own hand. If they'd left right after I went to the market, they could be anywhere by now. *How do you know I'm not crazy?* I heard her say as she dragged my daughter away to a rice field. To please her, QQ would stand still as the plants blazed up around her. I threw the groceries on the ground and ran out.

The village was surrounded by paddy fields. As I walked, I called my daughter's name. I was afraid of asking for help—*why would you leave your daughter with a madwoman?* I imagined them saying. As I treaded along the edge of the field, slick, long, and black water snakes creeped under the water. I shouted her name until my voice became raspy, my throat constricted. The golden rice had become a sweeping blur and still I couldn't find her. I asked a farmer in the field if she had seen a little girl with light brown hair, bluish-grey eyes and very fair skin. She was a mixed child, I added so the farmer could easily search her memory. She shook her head.

"I hope you find her soon," she said kindly. "Around here, girls, especially a beautiful mixed child, get kidnapped and sold into prostitution. When was she the last time you saw her?"

"I left her with someone," I said.

"Oh," she said. "Then why are you running around? They probably just went somewhere."

I turned around and walked back to the village police station. It was a small building, not much different than a house. The front door was open. Inside at a low, plastic table, two men in uniform sat playing cards. The younger one noticed me first.

"Can I help you?" he said.

"I need to report a missing person." I was choked up, unable to believe what I was saying. "My daughter."

The one with grey hair put three more cards on the table.

"How long has she been missing for?" the younger one said, not putting down either his cigarette or his cards.

"I don't know. Maybe two hours."

"Two hours? She's not missing." To the older cop, he said, "Mothers these days can't let go of their children for a minute. How are they supposed to grow into human beings?"

I decided to go back and wait, suddenly panicked at the thought that they'd come back but I hadn't seen them. When I got there, the bamboo gate was slightly open just as I'd left it, the tall grass just as dry and motionless. Inside, I sat down on the straw mat. Sweat trickled from my temples, my neck, under my arms, between my breasts. I lied down and recited her words from memory.

So what if I got hurt in the fire?
It was a blessing, can't you see that.
He never touched me again afterward.

My mind began to spin. I doubted it was possible for my friend to hate her father so completely. My own desire for a father made it difficult for me to believe her. She must have become dependent on his abuse and when he stopped, it must have been painful. She hated me for taking away everything, even her abuser. Then later she married my soldier out of spite, knowing that as a young girl it'd been my wish. So far she'd said nothing about his death. He would be about my neighbor's age now. A stroke seemed too easy. Perhaps—

I rolled onto my stomach and screamed in my hands. I rolled back and forth the entire length of the mat. A thought occurred to me—had it been me living in this village, in this broken-down house all these years? Was she the one that left me behind to go to the United States? Or perhaps I'd imagined her to deal with the boredom and loneliness of the camp. I scrambled to the stack of manga and opened them page by page to look for clues.

I'd read every single one of these books. A few I'd committed to memory. Between the pages of one book, I saw my father's death certificate, my gift to my friend before we could understand its implication, her death wish for her father. The color of the photo had completely faded, leaving only a shadow of his face. I became confused. Was it possible for her to have kept it all these years or was it that it'd been here with me all along? I thought my identity was dependent on what I remembered, but it seemed now insignificant compared to what I'd forgotten. My mind became a maze in which every thought carved a new path, on and on it went until every detail of my life became a question.

I got up and went out again. My shoes were soaked from walking in the paddy fields so I wandered the village barefoot. I was still semi-alert to the sound of children's voices. When I arrived at the banyan tree, I sat down under its retreating shade.

I didn't know how long I was there for, but when I looked up I saw the stars and her face. Though it was still emptied of expression, it looked softened and almost kind.

"There you are," she said. She took my arms gently and guided us down a moon lit path back to the bamboo gate, through the cracked door.

As soon as QQ saw us, she ran up and hugged me, unaware of my disheveled appearance. She talked constantly in pidgin, exerting a great effort to tell her story in Vietnamese, about the evening they'd had, the crickets they caught, the sour mango they ate, the kites she saw the other village children fly. She told me to close my eyes and put out my hand. A present. In my palm, she put a round, green fruit the size of a longan.

"Poison," she said. I kissed her over and over.

I didn't want my friend to see how shaken I was, so I showed her the groceries I'd bought, still scattered on the floor. "I bought those things but I don't know what to do with them. I've never cooked Vietnamese food before," I said to my friend.

"Don't worry. You got all the right stuff," she said.

I followed her out front. We built a small fire from the wood I brought back. She added water to the pot. We sat and waited for it to boil. The flame lit up only the unmarred half of her face. For a moment, I got a glimpse of the little girl, of who she might have become.

"It's been a while since I cooked too," she said.

"That's medicine, I don't think you should cook it with the food," I said, seeing that she had put a few medicinal twigs into the pot.

"Oh, what does it matter?" She poured the entire content of the brown medicinal bag into the pot with the fish, tamarind paste, and okra. "Kem is in love with Quoc Anh. You shouldn't have brought her here when you're just going to take her away."

"It won't be easy for QQ either, but children forget easily."

"Do they?"

The medicine added a slightly bitter, herbal taste to the soup. We gave some to our children and ate until the pot was clean. As the last of the embers died, my friend's face slowly retreated into the darkness.

"I married him because he was the only one who knew what the camp was like," she said. Her voice was strange, quivering and childlike, as if she was an echo of her past self. "We didn't exactly have the typical Vietnamese experience, you and I. Once my father and I left the camp, I met other kids. It was then I realized we had grown up in different countries."

"And after your husband died—" I began.

"There was nobody left to tell me who I was. What I do know," she chuckled. "Is that I'm a terrible mother."

"I'm not much of a mother either," I said.

She smiled, "I know. You left your daughter with me."

At night, Kem and QQ lay between us. They fell asleep the minute their backs touched the ground. We whispered so as not to wake them.

"I'm sorry," I said.

"For what?"

"Not trusting you."

"I'm sorry too," she said.

"For what?"

"For saying I had no idea who you were."

We'd put up a mosquito net for the night. They buzzed around us from the outside, a few grabbing their legs onto the minuscule holes of the net. A big one landed on a part of the fabric that drooped down to almost touching my nose. My friend slapped the net together, making a small splatter of blood where the mosquito was. All over the net were older brown bloodstains.

For an instant, I imagined our life together if I didn't leave her again, sitting together under the banyan tree during the day, sharing the straw mat at night with our daughters safe between us as the embers from our cooking slowly died in the yard. I wished foolishly that I'd never gotten the chance at a better life, though I knew she had to pretend to be mad if only to make hers more bearable. We lay for a while, the music of buzzing mosquitoes, crickets, and frogs growing louder around us. I thought she had fallen asleep so I whispered, "What if I stayed?"

"Then I would steal your passport, your daughter, and go live your life in America."

I smiled. "Let's swap lives."

"Still playing games. You haven't changed at all," she said.

"You were the one who came up with all our games," I retorted.

"I remember differently," she said. "I only followed along."

"That isn't true. You knew the camp better than I did. You—"

"Does it matter? We were both there," she said. "I feel good."

"Is the medicine working? We were supposed to cook it overnight."

"This is the best I've felt in a long time. Seeing you again was as impossible as seeing my husband again. I thought you were a ghost or an echo of my own thoughts."

"I wish I had come back sooner," I said.

"Why would you? You're the lucky one. I always knew that," she said.

4

I only had one day left in Vietnam so in the morning I decided to go to the address at the bottom of my mother's signature in the e-mail she sent me. We hadn't talked again since her vague promise of us meeting. I asked my friend to look after QQ again while I went back to the city.

On the way, I stopped at a café and ordered a beer. I drank it down quickly and asked for another. The waiter, a young man, looked at me with concern. He brought me a lighter-tasting beer than what I'd asked for. He was shy and tiptoed around me while I drank the second. I told him that it tasted like water and to bring me exactly what I'd ordered. He went away and brought back the correct beer in a smaller glass.

I was angry, "What's happening here? I ordered a regular sized mug. Why aren't you bringing me what I want?"

"I'm sorry," he mumbled. "You just look a bit tense."

"Are you a doctor?"

"No—but you have the look of someone—I'll bring another glass."

"That's okay," I said. "Thanks for worrying. I don't live here. I'm on vacation, that's why."

"Oh," he breathed a sigh of relief. "Men are supposed to look out for women. I'm sorry if I offended you."

I smiled, "Is this part of your job, to stop women from over-drinking?"

"At eight in the morning, yes." He blushed. "My grandfather

once told me that he who goes to sleep crying is a man, but he who wakes up crying is in deep trouble."

"I'm fine. I just need a bit of courage."

My mother's office was inside a high-rise building with large glass windows. The receptionist informed me that I could not see her without an appointment. The wall behind her was crowded with my mother's awards for her business, humanitarian, and political achievements. At the bottom was a picture of my mother holding a fluffy bichon frise. I decided to sit and wait in the lobby so I could catch her on her way out. The receptionist eyed me with curiosity. After almost an hour, she asked if I was a relative. I told her that I was and that I came from outside of the country.

"You look like a nice person, so I'll be honest as not to waste your time. She's not here today. She's rarely ever at the office. In fact, she only meets new clients here."

"Where is she?" I said.

"I can't tell you that, but I'll let her know you stopped by."

"Can I have a pencil and some paper? I'll leave a note."

In the letter, I wrote a brief summary of my life, or at least the summary of a life that I imagined she wanted for me. I told my mother that I worked in a law firm alongside my husband. I even added that it wasn't my most hoped for career, but I had a daughter to look after. I included a photograph of QQ. She was the only truth I needed to give. After I finished writing, I asked the receptionist to look over the letter for grammatical errors. When she finished reading, she studied my face, I thought, for any resemblance to my mother. She erased a bit at the top of the page.

"It's too formal. Nobody talks to their mother this way." I nodded and let her pencil in the more casual pronoun.

As I was leaving, she said, "I've worked here nineteen years and I never heard her speak of a daughter."

"Can you keep the content of the letter private? Don't let her know you've helped me with it," I said. She agreed and gave me a handful of mints from the jar on her desk. As I turned to leave, she called.

"Wait. I'm not supposed to tell you this, but she's giving a graduation speech at the International University. Do you know where that is? Let me write it down for you."

On the way to the university, I ate the candies one by one until they were gone. At the school entrance, students in white shirts, blue skirts and pants stood in groups, chatting excitedly. I could tell this was a wealthy private university, one funded by American or British donors. The students didn't have that haggard expression typical Vietnamese students often wore, caused by lack of sleep, nourishment, and an excess of both intellectual and physical labor. Here, their shirts were newly starched, their shoes still smelling of leather. Though they wore uniforms, they still tried to express their individual prosperity—the girls with brand name handbags, the boys with belts and shoes. I followed them to the school's courtyard, where a little of the Vietnamese hierarchy in education was still in place. Thousands of students stood in line. They would not be allowed to sit for the next four or five hours. I found a spot at the back.

The school dean introduced my mother. He listed her accomplishments, claimed that she was a visionary, an example for Vietnamese youth to follow. I was used to hearing praises about my mother since I was a girl, so that I couldn't rid myself of the feeling that I was still watching her through a screen. I was not anywhere closer to her now than when I read news about her in New York.

My mother walked on stage. She was in her sixties now, but no one would have known by just looking. From where I stood, she looked the same as when I last saw her at the camp.

She wore a knee-length skirt, high heels, and a jacket with shoulder pads that made her look larger than she was. As usual, she commanded attention easily. She spoke as if she were having a conversation with just a few people and not thousands of students. The cadence of her voice was perfectly measured—commanding at times, soft and intimate at others. She told an anecdote of her childhood, of her mother who had ripped up her schoolbooks to use as toilet paper.

"You will meet people who have no use for education. You may have to fight against them to get yours. They might be your own parents," she said. "But fight you must. Everything in this life can be taken from you—your home, your loved ones, even the clothes on your back—except what you've learned. Knowledge is so abstract that it is hard to appreciate, especially in our country where poverty has made us desperate for material wealth. Be curious. Be critical of how little you know." Then she singled out the female students, encouraging them to stay in the work force despite the cultural pressure to get married and bear children. My stomach tightened when she began speaking of her own life.

"If I had two lives to live, I would have done it differently," she said. "Anything worth having requires your sacrifice, even your personal happiness." She paused, as though suddenly at a loss for words. Someone in the crowd cleared his throat. My mother looked up from her podium, her proud, porcelain expression gone. "I had a daughter once. The only thing I taught her, the only thing I knew well, was how to be alone. The most important question about success—the one you should ask yourself—are you ready, when the day comes, to stand alone? You're all very young now. Someday you'll understand what I mean."

My mother looked down at her hands, her face half-turned into the shadows. She looked just the way she did in my childhood memories, bent down at her desk reading loose pages.

She was always alone then. Even after I'd spent hours outdoors with the little girl, I'd come back to find her in the same position, her chin in her palm, her other hand clicking the end of a pen. I'd never asked her if she suffered, never thought to. In my vision, the stage seemed to close in; narrower and narrower. I squinted my eyes against the sun—my mother, her thin smile, a few strands of grays that had escaped from her hairclip. I pictured her bare shoulders beneath her jacket, small and soft. I slipped out before the speech was concluded. I thought it would be cruel for her to spot me amongst the crowd, to be forced to look at the face of her personal sacrifice. I couldn't blame her because she was right. She was meant to do more than just be mine.

I went back to the village.

Kem and QQ pretended to be dead when I came in. It was a game my daughter loved. I put my fingers near their nose and checked for air.

"Oh no. My poor girls," I said. To this, they pressed their lips harder together to keep themselves from laughing. "I guess I have to revive you." I put my ears against Kem's chest and tickled under her arms. The girls kicked and roared happily.

"Mama went for a walk," Kem told me.

"Mama went for a walk," QQ repeated.

They squealed and hit each other. On top of the stack of manga, I saw a neatly folded piece of paper. I opened it. The handwriting was squiggly, the ink dark in unnatural places as though the writer was not used to holding a pen.

She deserves more than what I can give her. I don't only pretend to be mad. The voices get louder every day. It is only a matter of time until I am dragged away to a cell and locked up. I do not want her to remember me like that. No matter what you do with her, I trust your decision.

My hands shook. I wanted to run out and look for her. I

wanted to find her under the bridge, walk out to the pond until seaweed and lotus leaves clung to my chest. I wanted to be the one to drag her by the hair as she screamed and fought. I was furious at her insistence on being lost. Once again, she showed that she forgot nothing. She still hadn't forgiven me for leaving her behind. She'd now abandoned all of us for good. All that was left of her was a little girl, dark-haired and brown-skinned, not unlike her mother. Kem was crawling around the house quicker than a dog could run.

"Get up," I shouted. "Walk upright like a human being. I never want to see you crawl like that again."

The next few weeks were a flurry of paperwork, phone calls, visits to various government offices, more phone calls. I had no choice but to delay my trip back to the United States. In the meantime, I rented a motel room for the girls and I. My neighbor advised me from New York on how to speed up the adoption process. We found out that a birth certificate was not submitted for Kem after she was born, not an uncommon occurrence given the frequency of home births and mothers living in the countryside. I had to first obtain this documentation before I could begin the adoption forms. Because Kem's mother was only missing and not dead, I had to use her letter to me as proof that she wanted to leave her daughter in my care. At that time, the country was going through various changes. Efforts were made to prevent foreigners from adopting Vietnamese orphans due to the embarrassment it cast on the country as a place where children were cheaply sold. I learned as much as I could about the process. I explained my plight to Minh, my neighbor's friend, and he helped me procure a fake birth certificate. "Everything can be bought here if you know the right people," he said. In front of officials, my Vietnamese was professional and crisp from hours of practice with my script. I treated my American citizenship as a side note, not something they should be concerned with. I had to prove myself a full-blooded Vietnamese with not a drop of foreign influence.

During the first few days, Kem vacillated between not asking where her mother was to screaming, wetting the bed, and slapping QQ. I held her close and told her that a child has many mothers. The first mother was only supposed to stay with her child for an allotted time, until the second one took over. Being a mother was extremely difficult, I told her; that was why the job was divided amongst many women. This was also the first time I spoke to QQ about Lilah, who I said was her first mother.

"I'm your mother now," I said to Kem.

"Forever? I don't want a new one ever again," she said.

"Yes, forever."

"Who's Lilah?" QQ said, not understanding what I meant.

"Your mother. She passed away," I said.

"You're mommy," QQ insisted.

"I am now, but she was first."

This information didn't upset QQ as I thought it would. She pulled the blanket up to her chin and covered herself and Kem.

"Kem stays with me?" QQ asked me.

"You're sisters now. From now on you live together."

The girls were satiated by this news. They covered themselves up entirely with the blanket and whispered to each other inside their safe box of darkness.

Once I passed the initial stage of adopting Kem, my neighbor began to work on it in New York as well. I didn't anticipate so much time off work, and so ended up having to borrow money from the bank to pay for paperwork fees as well as gifts for less honest officials. I brought baskets filled with fruits, which sat on top of envelopes of money. On the phone, my neighbor warned, "It's going to be a handful with two girls."

"They keep each other company. It's less work," I said.

"You're too optimistic."

"People here raise five, ten kids with barely anything."

"You went from not wanting to have kids to having two," he chuckled.

I laughed at this too.

"I suppose what's yours is yours," he said.

5

Children don't forget easily. They only store away events that aren't consistent with their sense of self, conducive to their well-being. They are fierce survivors, loyal to nothing but their version of the story.

At school, Kem and QQ protected each other. One reinforced the other's lies. Their teacher told me the other kids taunted my daughters because nobody believed they were sisters by blood. Kem's skin was a dark brown, her eyes obsidian black, while QQ's skin was pale, her eyes a zaffre blue. A boy told them their mother must have cheated on their father. They bit his arms until he bled. They never shed a tear from being ridiculed by their classmates. Always, they went back to playing by themselves. Together, they rewrote their origins. Their imagination didn't allow them to deny those first memories of when they met, so they told themselves that I'd given birth to them both in a hut in Vietnam. We stayed there until they were old enough to travel. In their story, Kem's mother and I were one, haunted by a malevolent spirit. They feared this figure and avoided mentioning her. Whenever I was angry with them, they whispered to each other that the spirit had gotten into me again.

My neighbor was frustrated with me for not correcting my daughters' fanciful talk. He also knew that if he tried to, they would count him as another evil spirit, not to be trusted. QQ believed in these stories as much as she did in fairy tales. They were as natural to her as air and breath, but she didn't depend on them. In her mind, the circles of her reality and imagination overlapped. Unlike QQ, Kem repeated these stories like a mantra; I believed that deep down she doubted them. Once I told Kem of a time when she was younger and loved only to crawl even though she could walk, she immediately asked, "When I was a baby?" It was like she was looking for evidence that I had been there when she was born. In these moments, I gave a vague answer like, "almost a baby," or changed the topic. More and more I resembled my own mother as I withheld facts and became an accomplice in helping my daughters obscure their origins. I no longer remembered when the girls started calling my neighbor their father. He and I weren't bothered by this. We were even a little happy. A favorite moment—the four of us went to the movie theater for the first time. My neighbor had asked a woman to take a picture of us in front of the concession stand. I couldn't get the girls to be still. The photograph was a blur of QQ slinging popcorn at any moving object, Kem's face purple from trying to suck down a giant Slurpee, my neighbor and I looking on at the shutter pointed at us, helpless. We were, for so long, placeholders for someone else's wishes, surrogates to memories that weren't ours. At the press of a camera's button, its flashlight—our chrysalis—we were just *there*. Our own beginnings.

It was December again. Kem refused to get out of bed to go to school. I asked my neighbor to take QQ. I checked Kem's temperature and determined that she didn't have a fever. She was curled up in a ball on the bed. "Will you stay with me?" she said.

"Mommy needs to work. If you're very good, I can bring you to my office," I said.

"My mommy doesn't work. My mommy is a crazy beggar."

My hands trembled. She sounded less like a girl and more like a cruel old woman. It was the first time she'd let me know that she knew this about her mother. Even in Vietnam I thought my friend had managed to conceal the truth from her.

"That's not true, Kem. You see me go to work every day." It was all I could do to keep my voice steady.

"My mommy begs!" she screamed and sat up in bed. She looked at me as though she was about to leap up on all fours and pull my face off my skull. I stepped back. Ashamed that I was fearful of her, I came closer.

"Is that what you want me to do today?"

She nodded. I was still in pajamas, an old egg stain in the middle of my chest. Though she was a child, she had not asked me for anything. Everything she wanted, QQ would speak on her behalf. Perhaps I wouldn't have another chance to give her what she really wanted.

"You're right. That's what I'd rather do."

We left the house, both of us still in our night clothes, except she had on a winter jacket and I didn't. It felt good to be so utterly cold. Kem was calmer but doubtful. It seemed she didn't think her mother capable of coming back even in another form. We went down an alley. I found a piece of cardboard and Kem wrote on it, *Help us.* She underlined the words twice. It appeared she had been prepared for this for a long time. We sat down against a wall patched with chewed gums, torn ads, and graffiti. Around us were cigarette butts, necks of broken bottles.

"Do not say a word to anyone," I instructed her. "Pretend you are mute."

A few people passed us by. Kem's expression lifted as the coins fell at our feet. She was like a flower turned up to the rain. She bowed to the generous strangers. A man in disheveled clothing yelled at me, "That little girl needs to be at school!" His breath stank of alcohol.

"Mommy, I want to go home. Can we go home now?" Kem said.

I pretended not to hear her. She tugged on my arms, pushed me, bit my shoulder. I grit my teeth so as not to let out a sound. *I am your mother,* I thought. *I am. I am.*

A man in police uniform approached us.

"Ma'am, you can't be here. We need to talk," he said. Immediately I stood up, straightened my back and willed good sense back into my face. I told Kem to go sit on a bench a few feet away. The cop asked for my identifications. I told him where I lived and worked. I explained that my daughter received an assignment on empathy at school. It was her idea to pretend to be homeless. I was a mother. I was an expert liar.

"I couldn't just let her do it alone," I said, producing my business card from my wallet.

"Do you need to go so far for an assignment?" he said.

"She takes her school work very seriously."

For a moment, admiration flashed on his face.

"So have you gathered enough information? Let me take you home. It's a dangerous business," he said.

"Yeah, I live over there, but you could walk us so you know I'm telling the truth," I said.

"It's dangerous," he repeated.

"It always is, to pretend to be someone else."

It had started to snow, the first of the season. Kem's first ever. I looked at her on the bench, her eyes as open as the sky. "Mommy! Look," she called my name.

For a few days afterward, Kem clung to me, fearful of losing a mother once more. In the morning after dropping her off at school, I would assure her, "Kem, I'm going to the office now. I'll be right here when you two get out." Once, she grinned and said, "You won't give me away again?" like it was an inside joke between us. Not knowing what to say, I'd chuckled. Usually, she would simply wave goodbye and run off with QQ as though the image of her mother under the banyan tree was completely erased from her mind, as though in acting it out we had removed it from reality.

Now and then, I took out my friend's last words, which I kept in my wallet. I realized for the first time the difference between us—how I'd tasked myself, given my life to remembering, and she to forgetting. Had she managed to cross the river? Or was she trapped between worlds, unable to shut out past echoes, unable to move on? I pictured her as a young woman walking alone in the street, stopping to rest under the shade of a tree, walking again when it pleased her to. She ate when people gave her food. She slept in the middle of the day, whenever she was tired. After it rained and the dragonflies came out, she looked at them, her eyes laughing. Her surroundings no longer reminded her of anything. She thought nothing at all. She was no longer laden with ghosts; she was free of us all.

On Sunday, the girls were upstairs with my neighbor so I could study. I'd started to take classes at an online program. I was attracted to journalism because of how rare it was to find true facts. Like mining, a coal and quartz could both be called a stone, which was both correct and misleading. I took a break from an essay and went upstairs to talk to my neighbor. On the coffee table was a box filled with papers. He was reading and highlighting the documents.

"Is that Kem's birth certificate?" I whispered in case the girls were listening.

"And QQ's, a picture of you, Jon, and Lilah together. I'm putting everything in this box for when they're ready," he said.

I looked at the picture—Jon had taken it of the three of us while we were all in the kitchen at the beach house. He was closest to the camera, most of his face cut off so you couldn't see what expression he was making. I believed his eyes were smiling. Lilah and I were further away, behind the kitchen counter. We faced each other, our profiles draped by our long, dark hair. I put the picture back in the box. I went downstairs, took the tapes Mother had put in my backpack when I was leaving the camp, and gave them to my neighbor.

"What's this?" he said.

"The girls' story," I said. "Where are they?"

"In the garden."

I went to my neighbor's bedroom. The girls were asleep, shirtless on the ground, their foreheads dotted with sweat, their limbs tangled into each other. Their ankles were inked with colored markers. Dirt caked under their fingernails and in the creases of their necks.

They had devastated the garden. Uprooted plants, bruised flower petals, halved butterflies were strewn all around. They didn't look like my daughters. Their faces glowed with satisfaction. Like day and night, they had given birth to each other. I picked up a fallen butterfly, the edges of its wings yellow like daffodils, spotted with cyan. Apart from its stillness, the butterfly looked alive. I held it in my palm.

The largest light used to grow indoor plants had given out, its milky glass bulb a charred black, yet somehow the bedroom garden was still softly lit, a pale, orange dusk. I looked toward the window—someone had ripped off the curtains. On the torn fabric—small handprints. Probably a mutual effort. My gaze followed shafts of twilight back to the girls' faces—hushed still—eyelids fluttering as though at the same speed, as though sharing the same dreams.

Acknowledgments

This novel was born out of the aching pleasure of rearranging memories, reinventing the past—a personal need to solve my childhood's mysteries, figure out how I've arrived here, and to give myself emotional conclusions that real life doesn't afford. I am thankful to my mother Dang Thi Hoang Yen, an extraordinary and complicated woman, for your gift to me, the greatest gift that could be bestowed on an artist—a strong start. I'm grateful to Ngo Vu Minh Chau, my first friend, for being a steadfast companion during the loneliest years. Thank you to my sisters Ashleigh Mayfair and Katie Dang who inspire me every day with your arts, your talents, and your huge hearts. To Tristan Shands, thank you for your infinite patience, your wisdom and consolation, for the hundreds of meals you cooked for us while I wrote, for showing me beauty more astonishing than I knew possible. Your love allows me to imagine this book's ending.

I'm indebted to my agent Stacy Testa, thank you for your tireless pursuit in finding my work the perfect home, for your unwavering belief in me and in this book. Thank you to Kent Carroll for making my dreams a reality. And thank you to the team at Europa Editions, especially Jessie Shohfi for your passionate work. This book would not be possible without James

Cañón; thank you for giving me the encouragement I needed to see the project through to the end; your insights helped me give form to a shapeless mass of words; your compassionate guidance brought forth the best in me. Thank you to Melanie Shaw, Mark Chu, and Kayla Maiuri for reading the early drafts. Thank you to William Boggess for your precise and surgical edits. Thank you to Tracy Ly for reminding me that I was a writer above all else in times of doubt. Thank you to Yang Liu for soothing my tears on multiple occasions and allowing me to be unapologetically myself; your friendship is magical. I'm grateful to Craig Wright for being among the first to see worth in my writing, thank you for your sensitive and soulful teaching. To Southern Oregon University, thank you for being the oasis you were while I was still discovering my voice. Thank you to Columbia University, to my classmates and teachers, for being the toughest critics I've encountered and for making me a better writer.

Thank you to the one who inspired the little girl character in this novel. You showed me the solace of the imagination, the joy in isolation, and the power of things unnamed. This book is for you, too.